LAS

Ronald Sukenick

Last Fall

✯ Invisible Starfall Books

Copyright © 2021 Julia Frey for the Ronald Sukenick Estate
All rights reserved.

Invisible Starfall Books
isbooks@chello.at

Ronald Sukenick Edition 08

Edited by Thomas Hartl
Cover and book layout: Thomas Hartl

First Invisible Starfall Books Edition, November 2021

For enabling The Ronald Sukenick Edition, I am very grateful to Julia Bloch Frey (now Julia Nolet, www.juliafreyauthor.com), widow and heiress of Ronald Sukenick; the Fiction Collective Two/FC2 (www.fc2.org), particularly Joanna Ruocco as Chair of FC2's Board of Directors; the University of Alabama Press (www.uapress.ua.edu), particularly Daniel Waterman as Editor-in-Chief; and the Harry Ransom Humanities Research Center (www.hrc.utexas.edu), University of Texas at Austin, housing the Ronald Sukenick Papers 1941-1999.

ISBN 9798764073712 (pbk.)

LAST FA

realtime c. 9/01/00:

It was a matter of theft, but the problem was that nobody knew what had been stolen. The museum was banking on my expertise as a professor of post-contemporary art both to identify the stolen work and, if possible, to get it back.

None of this had been made public and, in fact, even the personnel of the museum were unaware, except for a vague feeling of unease, which was itself part of the evidence. Because the feeling that something, something important, was gone was a factor. That is, how else, other than through feeling, were they to know that something was gone when they didn't know what it was?

The importance of feelings in the case, it turned out, was one of the reasons they hired me. The director of the museum, a woman, felt that a woman would be more attuned to the nuances involved. In fact, the sense of an absence was something I had been increasingly feeling within myself, and I didn't have to be a clairvoyant to suspect that something intangible but real had been stolen from me also.

Evidently, this had been an inside job, and records had been altered to obliterate any reference to the work in question. And yet, the people who worked in the museum remembered ... something. I was advised to interview Brewster Fynch, who had endowed the museum, as my first step.

Fynch lived in a Tudor mansion in a wealthy suburb up the Hudson. I was surprised he was so young, correctly so, because the virile looking man with the black shadow of a beard who opened the door turned out to be staff. He looked me up-and-down with an intensity that was more than professional—for a moment I thought he was going to frisk me, and if he had tried I don't know what I would have done, but he didn't.

Fynch, I knew, had made his money manufacturing time pieces, and in fact had a very precise manner. It was impossible to guess his age—somewhere between 60 and 90?—but he looked as tensile as bone china. I was predisposed to a kind of reverence for him on account of the spiritual reach of his project.

"We thought of calling it the museum of temporal art," he explained carefully, and paused. "But that seemed elitist and pretentious. The Museum of Temporary Art brings in the effect of time anyway but that, in the sense that a temporal artwork can't be fixed, that fixed just means static, created the problem we have here."

"Which is?"

"That if its collections are supposed to be fluid, transitory, how can we say that something which is no longer there is missing? No, Austyn, if I may use your first name, the whole damned mess is based on a paradox."

He projected the impression of someone who was endlessly caught up in the convolutions of his own mind. I gave him a somewhat evasive response, hoping to parry, playing for time.

"Well, Mr. Fynch, I find that paradox is usually the result of insufficient understanding."

"Very glad to hear you taking that tack, Austyn, because that in a way is what we're paying you for. I can tell you one more thing, that is, I felt much better about the Museum before this happened. I thought of the temporal as spiritual opportunity. I thought time underwrites change, it means there's time to change your life. As I have changed mine, as I have dematerialized my interests, so that some people think I've gone crazy, especially my family back in LaFange. That's Minnesota. Worried I suppose about being disinherited. But if the liquidity of a time-work can be stolen then time itself can be hijacked, possessed and bought and sold. While my whole conception is that time is the one element in our experience that is uncontrollable, untouchable, pure reality."

I empathized with the man, he seemed sincere, while at the same time I wasn't entirely sure what he was talking about, and even wondered whether he was a little wacky. But very quickly, he pressed a button, and the individual with the five o'clock shadow came to show me out, introducing himself as one Pyhl, Fynch's factotum. He was one of those blade thin but robust types, trying his best to seem transparent rather than devious, and I wasn't sure whether I didn't like the way he looked at me or whether I did.

He offered me a ride to the train, and ushered me into a long black chauffeur-driven limo. He sat a little too close in my opinion, and on the way I was extremely aware that he took every opportunity to touch me, if politely. He also made it clear that though he was employed by Fynch he was skeptical about the Museum of Temporary Art.

"It was all done already by Marcel Duchamp," he said. "Art is how you look at it, Austyn, like the famous urinal, presented as an art work, is an art work."

"The urinal," I replied, "was an art work—for five minutes. And for five minutes again for anyone seeing it the first time. The Museum of Temporary Art is Duchamp plus time." But as I said this so glibly I realized I had no idea what time is and actually had a tiny moment of panic, one of her fits of nothingness as she calls them, as if the ground underneath suddenly disintegrates language breaks up . . . the Incident . . . memory vortex . . . arrested by syncopating recollection, Kenny Clarke, the jazz drummer, playing in a club in some way transmuting stream of pure time to now, a rhythm that seems to surf on time itself dreamy, floaty, blissed, blessed . . . like Miles Davis at his best, or Charlie Parker any time . . . horns of plenty . . . like:

Pyhl was inviting me to a gallery opening next day in SoHo of an exhibition by a painter named Jimmy Lochs. I'd heard of him, he was talked about, controversial. The Temporary Museum was going to do a Lochs show.

"He's a sort of a negative force, more self-negating than anything else,—you'll see. And possibly dinner afterward?"
"Possibly," I parried, feeling tempted if a little rushed.

But I did go to the opening and I was glad I did, because Lochs's works were something special. They were in a digital medium designed to decay and already starting to disintegrate, consisting of no more than colorful texture on canvas, but that in itself was not very interesting. What was interesting was the language deployed on them to tell you what you were supposed to see in the painting—"nude woman bending forward," for example—the play between the visible and invisible in other words, the photo in the mind emerging from the negative on the canvas. Pyhl was there, and renewed his invitation, and though, or maybe because, he still seemed sexually dangerous, I accepted.

And besides, I sensed in him a challenge, as from one whose best instincts were still dormant, who hadn't been awakened yet. What must have been in my mind also was that if he had put me on to one good thing, others might follow. He took me to a bar-restaurant in the neighborhood, and we were having a few preliminary drinks waiting for a table, when the crowd from the gallery came in and Pyhl singled out Lochs.

I was immediately put off by him, I didn't like his looks. Jimmy Lochs was a tall, big-bellied, broad chested redhead with an aggressive way of moving, and an obvious ogling interest in any female who happened to pass by—definitely bad news. I put him out of my mind and focused on Pyhl.

He had a way of touching me as he talked—on my arm, on my shoulder—that created a certain, how can I put it, corporeal intimacy, and I could hear my voice softening, dropping its professional certitudes for a certain girlishness. I was beginning to wonder where this would end up, when Lochs suddenly appeared to greet Pyhl, who in turn introduced him to me and my first impression of Lochs was swept away.

It was his voice. His voice was low and throaty, like the rumbling purr of a big cat. His voice immediately undercut the aggression signaled by the way he moved.

It was true that his gaze made me super conscious of the low cut dress I was wearing, but it was a child's gaze, full of erotic curiosity. Nevertheless, he was disrupting the current already sparking between Pyhl and me and I found myself wishing that he would go away. Besides, grown-up children are always big trouble, and on top of that he smelled funny.

But he invited himself to sit down at our table when we got one, and I suppose Pyhl couldn't refuse, since he was Fynch's representative at the Museum. During that whole start of what became a, to say the least, significant evening, I to this day have no sense of what Lochs said, because I was listening to his voice not to what he said. Or to put it differently, his words were saying one thing while his voice was telling me another, tune undercutting lyrics.

All I remember of that dinner was that halfway through it Pyhl excused himself to go to the men's room and as soon as he was out of sight Lochs said, "Let's go," and I went. Lochs, to my astonishment, picked up his half-finished steak with his fingers, and slipped it into the pocket of his black leather jacket. "The Museum can pick up the tab," he said, "the waiter can pick up Pyhl."

All my life I've felt in myself, and believed that other people feel, a blind inner force for the good, a sort of "weak force," I don't know where it comes from, that in the long run is stronger than anything else. So it's ironic, to say the least, that I went off with someone so aggressively destructive if not worse. He treated everything and everyone as part of a game which he had to win by any means, and there was something two-year-old about him that, perversely, appealed to me.

From the very beginning he took physical control of me, steering me by the elbow or waist, or with an arm around my shoulder, even getting me where he wanted me to go with his hand on the back of my neck, which for some reason I didn't resist. All while he talked endlessly, my impression was he would say anything, even nonsense, garbage—some kind of spoken stream of consciousness. His loft when we arrived was like that too, scrambled, cluttered with miscellaneous objects, filthy, laundry and painting tools on chairs, pervaded by the same rank animal odor that surrounded his person like a nasal halo.

A pattern of patter began to emerge.

"You have to market your concept to the media," he said. "It doesn't really matter what's on the canvas, that's not where it's at. My work exists in the public mind surrounded by the aura of celebrity, because nobody knows how to judge the concrete work in itself. It's all ideas today, you can't get around that."

Later I would find out that it was just talk, language he'd picked up, it didn't mean a thing to him, it was just distraction while he had other things in mind. It was a warm night and I wasn't wearing many clothes. Without preliminaries he started pawing my body, had me undressed almost before I knew it, before I could decide to say no, and then it was too late to say no, because I didn't want to, or I did but didn't, his finger already invading me, probing with remarkable accuracy, right on target and then I managed to say no and repeat it over and over and even when his shaft slid into me too big it hurt I tried to shake him off and then gave in, no other choice, pinned. And just as my vagina started to relax and it began to feel really good he came, throbbing and thrusting, and he never kissed me.

And the first thing he said to me after he pulled out and began to drowse off, his boozy breath in my face, was, "You can go now." Which I did, hurt and humiliated, wondering why in the world I gave in to him, and loathing myself for it.

Next day at the museum I had to face Pyhl, because he was talking to the Director when I arrived at her office.

"I was glad to see you taking such good care of one of our artists last night," Pyhl commented acidly as he left, "we need to keep them happy."

"I think he keeps himself happy," I answered.

The Director, L. L. Achs, was a sharp faced woman of a certain age who appeared to be a fountain of information and goodwill. She had asked her staff to make some notes on what was missing in the Museum, without specifying what the real problem was. She wanted to talk to me about the results.

The results were surprisingly unanimous—instead of specifying lacks in this or that collection, the staff mostly commented on a change in the spirit of the institution. As one person put it, prefacing the remark by noting the inevitability of such a development in any institution devoted to accumulation, "we began by emphasizing the flux of life over the static art object and we switched to valuing the art object more and more relative to the life it's part of." Another person wrote, "something is missing in the museum and it's missing in myself."

Another: "why are we now talking about art when art is just sliced life [sic], sliced to reveal its content." Another: "There's an empty space here, something more than real but real too, whose absence is stupefying." I don't pretend to understand these remarks as such, but the sense of absence they expressed I recognized and empathized with immediately.

I went back to my apartment pondering the sense of absence in myself that had been growing in my consciousness. No sooner did I arrive than a messenger showed up with a small package from Lochs. When I opened it I found this drawing:

which demonstrated two things about him, confirmed later— he couldn't write and he couldn't spell. That is, he was dyslexic. But, curiously, this revelation, rather than evoking pity in me, provoked a sort of fascination.

And I suddenly realized that written language, for me, had become hollow. Had become dead, an extension of death. At that moment the phone rang—he didn't announce who he was and I didn't need to ask—in his feline voice now with something anxious and raspy in it, wanting to know if he could see me tonight and of course I said no.

But what I was feeling was something stronger than refusal and it surprised me: some kind of destructive, nasty rage that made me want to do something really evil to the man. So I said, "Wednesday night." And immediately had second thoughts about it, because I felt he would sense what was in my mind and then we would be playing his destructive game of win and lose—but this time, I wasn't going to lose.

The next day began in conference with Pyhl and Achs.

"The Museum of Temporary Art," Achs explained in her staccato voice, "conceives painting as a kind of music that exists only in the moment of perception—that was Fynch's original idea. Of course the work exists beyond that—beyond time, that is—but it's only the static score of a potential live interaction. And in some cases there is no score, which is the problem we have here."

"If the tree falls in the forest and nobody hears, did it really fall?" observed Pyhl.

"Not exactly," corrected Achs. "The question is, was there ever a tree?"

I remember then a jolt of fear. Was there ever a tree, or was there nothingness? Art is an arrangement against nothingness. Arranging the right things in the right order, the right constellation, the right words symbols sounds, the right magic to induce meditation, summon the spirits, cast spells, lay curses, invite visions, prophesy the future, pattern the present, distinguish right from wrong.

When I used to join wholly in the spell of prayer, engage my soul, let myself go to my holy ghost, my spirit, relinquish control, then voices would come like poems, come out of nothing, mystery. They would enter me with pleasure, like a lover, and like a lover they articulated themselves in me. I know this doesn't sound normal, but the problem is I've never been a normal person.

In any case, Achs picked the right person for this job. I have a certain familiarity with absence, with nothingness, with whatever is missing. I told them my first move would be to examine the books, because though the provenance of the piece is deleted from the records, there might be a paper trail of the financial transaction.

And sure enough, after a lot of digging, I found a mysterious notation for a major expenditure, referred to only as "The Concept." The purchase price was listed mysteriously as: "$000,000." When I asked Achs about it, she said it must have been before she became Director and that possibly it was a contemplated purchase.

"Isn't this a highly irregular entry?"

She considered the question. "Unusual, yes, irregular, not necessarily, considering that we have an institution here that deals you might say, normally, with the intangible."

"But I feel we may be on the right track here," I said.

"Well, your capacity for feeling is a part of your expertise we're counting on. Where does it lead you?"

I let my mind go blank. "I'm getting nothing," I said.

"That's a little disappointing, Austyn."

"Does nothing mean nothing to you?" I asked.

"What do you mean?"

"Nothing, zero, naught, not?"

She closed her eyes, frowned, "Zero, I think it was a musical piece by that name."

"Yes?"

"I heard it was once commissioned, that's all I know."

Logically, I should have done a little research next. Instead, I did nothing, or as little as possible, just sitting around keeping the mental doors and windows open, unmethodical, waiting for signs, totally responsive to the situation as it unfolded. Waiting, possibly, for the occult hand to pull the genetic strings.

Back at home, I fell into a kind of aimless sexual reverie, without content, that expressed itself only as a hot pink spot in the middle of my mental screen. I drifted into a totally receptive, even submissive emotional state, a yearning to relinquish all responsibility, even for myself.

And then I remembered there was someone I met recently who I felt could bring those feelings out. It was at a reception at the Temporary Museum, it was someone dressed in black, priestly, bald, and he was a musician, and he worked in a form that he called "conceptual music." And the odd thing was he had a cane and dark glasses and I couldn't tell whether he was blind—I only talked to him for a minute—but his voice sounded as if he were blind. I don't know exactly what I mean by that.

He called himself by the single name Notley, and when I asked him about it he said, mysteriously, it was because he spent several years in Japan in a Zen monastery. I called Achs and asked whether he could have something to do with "zero." She said his idea of conceptual music might have something to do with the phrase, "The Concept," and that it might be worth a follow-up.

I asked her what conceptual music might be and she said, "It's John Cage without duration." I knew exactly what she meant. Instead of, like Cage, conceiving a musical piece as the duration of a certain time of silence, conceptual music must be a complex of sounds taking no time at all.

I wanted to talk to this man. Achs had supplied me with Notley's number and I called. But I wasn't prepared for the voice that answered the phone, a toneless voice, without cadence, muted, almost a whisper.

It had the effect of making me mute, tongue tied, it seemed to suck the meaning out of words. It was after the Incident when I first started having trouble with language. I can remember exactly what happened. I call it the day that language left. It was nothing really, somebody at school asked me what time it was, but it was like the words echoed in my head and kept repeating until they were meaningless. I couldn't figure out what the word "time" meant, and I panicked.

But more and more frequently, the same thing started happening with other words, blown to alphabet soup, sentences exploding. It was as if the texture of language were being eaten by moths, and I was thinking Alzheimer's, psychosis, dementia praecox. Then I found the antidote.

I was walking down a street on the way to an appointment which I knew I was late for, but I didn't know how late and I couldn't get myself to look at my watch, because looking at clocks during that period nauseated me. I passed a church and heard, faintly, the sound of organ music, and for some reason—I've always liked organ music—I went in. Someone was playing Bach's *Toccata and Fugue in C Major*.

The only way I can describe what happened then is by asking you to image, say, the word *tree*, without color, missing some dimension, sensuously disconnected because there's no way to connect. And then suddenly the color comes back, the solidity, the branches swaying, the leaves turning in the breeze. Problem is it's not a permanent cure, the vertigo comes back, nausea, my fits of nothingness, and Bach doesn't do it every time, sometimes it's another composer, but sometimes it's pop or jazz or rock or even rap, there's no telling.

And it happened again when I called Notley, this craziness with words, but I managed to stutter out my business. It turned out he had written a piece called "The Concept." So I asked him how I could hear it.

> "I can't tell you that," he answered in his ghostly, hollow voice.
> "Why not," I asked.

"You have to see it," he said.

"You mean, it's an opera or something?"

"You have to see it."

"All right, how do I see it?"

"I'll give you my address." And he gave me an address at the tip of Manhattan.

"When should I come?"

"When you want."

"Well how do I know you'll be there?"

"You won't," and he hung up.

It was walking distance and I immediately got myself out and went down there. It was an office building in the Wall Street area, but facing the Bay and I couldn't imagine there'd be an apartment in it. The doorman, however, indicated Notley, top floor, so I assumed it was a luxurious penthouse.

Far from it. He opened the door, still in his black costume like a priest, black slacks, tight black T-shirt, dark glasses, large round gold earring, shaved head with ∞ tattooed on scalp, and I was in a small, cell-like space maybe ten feet by ten feet. The walls were white and everything in it was white: one chair, one dresser, a bed, one small desk with a computerized keyboard on it. I waited to be shown into the rest of the apartment but nothing happened and after a while I realized that was it.

He pulled the white wooden chair out from the wall and carefully placed it close to the bed, or rather, cot, which was covered by a white quilt on which he sat down. Given the cautious way he moved, I was still convinced he was blind. I took my indicated place on the chair in front of him.

Our knees were almost touching. It was hard to see his face because his head was framed by the light coming in the one window of the apartment, through which I could see the Upper Bay, the Verrazano Bridge across the Narrows, and beyond that the widening expanse of the Lower Bay.

"Now what is it you wanted from me?" he asked in his whispery voice.

"What is 'The Concept?'"

"What it was yesterday is not what it is today, and what it is today is not what it will be tomorrow."

"Okay," I asked, "what is it today?"

"Today it's everything happening at once. Let me feel your face." His hand groped the empty space in front of him.

I took his hand and guided it to my cheek, and he began to slowly trace its contours with very sensitive fingers. He moved his hand up over my temple to my forehead, took my head in both hands, then traced my eyebrows with his thumbs, ran an index finger slowly down the bridge of my nose, moved it to my lips, running it caressingly across my upper lip and then back and forth along my lower lip.

Frankly, I was getting turned on. It was partly the idea of someone who could feel me but not see me. I don't know why that was so sexy. I had no intention of making love with the man, but I was beginning to feel it had gone too far for me to want to resist. But most of all I felt at a moral disadvantage because of his blindness, and so allowed him to guide me onto his cot, lay me down, and gently pull off the rest of my clothing.

Then he started massaging me between the legs for what seemed an excruciatingly long time. Finally he leaned over and opened a dresser drawer, looked through its contents, selecting a packaged condom which he ripped open and, adroitly releasing his cock from the confines of his clothing, expertly rolled down his stiff organ. Something about the nimble way he moved disturbed me, but I was by now so abjectly at his disposal that I couldn't think about it.

He mounted and thrust himself hard into me and I could tell it was going to be wonderful, but just as I started thrusting back I remembered that this was something I really didn't want to do, for professional as well as emotional reasons and then I realized what bothered me about the way he had found and put on his condom.

"You're not blind," I managed to whisper.
"Who said I was?" he replied, his voice even more muted and flat. I could hardly hear him. He got up, zipped his pants.
"You deliberately misled me, you prick." The words tore out of me and I immediately felt apologetic.

He went over to the electronic keyboard and began fingering the keys without sound. To this soundless accompaniment he added a rhythmic succession of mournful moans and groans, gasps, and finally growls and low howls. It was the most disturbing thing I ever heard, I wanted him to stop immediately. This chant, I guess you would call it, issued before long in song, but song without words, or without intelligible words, yet surpassingly sweet and sad.

He came back to the bed and stood over me. I apologized, saying the misunderstanding was not his fault. I focused on the view out the window, the wide expanse of water, the bridge, the distant horizon, thinking Notley embodied what I called the weak force, and the weak force was strong.

Meanwhile, Notley was standing over me in a recessive, attentive way, waiting. "Take off your glasses," I told him, and he raised the lenses to his forehead. His irises were so pale a blue they were shockingly almost white, and the eyeballs were pinkish. He lowered his dark glasses over his eyes, leaving me to mull the possibility that he was an albino or something like.

Then, I noticed something else that was strange. I have a very sensitive sense of smell, and though he was standing right over me, he had no scent. And I suddenly flashed on him as the photographic negative of himself, a visible absence, and I knew that it was going to require further developments to discover his real presence.

I went into his bathroom to dress, and when I came out he was fingering his electronic keyboard again, his lips shaping silent utterances. The thought occurred to me that he was mad, but I felt something ineffably gentle about him that was very magnetic. There was a small drawing, framed above the desk with the computer on it, the only decoration gracing the room, consisting of a thick black squiggle looking like this:

I was attracted by the drawing and asked who did it.

"It's by my teacher," he said. "It means 'writing emerges from drawing and disappears in music.'"
"Who is your teacher?" I asked.
"I don't talk about my master," he answered, or rather, didn't answer. "My master never speaks to me, and has taken a vow of

silence toward me. My master believes that silence puts you in touch with the invisible. My master believes that music is organized silence and drawing is organized emptiness. My master believes you have to empty yourself of language before you discover the invisible. My master believes that language stains the white radiance of eternity."

We were quiet for awhile, a long while it seemed to me, during which I was thinking how much Notley's sense of the invisible seemed to correspond with my sense of it. But whether or not, I sensed some sort of bonding growing between us at some deep sub-vocal level, as if his DNA were groping my DNA. I felt compelled, though, to ask him about "The Concept" again.

"Concentrate and listen," he said. I focused my attention on my auditory sense, and maintained it for some minutes. I heard nothing and said so.
"Then you didn't hear it," he said. "But trying counts."
"I have to go," I said finally, "but I hope I'll see you again."
"Don't worry," he said in a voice that was almost a whisper.

When I got outside it was dark, the twin towers of the World Trade Center looming luminously over the downtown streets, illuminating clouds from the inside.

In the morning from my office at the University I called the Temporary Museum. Achs was tied up so I got Pyhl.

"I may have found it," I told him.
"Found what?" he answered.

"Exactly," I said, "I don't know what, but I may know where. Locked up in someone's head."

"Whose?"

"Do you know Notley, the musician?"

I heard Pyhl exhale loudly: "He's just a John Cage knockoff, Zen, silence, the whole bit. I hope you didn't buy that baloney about his silent teacher—I'll bet he never had a teacher, that's why he's silent."

"You know this man?" I asked.

"Not personally. He's tried to sell things to the Museum, probably has sold things to the Museum, and always at the direction of his famous teacher."

"Well if you don't know him, how can you judge him?"

"I take it you know him. Though not as well as Lochs, I presume."

"I think that was a very unprofessional remark."

"I think that was very unprofessional behavior."

"Are you referring to the restaurant? Who I choose to eat with is not part of my professional behavior. Dating is not part of it either."

"All right. I'll tell Achs your scholarly conclusion is that the missing item is to be found in Notley's head. I'm sure she'll be gratified to know you're as much of a nut cake as he is."

I hung up. And what was I going to tell Achs? I suddenly wondered. I had made an appointment with her at 4:30, an hour and a half before meeting Lochs.

I looked at a clock, it was 2:05 p.m., but that suddenly seems arbitrary. And then it happens again, she feels dizzy, her stomach begins churning, it's as if she's getting sea sick. The time seems wrong, or rather relative, though her sense of the real time is elusive.

She quickly puts a Miles Davis CD into her player. Davis's first reedy trumpet solo soothes her, but not by its sound, it's the way it looks that stops her nausea, its solid invisible architecture which she can't describe, even to herself, and though she begins to feel better she wonders at the same time about her sanity.

I took a cab to the Temporary Museum for my appointment with Achs, who was eager to know what I had discovered.

"Well, I saw Notley. And what I discovered is what's missing is an absence."

"Meaning?"

"Meaning that Notley is sort of crazy, and I don't exactly understand what he's getting at with 'The Concept,' but I think he's making the point that we lack something."

"Isn't that where we came in?" Achs observed tartly.

"What I mean is," and since I didn't know what I meant, I hesitated, "is that his project is to give the appearance of something that has disappeared but is really there."

"I'm afraid I'm not following you," said Achs, who had little patience with the indefinite, the undefined, and the perhaps undefinable.

"He's started a whisper that something is gone that could not be gone."

"And what is this thing that's gone?"

I took a big breath, because I knew this wasn't going to go down well with Achs, and said, "I think it's what we used to call," I paused.

"Go on," she urged.

"God," I blurted.

She stared at me and asked: "Is that an exclamation, or a profession of faith?"

"Not that I believe in God," I reassured her, "but . . ."

"Yes?"

"I do believe in . . . something."

"And what would that be?"

"That's the problem," I told her, "I don't know. God or gods or godliness. Or demons. Or evil."

Achs sighed mournfully, "Let's move on. I believe in something also—nasty people pursuing their own nasty purposes, usually for profit. There are people who would like to see the Museum of Temporary Art fail. They believe it challenges the validity of the art market, and therefore of the gallery scene. Because the way we deal with art here is the reverse of mercenary, since how can you place mercenary value on art that is going to evanesce? The message we imply is that art is not something to collect but something that makes you recollect what you are about, where you come from and where you want to go. So I've been making a list of the Museum's ill-wishers who might turn out to be evil-doers." She handed me a piece of paper with the names of quite a few biggies in the gallery world.

"This is top secret," she said. I could see why, given the eminence of the persons named, but the most surprising name of all was that of Pyhl.

"Jack Pyhl, is that a mistake?"

"Pyhl," Achs responded, "has the confidence of Fynch, but doesn't merit it. This is strictly confidential. Pyhl thinks that Fynch's idea for the museum is blatant nonsense. Pyhl is always trying to persuade us to establish a permanent collection, in direct contradiction of our mission to house the transitory and ineffable."

"And what do you want me to do with this?" I asked.

"That's up to you, Austyn, but you might use your intuition to determine who gains the most from the rumor that something important is missing from the Museum."

"And if I can pin it down?"

"Then we'll see, but if it's Pyhl you'll have to go to Fynch. Because that means Fynch's daughter is involved. They are good, let's say, friends."

I had agreed to meet Lochs at his studio but because my meeting with Achs ran over I was a half hour late, though I have to admit, I didn't rush. Much to my surprise, I found Lochs distraught over my tardiness.

"I called your home, I called your office, I was sure you weren't coming. Figured it was because you're pissed at me."

"I am pissed with you, but when I make appointments I keep them." His odor was, if anything, more pronounced than before, something like rotting meat, and I couldn't help but think it indicated something about the man's soul.

He took a half filled Styrofoam container of coffee off a bar stool and wiped its scarred vinyl surface with his sleeve: "Have a seat," he said. "Would you like something to drink?"

"Thank you, no. Why did you want to see me?"

"Because I like you, why did you think?"

"You didn't treat me as if you liked me," I observed.

"I know I have bad manners. Where I grew up, having manners was two strikes against you."

"And where did you grow up?"

"Where isn't the point, it's how."

"Or if?"

"Come on, I know I was being a swine."

"You stopped?"

"I'm trying."

"I guess you have to try hard. Tell me about yourself," I continued. "Where did you go to art school?"

"I didn't go to art school, I started drawing in jail. Jail was my art school."

"What were you in for?"

"Robbery, I used to rob houses. When I got out I took studio courses."

"Speaking of studios, it's warm in here," and I slipped off my suit jacket. I was wearing a tight, low cut sweater. I thought he would notice, I didn't think it would make him crazy, but it was like a red cape to a bull. He made a grab for me, but I slipped off the stool.

"You haven't learned any manners either," I told him.

"What do you want to turn me on for then?" he spat.

"Did you ever hear of self-control?"

"Then why are you here? Why are you wearing a sexy sweater? What do you expect?"

"I expect you to act like a gentleman, or at least like a grown-up."

"I'm not a gentleman, but at least I know how to treat a lady who dresses like a whore."

He went over to an open drawer, fumbled around and came back with two fistfuls of hundred dollar bills, threw them both in my face with a motion that seemed somehow childlike, and stood there red faced, looking confused. Then suddenly he leaned against a wall and buried his face in his arms, saying he was sorry.

"Go ahead," he said, "go ahead and leave, I know that's what you want to do."

But to my surprise, this had a reverse effect on me, and I went over to him and put my arms around his waist, turning him around, and he kissed me, long and hard, and I responded, and it was as if our clothes just fell off, and he had me on his bed again, he was between my legs like a pole. He plunged into me brutally, without prelude, I tightened up and it hurt, then I became aware of his odor and I flashed on the Incident again. He must have sensed it, because suddenly he wilted, groaned, and flopped out.

"You choked and went slack," he said. "I could feel you turning off, no but it's my fault, you're scared of me, I'm an animal, I know it, shit, shit, why do I act this way?" He threw himself on his back. "This always happens, I turn women off and then I turn off, I'm not even a man, I'm finished, washed up, I might as well slit my throat."

We got up and I slipped my panties and jacket back on, he stayed naked, and I noticed a jagged red scar on his chest. He poured us some drinks from an open bottle of single malt in front of the television set, which as far as I could tell he always left on without the sound.

"Why do you always leave it on?"
"It's my religion," he said.
"You're kidding."
"No I'm not. When I turn on the sound it's like a ritual, or prayer. I almost know it by rote, I know what they're going to say and I can repeat it with them. The tone of the commercials especially, they promise to save me, they promise to change my life."
"You're not kidding."
"I don't kid about stuff like that." He took a big gulp of his single malt. "In prison that's all I had to do, watch TV, it kept me sane. That's how I started drawing, I started sketching what was on TV. That was the only time I stopped being scared, when I was watching TV. I didn't think I was going to get out alive. And I almost didn't, you see my stigmata? A homemade knife meant for my heart that just missed and collapsed a lung. So TV was my salvation, mentally, because everything inside began to get translated visu-

ally, out where I could see it. And what saves you becomes sacred I guess."

I still couldn't tell whether he was kidding, but he was staring vacantly at the TV, absorbed now by something for sure. Scarred scared sacred, I thought.

"It makes everything visible," he said.
"And leaves out everything that's not," I added.

We were watching a long commercial break in a sitcom. He turned on the sound. He was drinking single malt now shot after shot. An ad for deodorant featuring a sweaty man was succeeded by a brassiere ad with a happy woman followed by a fast food ad with a contented family finishing with an exerciser ad with a smiling young man showing off his hard body.

I noticed movement in the neighborhood of Lochs's lap during this sequence. As it proceeded I was fascinated to see his penis rear its head, slowly elevate, and finally stand as hard as the hard body in the commercial. Impressive in a man his age. Resurrected it was sort of wedge shaped, not very long but extremely wide, which explained why it had hurt me.

"Do you always drink this much?" I asked him.
"Anyway, I'd rather drink than fuck," pouring himself another.
"Come on, you don't mean that."
"Like hell I don't."
"Well what am I doing here?"
"I was just wondering," he answered.

I got up, he got up too, erect in both senses now I couldn't help but notice. I went to get dressed, nervous because he stood there watching me, a contemptuous look on his face.

"I'm so glad I came," I said, "I feel I've really gotten to know you. Impotent and drunk, in that order."

He threw his glass at me, hitting the wall next to my ear and splattering my jacket. I headed for the door. He grabbed his balls with one hand and shook his still erect cock at me with the other.

"Don't let anyone say I couldn't do it to you if I wanted to. Bitch," he yelled, as I went out the door, slamming it behind me.

When I got home I found an e-mail from Pyhl: "Checking around the gallery scene I've discovered Notley has the reputation of being a shrewd businessman. And more. You can call me at home."

I called Pyhl and got his answering machine.

"There's nothing wrong with an artist having a practical side," I told the machine. "I should think we're beyond infantilizing creative people as helpless. A little business sense is absolutely necessary for an artist these days. You're still trying to unfairly discredit Notley, for reasons I don't understand."

In a little while Pyhl returned my call:

"I also found that his famous teacher is widely believed to be a press agent," he said without prelude.
"Get in touch when you have some real information about Notley." I hung up.

There was a profusely apologetic message on my machine from Lochs, which I had half expected, but not so soon. I didn't answer it. And there was a message from Notley asking me to meet him at a macrobiotic restaurant for lunch the next day.

I seemed to be getting popular but I was troubled by his invitation, given the controversy at the museum. I worried the issue a bit and finally decided to go since I might learn something. The restaurant was in the Village and when I arrived Notley wasn't there. I waited 15 minutes, twenty minutes, after a half-hour I was about to leave when he finally showed up.

"I was with a patient who couldn't come," he said by way of excuse.

"You were playing doctor and you were going to bring a patient with you?"

He laughed. "No, no," he said, "I do musical therapy, and this woman had a sexual problem. She thought she was becoming a nymphomaniac because, though she was perfectly happy and in love with her husband, she was having intense affairs with two other men, and on top of that was falling in love with them too. I was trying to get across to her that conventional morality does not necessarily correspond to the physiological reality of a woman's body.

"What," I asked, "can you learn about life from music?"

"Everything!" he insisted. "The structure of music is the structure of life, only more refined and abstract, more intelligent if you want. It corresponds to the structure of the brain. That's also how I explain my mantic abilities."

"Are you telling me that you have the power to predict the future?"

"Once you've captured the structure of experience," Notley explained, "you can tell how the structure is going to evolve."

I must have been looking at him skeptically, because he immediately added, "It's not mystical, it could probably be done by computer eventually. And besides, I'm not very good at it, I'm just a beginner."

"Well, can you give me some tips?"

"Stay away from tall buildings."

When I arrived home that evening I was shocked to find a disreputable looking Jimmy Lochs slouching against my apartment door.

"How did you get in the building?" I asked, associating immediately with the Incident trauma and feeling the beginnings of hysteria.

"I got in," he answered.

"Well now get out."

"Okay, okay, but first there's an explanation I owe you. What you don't understand, about the other night. When I was drunk?"

"Go on."

"That was the first orgasm I've had in almost a year."

"Notley says you're married, so what's wrong with your wife?"

"What's wrong?" He laughed. "Where do you want me to start? With our fights? With our sexual problems? With her boyfriends? With her money demands? With the fact that I have to call her for dates? With her contempt for my art? What else you want to know?"

"That you're married. That much I needed to know."

"You can ask me anything you want, I don't hide anything."

But it was things he didn't hide on purpose I was worried about, because I was picking up some strange undertones. First of all there was the odor. I don't know whether Lochs absorbed the smells of the painting supplies he worked with, but I became aware of an odd chemical scent hovering around him, acidic, sulfurous, rotten-eggy with possibly a hint of urine. Then it was as if the smell began to crystallize in images, images of what's going on in his head: black bubbles boiling up from the brain stem polluting my mind with pure anguish—and suddenly I'm wondering whether he's in my head or I'm in his nightmare, whether this is my effect on him, frightening, and I feel guilty.

"Hey, did you see the article on me this morning in the *Times*?"

"I haven't had time to read the *Times* today, why don't you tell me about it?"

"If you insist. It pegged me as the shooting star celebrity of the gallery scene."

"Is that the same as the world of art?" I couldn't keep the contempt out of my voice.

"So it's hype," he said, "who knows the difference? Admiration is a curse if you don't get off on it. Unless you get off on pure admiration."

"You don't get off on praise?" I asked.

"Shit, I probably get off on it too much. It excites me more than money."

"Well then, I hope you get enough of it."

"You never get enough. Prestige. Power. Praise. I don't even know what it's all for. I do what I do. I'm not even sure what they like about it. It never makes any sense to me, what they like. One day I'm an ex-jailbird doodling to keep himself busy, the next day I'm a famous 'outsider artist,' whatever that means. Who the fuck understands it? But why ask questions, I just hope it keeps up. How about going out to lunch, I know a bar around here."

"No thanks, I already had lunch."

"Gee, you eat early. It's only 11:30," he said.

"No, it must be after two o'clock."

"Your watch must be fast, look at your clock there."

He was right, but I had met Notley at noon, how was it possible? I checked my watch, it said 11:30. Did I lose a day?

I felt a fit of nothingness coming on, vertigo, faintness. "What's wrong, you're turning pale," he asked, but she can't talk, she feels sea sick, she spirals back to the Incident, time stopping for three hours, she's going to throw up she manages to think Kenny Clarke then she goes blank she's on the floor she sees Lochs shaking her.

Slowly, I woke up, Lochs bending over me looking agitated. "How long was I out," I asked.

"Just a second," he said. "Are you okay?"

"It's not serious, it happens to me now and then," I assured him.

"You ought to see a doctor. What does it feel like?"

"It feels like . . . losing my soul," I found myself saying.

"Is that all?" He laughed. "I lost mine a long time ago."

"It's not a joke," I said. "How do you get through the day?'

"My devils tell me what to do."

"You don't seriously believe in devils. Come on."

"Damn right. I was brought up religious, and if you believe in God you believe in devils."

"What religion?"

"My foster father was Catholic, but my foster mother was Jewish, and they were both very religious. I kept changing back and forth, because they got divorced, then my foster mother remarried a devout Baptist, so it depended on who I was living with. I was christened, baptized, circumcised, confirmed, bar mitzvahed, and took my first communion."

"And what did you get out of all that?" I asked.

"I forget," he answered, "it's one of the things I choose to forget."

"What else do you choose to forget?"

"I like to forget what I forget. Prison is something I can't forget, but at least I can forget certain incidents."

"Why can't you forget the whole thing?" I asked him.

"I learned too much. Prison was my college education. I got out at 22, and now even at my age I still think the most important thing in life is to be completely free. Nothing prevents me doing what I want. When they let me. But I myself never know when that will be until they tell me. The important thing is to keep them locked in my head, otherwise there's trouble."

At that moment there was a rustling sound, like a huge sail unfolding, floppy, flappy, as if I had heard an invisible bird taking off through the window, which was closed, and as the bird dissolved into light and air, I imagined I got a glimpse of it:

When I looked at Lochs I saw that his eyes were glazed, his body rigid and erect. "I have to go now," he said in a strange slow voice, and he walked out of my apartment like a zombie.

I hadn't figured out much about the theft so far. But it was clear that I had to figure out Fynch's daughter, Jocylyn. I called Achs to find out how to reach her.

Achs gave me her private number. But warned me that Jocylyn would have to feel there was something to be gained by talking to me, otherwise, forget it.

Well, I figured I could offer Jocylyn information, information about the Museum and the theft. If she were hoping to divert money from the Museum back to the family, that is, to herself, any scandal about the Museum would be helpful. I, on the other hand, might learn something about her designs on the Museum.

I got a machine, but when I identified myself, she picked up the phone.

"I've heard so much about you, Austyn," she cooed. "Most of it negative," this in a deeper voice, almost a baritone.
"You must have been talking to our friend, Mr. Pyhl."
"Among others. You're not well loved in the gallery world, you know. What exactly is going on over there at the Museum?"
"We should talk," I said.
"What do you think we're doing now?"
"I mean really talk," I insisted.
"Get over here then. I have an hour."

Though I knew I'd never seen her before, Jocylyn looked naggingly familiar. I was shown into what was obviously an office at home, sparsely furnished, bare white walls, illuminated by a small, high window, all of which made me feel as if I were in a prison cell. Suddenly, it struck me why Jocylyn looked familiar.

The wide eyes, the straight nose, the classic lips and firm jaw, she looked like the Statue of Liberty. She was blond and buxom, queenly, and wore a toga-like dress and a lot of expensive jewelry. And, like the Statue, she was spikey.

"I want to tell you," I began, "that something important has been stolen from the Museum."

"I know all about that," she snapped. "I probably know more about it than you do."

"What do you mean?" Against her deeper voice my own sounded almost timid.

"I mean that what was stolen is a forgery," Jocylyn declared.

"How can that be, when . . ."

"You mean, when what we're talking about is strictly ephemeral. It's because the concept of it is strictly phony. As is the whole crazy idea of a museum of ephemera. And I have proof."

"What do you mean, proof?"

"Let me just say that we've been watching your friend Notley, and at a certain point, if necessary, we're prepared to expose financial collusion between him and the Museum. Including the six-figure payment for, basically, nothing. Now, what can you tell me to ward off that eventuality?"

"This is blackmail, but it's blackmail over nothing, as far as I can see. Suppose I tell you that what Notley sold the Museum was invisible. As music is invisible."

"I'd say it's nonsense. While a hundred thousand dollars has a certain blunt truth about it."

"Is money the arbiter of truth?"

"I'd say, basically, yes. Money is the measure of everything, yes. Bluntly. Isn't that art's dirty little secret?"

"Not mine."

"What is yours? Why don't you let me guess? The measure of everything for you is cultural prestige, the best that is thought or written, or painted, or composed, or e-mailed, or faxed. And who decides what's best? Those who can pay for it, finally. Everything comes to market, I think Robert Frost said that."

"Which brings us to back your father's museum."

"Father Time. That's what I call him."

– 35 –

"Do you dislike your father?"

"Dislike? It doesn't apply. He's the condition for my existence."

"Like time."

"Time, in any event, to get to the point. The point is, unless he retires Achs and turns the Museum over to Pyhl and myself, we go public to the tune of six figures."

I found, when I got home, that I was inordinately upset by my conversation with Jocylyn. So I tried an exercise Notley had taught me called "betterness." I tried to concentrate on what I would have preferred Jocylyn to be like and what I would have liked to happen in our conversation.

And I discovered something interesting. I discovered that I wouldn't have liked anything to be different, neither Jocylyn nor what she said. Because I felt something was being played out and she was part of the play.

Instead I felt the need to understand Jocylyn more deeply. I wanted to see where her point of view was coming from. And I wanted to take another look at the Statue of Liberty.

An e-mail from old friend Hymi, his characteristic semi-coherent one-liners:

revelation of the day, I'd been going through some old letters between my parents, you know they're both dead long since

turns out my parents?

may not have been my parents, probably were not

it seems there was some kind of mix-up in the maternity ward that they only found out about when I was twenty-one

by which time they figured it was too late to tell me.

besides, it wasn't certain, what could they do?

but who am I?

I called up Notley and met him at a place in the neighborhood. I wanted to ask him about "The Concept"—I knew it was inaudible, at least to me. Was it, then, in any sense visible?

"It's both inaudible and invisible," he answered. "To those who can neither hear nor see it. And it's also unintelligible."

"To those who can't understand it, no doubt. What about the money?"

"What money?" he asked.

"Didn't they pay you? The Museum?"

"They paid me in-kind," he answered. "In the same coin."

"And what kind of coin is that?"

"Credit. Liquid assets. Soft currency. Legal tender. Wampum. Promissory notes. Payable on time, in time, some time."

"Could you be more specific?"

"No."

We were having drinks in a cocktail lounge in the World Financial Center, across from the World Trade Center and Wall Street. The bar was in a telescoping glass structure ten stories high through which you could see the towers of the World Trade Center leaning precariously over you, and on the opposite side through a plate glass window, the Hudson and the Statue of Liberty. I was thinking of Jocylyn Fynch.

"Did you know," I asked, "that the same sculptor who did Mount Rushmore also repaired the diadem of the Statue of Liberty? The two biggest objects of idol worship in America."

"So? What have you got against idol worship?" he asked in his whispery voice. "Idols freeze our values and give them stability. They bridge the gap between the invisible and the visible. They do what music does for silence. They express the inexpressible. They objectify values so they can be traded in the open market. Miss Liberty is a libertarian."

"Funny, I didn't expect you to say that."

"It's not only the three little pigs that come to market," he said.

"That's just like something Jocylyn said."

"Jocylyn's got a head on her shoulders."

We finished our drinks and walked out of the lounge through the building with its massive overbearing black pillars, "like Karnak," Notley remarked, "the crush of power." He called the whole complex along the river, the World Financial Center, Battery Park City, "Luxor on the Hudson."

"With the World Financial Center, the World Trade Center and Wall Street, it really is the center of some universe. Not mine."

"We seem to be heading toward your place," I observed.

"I wanted to give you another try at listening to 'The Concept.' You accept?"

Of course I did. Urgently. Since speaking to Jocylyn there was a real issue about whether there was something tangible there that you could put a cash value on.

– 38 –

So I found myself in his white room again, sitting on his cot. He did something complicated on his computer. Then he came and sat down on the cot next to me.

"This time let me suggest something. The key is giving in to it. You have to become absolutely passive before you can hear it, otherwise the noise of your ego gets in the way. You have to let yourself be overcome, submit to the experience, relinquish your will. Obey the prompting of your libido."

"What's libido got to do with it?" I inquired.

"Because we're dealing with a creative work and Eros is the creative force. And the destructive force too. No creation without cremation."

"It sounds risky."

"It is risky. You have to be willing to take the risk. That's part of 'The Concept.' Are you ready?"

"Can I trust you?"

"No. That's part of the risk. Take off your jacket."

I was dressed properly for once, a tweed jacket and skirt, pearls, and a cashmere sweater. Though I wasn't wearing a bra and the sweater was quite tight. I did as he said.

"You have to give in to the experience," he added.

"Experience? I thought I was supposed to hear it."

"Ideally, you'll not only hear it, you'll see it and feel it and maybe even taste it. Now, lie back on the bed and relax." He disappeared into the bathroom for a few minutes, coming back with a glass of water and something cupped in his palm.

"What's this?"

"Pills. Don't ask questions, just take them."

And I took them, though I was a little frightened frankly. But I figured that was part of it, like the thrill of the roller coaster. Pretty soon I began to feel a little sleepy, but it was a delicious sleepiness, very sensual.

"How do you feel?" he asked.
"I wish somebody would pet me, like a cat."
"Be a good girl, take your skirt off for me."

I groaned in protest, but I complied. I squirmed my skirt up on the bed, and he lifted my sweater over my breasts. I threw my arms back over my head, and whether my posture turned him on, or what, he began caressing my thighs in the space left between my stockings and panties.

"What are you hearing?" he asked.
"I'm not hearing anything," I answered, "but keep doing that."
He kept doing it, but soon I was eager for him to do it between my legs. And he wouldn't. So I asked him directly, explicitly.
"No," he answered.
"Why not?"
"Just no."
I was beginning to get scary reverberations of the Incident. "You want me to beg?"
"You can try," he said. "What are you hearing?"
"I'm not hearing anything, damn it."

Then something cracks in her, she feels a sickening, sensuous flowing sensation in her lower belly, she doesn't exactly faint, swoons would be more like it, and she does hear something, something like a rich, timeless, indefinite chord.

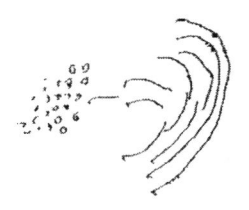

"What are you hearing?"
"It sounds like—Richard Wagner. But atonal."
"That's all?"
"What else should I be hearing?"
"Some of it may be beyond your range, like a dog whistle beyond the range of normal perception. Go with what you can hear," he instructed, "and that may lead to further sensation."

The sensation it seemed to be leading to was intensification of the feeling I had before, with waves of eroticism rippling through my body, amplifying as the mysterious chord slowly magnified in volume. I was in some sensually agonized place that was not satisfying either erotically or spiritually. If I was supposed to divert the energy being generated to spiritual ends it was not diverting, in fact I felt there was a kind of torture involved.

"You're getting off on this, aren't you?" I asked.
"I suppose if there were no gratification involved, honestly, I wouldn't be doing it. But that doesn't invalidate what I'm trying to do for you."
"I think I'd get more enlightened if you hit me on the head. I once had a very unpleasant experience like this that I'd rather not remember."
"Would you like to tell me about it?"
"No, I can't talk about it. I can't even think about it."

"Well unfortunately, 'The Concept' is precisely about what you can't think about. So that more or less ends our session."

"I didn't know it was a session," I said, sitting up and pulling my clothing back down.

"Till next time?" he asked.

The next day I had a meeting with Achs, and I tried to convince her of a connection between the theft and Notley, but she was not impressed by the evidence. Instead, she cautioned me about his reputation for attracting press, positive or negative. She warned me that he was known in the art world for his marketing ability.

"Behind that ascetic pose there's a very sharp customer. Publicity and self-promotion are his games," she warned.

"That's odd, because I find him rather benign and paternalistic."

"If you find him paternal, it may be that you need a father."

I was a little offended by this. "First of all, I was brought up by step parents, and had more than enough of my stepfather to last a lifetime. My real father was supposed to be a drunk. Before he disappeared. I never met him."

"I am sorry," said Achs, "I didn't mean to be personal. How about your mother? As long as we're on the subject."

"I never knew anything about my mother," I told her. "Maybe it's just as well."

"No telling," said Achs. "Meantime, I have some advice for you, more than advice, a request. It's time to speak to Pyhl, because whatever Notley's involvement, if there's money involved, Pyhl's involved. It's high time to confront him and see what he knows."

Pyhl agreed to see me that same afternoon. He lived in a loft in Tribeca whose entrance and elevator looked like those of an old industrial building. But his loft was dazzling, it was rich, it dripped wealth.

The space was huge, a floor through, with a view of the Hudson. One side of it was divided into rooms, the other side, unencumbered by walls, served as a gallery for an impressive collection of contemporary painting, sculpture, installations and conceptual work. He gave me a guided tour of its contents, becoming in turn eloquent, persuasive, and contagiously enthusiastic, so that I was absurdly tempted to buy something, even though I couldn't afford anything and as far as I knew nothing was for sale.

I had expected him to be rather hostile, but on the contrary, he was cordial, even warm, even seductive. He sat me down and offered me tea, he offered me pastries. This was a new, genteel, upper crust Pyhl revealing himself, a self more appropriate for art collectors, dealers, and museum executives rather than employees. Even before we began talking, he invited me to lunch at the Four Seasons some time, as if we weren't actually there in his loft, in two easy chairs, looking at one other yet, as if my real presence had to be framed by lux for my true identity to manifest itself.

I declined, and I was flattered, actually, despite the fact that I knew it was cheap to set my value by what I cost. And there was something else. I was lulled by the feeling that I was in an ambiance in which I could relax luxuriously, in which somehow everything would be taken care of, in sure hands in which I wouldn't need to make any effort or troubling decisions. At the same time I realized that I was being narcotized by the aura of power.

On top of which, he was very complimentary, saying that he was hearing good things about me from Achs, and telling me how well

I was looking, while at the same time taking every discreet opportunity to touch me, as if to establish complicity. Under the circumstances, it was very difficult to begin the subtle cross-examination that my mission required. I finally broached the subject of the theft.

"Of course, I know it's your job," he said, "but still it might be better if you didn't obsess about the theft. First of all, as you're well aware, this does not fit the MO of ordinary art thieves. The theft is metaphorical."

"Metaphorical for what?"

"You understand, I don't know anything about it. I believe Notley is the chief suspect. But what's been stolen is not art so much as value. Or to put it another way, art is value, purely agreed-upon value, and nothing else. You don't even need a particular object. And how do we measure value? Basically in terms of money, power and sex, and in reality they're indivisible. Money is power, and the ultimate power is sexual control over another person."

"How do you figure that?" I found his attitude repulsive. And I could feel myself starting to get horny.

"Think about it. There's nothing so intimate, so total, as forcing someone to submit of their own free will. What is that worth in terms of money?—well, everyone has a price, and everything has a price, and when you make someone pay your price for a piece of art, it's also an act of sexual conquest."

"What is this," I blurted, "the fascist theory of art?" I was speaking louder than I should have been, but I was unnerved by his ideas because, though outrageous, they had a speck of truth.

"On the contrary, it's very democratic. Money is. Anyone can exercise power with it. It breaks down rigidities of class, of manners, of opportunities. What would your price be, for example? What would it take to break your rigidity? Would it be the solution to the riddle of the theft?"

"Try me," I said. And as she says it she begins to get scary echoes of the Incident, fragments, phrases.

Pyhl gets up and puts his arm under hers, lifting her out of her chair. He's quite strong. He leads her over to a couch and sits her down, sitting down next to her and putting his arm around her shoulder.

"Suppose I told you," he says, "you're the hapless dupe in what is essentially a family quarrel? Suppose I told you that there never was a theft? Because there was never anything to steal?" he continues, putting his hand on her thigh, and she knows she should get out of there but she can't do it because of what's at stake and because as soon as he touches her there she goes into a sort of hypnotic state like a rabbit in face of a predatory snake.

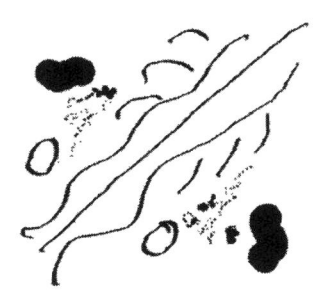

And she sees herself being pulled gently toward him, but she knows this is not really her because she wouldn't allow it, until her head rests in his lap, while at the same time she knows this is a hallucination because she doesn't submit to this kind of treatment, because she doesn't do things like this, and therefore it's not her doing them. Blackout.

The next thing she remembered Pyhl was offering her a snifter of cognac.

"Let's talk a bit about the Museum."

Austyn nodded yes.

"You know this business about a theft is just a wild goose chase."

Austyn nodded yes.

"And you know the premise of the Museum, the idea of art without artifact, or even without the language to talk about it, is nonsense."

"You think I should quit?" Austyn asked.

"Definitely not. I think you should exercise your influence on Achs and Fynch and get them to give up on their odd ideas."

"And give up on the Museum?"

"I wouldn't want you to do anything against your better judgment," he said. "What's 'The Concept?'" He brought it up out of nowhere, the flash of a concealed blade.

"I don't know."

"Is it worth money?"

"I don't know."

"If it were worth money how much would it be worth?"

"I've heard six figures but . . ."

"High or low six?"

"I didn't hear anything . . ."

"I want you to find out for me. You can go now, but keep an ear open."

She got up, a little wobbly. "Thanks," she said vaguely.

He patted her behind, "Don't mention it. Please. Especially to Achs."

Walking away from Pyhl's building, I wondered how Fynch allowed a man so set against his interests such an influential position with regard to himself and the Museum. Then I wondered how he got my number so precisely, what kind of power did this man have?

— 46 —

I knew enough about Pyhl to know that he was a moral disaster and a spiritual black hole. But I had the intuition that, like a black hole, he sucked things in to his aggressive darkness only to release them transmuted into some other dimension. I still have enough of a religious sensibility to feel that, somehow, in whatever convoluted way, things get better and salvation is possible.

I thought of asking Notley about Pyhl. Or Lochs. He seemed to know Pyhl better. And then I thought, why not ask them both, and actually why not both together? I thought it might be interesting to see what chemistry developed between them, and what ideas they came up with about the situation at the Museum, though I have to admit that getting them both together with me seemed to be an impulse from my dark side.

Speaking of my dark side, I heard from Hymi when I got home, by e-mail of course, in which he tended to communicate in a series of rambling one-liners:

maybe you need a stitch in time like I had, that followed my adoption of The Boy

through the surrogate program of the so-called Improvement Society

matching boys who need fathers with men who need sons

imagine a seven foot hulk, sullen, with a temper, chronically down on his dad

forbidden to communicate by phone, since that always led to vicious arguments, limited to e-mail yesterday he wrote:

>It's all your fault
>don't ask me what
>it's whatever you did
>and costs whatever you got
>so don't complain
>—and call me a pain
>cause I'm the one who's got the issues
>you shed the tears and bring the tissues
>you suck so much
>I'm feeling bad
>I still have to call you
>Dad

how's that for a morning eye opener? Let me hear from you.

I hit reply and wrote: Your Son, The Boy, is a projection of an unstable thermonuclear family. You're in trouble. But I have to admit to you I'm a mess too, fits of vertigo, sleeping around, on pills, living on credit cards, losing faith —Austyn.

I called Notley and asked him to arrange to see me with Lochs to talk about museum matters. A short time later I got a furious call from Lochs who opened the conversation without even a hello.

"You're screwing Notley!"
"So?"
"At the same time as me?"
"I don't belong to anyone."
"I love you."
"So what?" Nevertheless, this was interesting news.
"What do you mean, so what? You want me to think of you as a whore?"

"Think of me as a whore then, if that pleases you."
"It doesn't please me."
"It must, since there's no other reason for it."

Soon I got a call from Notley. They were coming over. Together. Now.

My apartment is not very big, a studio with alcove, basically a bed, a desk, two chairs and a kitchenette. So when they got there and Notley announced they had decided to work it out among us on a physical level, my first thought was like, where? And my second was, how?

My second question was immediately answered as Notley quickly took his shirt off and Lochs unzipped his pants. She panics, heads for the door, Lochs grabs her, pants down around his ankles, tries to unzip the front of her jump suit, she goes limp, loses balance, falls.

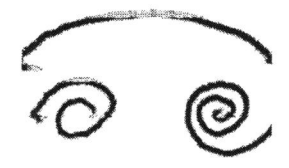

Comes to in Jimmy Loch's arms.

"Hold on," said Notley, "let me explain," me struggling again to get out the door.
"Get dressed, both of you," I screamed, the Incident reverberating. "You're crazy."
"We were just...," began Notley.
"Completing the triangle," continued Lochs.
"That's the solution to our little problem," said Notley.
"That we all know we have," added Lochs.

— 49 —

"And work it out with our bodies," said Notley.

"Not up in our heads," concluded Lochs.

"You could have let me in on it," I said.

"We thought you'd understand," said Notley.

"You scared me witless," I said as they started to get dressed. "It's no way for sixty-year-olds to behave."

"It's no way for fifty-year-olds to react," said Notley. "I need my dose of Prozac."

"I guess I shouldn't have taken my Viagra," said Lochs.

"I need to take a Ritalin," I said, "I'm so edgy. It must be that dash of testosterone they're putting in the estrogen cocktail."

"Chemicals aside," said Notley, "are we still coupling, or are we triangulating? Because coupling separately isn't going to work. It's a mathematical problem that can be solved elegantly only through geometry."

"What do you have to say about it, Austyn?" asked Lochs.

"I was wondering when you'd start dividing me up and asking for pieces of me. First of all, as far as I'm concerned, we don't have any couples here. Aside from a couple of old men with loose screws and wobbly nuts. So maybe what you need to do is pair off together and leave me in peace. And in one piece."

"I think I see where you're coming from," said Notley. "How about it, Lochs?" he asked, putting a hand on his shoulder. Lochs shook it off.

"Keep your hands to yourself or I'll let you have it."

"You two shouldn't be rivals," I said. "The situation you're in at the Museum, as contributing artists, you have interests in common. Above all, against Pyhl trying to sabotage the Museum."

"Does Fynch realize what Pyhl is up to?" asked Notley.

"I'm sure he does," I said, "Fynch is a very smart man."

"And at his age, I guess he's seen it all before," said Lochs.

"Which means he must have something in his misty mind," I said.

"Achs says what he has most in his mind is you, you seem to be some sort of key for him, god knows why," said Lochs. He flipped out a small camera, "Hold that," he said and snapped my picture.

"What was that for?"

"It's for Fynch, I want to hear what he says when I show him his key informant."

"Not with my hair messed and my jump suit half unzipped you won't," I reached for my zipper but Lochs beat me to it, grabbed and pulled it all the way down to my crotch, baring my body and snapping his shots when Notley intervened, knocking away Lochs's now encircling arms. The two started pummeling one another, but it was all pretty feeble and soon they stopped, breathing hard, while I zipped up.

"Sorry," said Lochs, panting, "I lost control."

"Will you guys just get out. And lighten up already," I said.

"What do you mean?" asked Notley.

"By that?" asked Lochs.

"American men. Women are blank books to be opened up and written in."

"As opposed to what?" asked Notley. "Ethiopian men?"

"But the writing is in code," said Lochs, "and it's a code that even we don't understand. It's more like the code writes us."

"Sounds like something Fynch might say," Notley commented. "I once asked him about his taste for the cryptic. What's the key, I asked."

"And . . .?" I asked.

"He said, 'Why.'"

"Is that a question or an answer?" I asked.

"Maybe it's both," said Notley.

"Enough of this shit chat," said Lochs to me, "what's your angle? I mean which leg of our triangle do you prefer?"

"Suppose I prefer both?"

Lochs and Notley looked at one another for a long moment, taking this in, like revelation. Lochs began stroking my hand, and Notley caressed my cheek gently, then things began to move more quickly, Lochs unzipping my jump suit again, each taking a breast in his hand, and it was amazing how different they felt, Notley weighing it in his hand, Lochs squeezing the nipple roughly. Then Notley pulled my pants down carefully, slowly, and slowly began spreading my thighs, and Lochs put his hand on my vulva and squeezed, sending waves of pleasure through my legs and lower body.

I don't know how long this lasted, but the next thing I knew, Notley was lifting my buttocks and sort of offering me to Lochs, who had his pants down again. I was so excited by now it didn't take long to spasm, a breaking wave, and then I heard him grunt and could feel him jerking around inside me.

When I finally opened my eyes I found Notley with his penis in Jimmy's mouth. I got up and left them there.

The next day Hymi appeared at my door. I almost didn't recognize him, now nearly bald, bearded, gray, wearing spectacles, he said he'd been abroad and didn't want to talk about it, he said he considered me family. He invited me for a walk.

The city at night. I remember walks through it with Hymi when we were first lovers. His favorite area was down near where Notley lived, Battery Park, Wall Street, the World Trade Center.

It was at night, he said, when the buildings and streets assumed their real identity, beyond their pragmatic use during the day. They became titanic sculptures as well as monuments to ghostly and insignificant utilitarian abstractions. The narrow, irregular, alleylike streets were a kind of Cyclopean hieroglyphics, he said, that was beyond our understanding but whose meaning made itself felt perhaps more powerfully for that.

Just, he said, as the pattern of lighted windows in the double grid of the World Trade Center towers were messages in a code we could not comprehend. And occasionally, also, the wind that ripped through the steel and concrete canyons made of the buildings musical instruments howling mournful and ferocious songs whose meanings we could grasp at but never verbalize. All this proved, Hymi liked to say, that we live in a meaningful world packed with significance, though we don't know of what.

For example, he wanted us to marry, but he wanted us to keep our marriage secret, so as not to compromise our other sexual activities, especially mine. Because he had the idea that women are biologically meant to have multiple partners providing multiple orgasms to satisfy them, whereas men are one shot creatures destined for monogamy.

He was very insistent about this, said it was proof he loved me, so I developed the habit of inventing lovers and telling him about them to turn him on, which worked just fine. Until one night he discovered I was actually alone in the motel, enjoying some peace and quiet, where I was supposed to be entertaining my lover, and he accused me of betrayal. One time when I actually did have a lover he, the lover, came to the house unexpectedly and caught me in bed with my supposed husband whereupon he, the lover, got furious.

Clearly this wasn't working out and eventually I found it impossible to live with Hymi and his ideas. He himself, he said, was acutely aware of how difficult he was and said it was that he was orphaned as a baby and brought up in foster homes. He said he was substituting for the father he never had by having a child, The Boy.

"I was told my parents deserted me. All I know about my family is that I have an uncle who I never knew," he said. "I suppose he is out there somewhere."

This was oddly similar to Lochs's experience, who mostly grew up in institutions and was dimly aware of phantom siblings. But the similarity was no surprise, since now often he seemed to passively absorb and store others' experiences like a sponge and repeat them as his own, so that sometimes I wondered whether he had any of his own.

Lochs's and Notley's interest in one another, however, did not prevent the two of them from squabbling over me. Like non-identical twins, they always wanted the same things but at different times, or in different order, or at different ends, or at the same time, which was usually impossible. Each was always trying to see me alone, and when one succeeded in doing so the other was terminally jealous and insisted on debriefing me in the most intimate detail.

It almost seemed that the one thing they had emphatically in common was the Y chromosome. Both had a boring male need to dominate the Situation. Jimmy Lochs did it through aggression, Notley by a stubborn passiveness.

Between Jimmy Lochs's uncontrollable energy and Notley's contained passivity somewhere there was a whole person. Just as, between Hymi and The Boy, there was a wholeness, a crazed inverted familial affection, demonstrated in the latest e-mail from Hymi.

Austyn, The Boy is waxing almost warm in his last, here forwarded:

> as a member of this family
> I'm really an anomaly
> I've only been imported
> I should be well supported
> but I'm not
> I'm treated like a snot
> praise is all I get
> you bet
> well you can shovel it
> or shove it
>
> cause I'm above it
> don't tell me what to do or how to do it
> I'll do it my way not your way or screw it
> or screw it
> or screw it
> so if you want me acting like honey
> give me your money
> your money
> money
> money

The next day I got a call from Achs, early, asking me to come in to the Museum right away. There had been an important development in the case. The insurance company for the Museum, I learned on arriving at her office, had received a ransom note for a piece missing from the Museum collection, but they didn't know what it was. They wanted to know what it was and what value was to be placed on it.

"Who put them onto this?" I asked.
"I heavily suspect Pyhl," answered Achs. "Any suggestions?"
"Why don't we tell them?"
"Good, but tell them what? That we don't know what it is?"
"That we do," I answered. "Within limits."
"Go on."
"We know that it's ephemeral, not material but spiritual, that it keeps changing so that it's hard to maintain contact with it, and that it's the property of everyone and can't be owned by anyone. Not quite a concept, though it can be put that way, it's more an example of an impulse. As to it's worth—priceless."

"I see, it's intellectual property, in other words. Can you insure an impulse?"

"Why not?" I asked. "Ideas are worth money in Hollywood. If the movies can sell ideas, we can claim an impulse. And I'm convinced now that what's missing from the Museum is the impulse it started with."

"Which was Fynch's impulse to dematerialize the concept of art. And everything else. Pare everything down to its concept, and then get rid of the concept."

"You knew Fynch quite well, didn't you, when he was developing his ideas for the Museum?"

"I've known Fynch quite well forever."
"Forever?"
"Yes, we've been quite close for, it seems, ever."

"Since you know him so well, may I ask you something? Why, if he knows, as he must, that Pyhl is trying to sabotage the Museum and all it represents, why does he allow him so much influence in it?"

"I can only tell you that Fynch is very fond of Pyhl. He doesn't trust him, but he is fond of him."

"Why?"

"I don't know, but Fynch wants you to call him."

I called and asked him what to do, but he said do nothing. He said he would be glad to pay a ransom if there were anything tangible involved, but he said that what was missing could not be bought or sold or even possessed, so the ransom request was somebody's bluff or probe. The best thing to do, he said, was to ignore it.

"Whoever is involved in this fiasco is suffering from a hallucination," he said. "As an art thief he is seeing something that's not there. Art is something that exists in people's heads, nowhere else. People who believe otherwise will be sucked into a spiritual vortex."

I could see that Fynch was in his cryptic mode. "You mean, no two people see the same work?"

"What color are my eyes?"

"As I remember? Green."

"Gray," said Fynch. "If you see what I mean."

"I'm not sure, I'll have to think about this."

"Do."

In the restaurant, Jimmy Lochs ordered pie a la mode, followed by bacon and eggs.

"Why do you order dessert first?" I asked him.

"Because I like it best."

"But then followed by breakfast?"

"Because I haven't had breakfast yet. Does it bother you?"

"No, no."

"Because if it does, fuck you. What am I doing wrong?"

"Well, you could improve your table manners. You tend to slurp your food like an animal."

"I'm not talking about that. I'm talking about selling art. What I do isn't art. Why is it selling?"

"Who gets to say what art is?" I asked.

"As far as I can see, it's rich people. And if not rich people then their pimp intellectuals."

"Do I hear paranoia?"

"Come on, come on. Let's go, my car's across the street."

"Where do you want to go?"

"Fynch wants to see me."

"Why?"

"Don't know."

He had a huge old Cadillac, tail fins, eight cylinders he said, but awful condition, bumpers missing, windows cracked, paint shot, body rusting out. A real old tank, but powerful, you could feel it when he accelerated.

"Should we pick up Notley? We could have a party," asked Jimmy Lochs.

"No, no party today."

"You see him much?"

"Not without you. I'm what you two have in common."

"But you see Pyhl alone, don't you?"

"None of your business."

"I can see your attraction to Notley, at least he's alive. And I manage to stay alive, even if it's going to kill me some day. But Pyhl, he's like a dildo compared to a prick."

"There are advantages to dildos."

"Yeah, but it's dead matter. And the ball game is all about staying alive. You know? Inside."

"Well, suppose it's the drive of that dead matter that makes me feel alive, you know, inside?"

"I can understand why dead matter needs to feed on life, but why you need Pyhl to make you feel alive is beyond me."

"Because death is the most powerful force around," I said. "Those who are willing to use it, to turn it to account, have something like the power of a magnet to organize iron filings. And I'm attracted to that magnet. It's death as a creative force."

"When death starts looking attractive, watch out. It's a vortex that pulls everything into it," said Jimmy Lochs.

At the Fynch mansion, a man showed us into Fynch's study. Fynch was sitting in a high architect's chair in the middle of a darkened room, the floor littered with books, staring into space. He began talking as soon as we walked in.

"You," pointing at Jimmy Lochs, "you gave the photos to Pyhl, proving that the power of your needy ego outstrips your rusty intellect. Show her the photos. Or I will."

"Why should I," said Jimmy Lochs.

"To show her their power is not in the image but in the impulse behind it."

"Well," said Jimmy Lochs, fumbling his pockets and coming out with several photo prints. "Shit," he mumbled, handing them to me, "I was going to show them to you anyway."

At first I was shocked and disgusted. Clandestine shots of me as erotic apex of our triangle. But then quickly I felt myself getting turned on, and it wasn't the images in all their captured detail, it was the awareness that someone recorded the images, saw me doing these things, saw them and recorded them, that anyone could see them. The erotic exposure, the obsessive idea of it, it was a spectral kind of love.

"This is an assertion of power, but it's also a kind of homage, of worship, isn't it?" demanded Fynch. "At best? Coming out of something like, some crude form of, the religious impulse. The worship of Venus."

"Are you a religious man?" asked Jimmy Lochs.

"My people were religious in the old country, but they lost it and everything spiritual raising hogs in LaFange, Minnesota. It took me a lifetime to crawl out of that mud."

"How did you do it?"

"At first selling watches to the Army in World War I. Fynch and Lynch, Inc. Keeping time, you might say. Now I want to let it go. I finally liquidated my interest by selling the company to Lynch, who's currently vending stock in it, anal shares of death in my opinion. But the paradox is that the key to temporary art is preservation against time."

"Is that why someone is forging permanent versions of my fluxiest works?" asked Jimmy Lochs.

"Your disappearables? We're as eager as you to find the forger. The Museum has no interest in permanent versions, the more so since we know all there is to know about preserving invisible art."

"How do you do it?" I asked.

"It's all in the head," answered Fynch cryptically. "In the mind and the soul, that's where things are kept alive."

"So now we have two problems at the Museum, theft and forgery. Is this unusual?" I asked.

"No more than at any other museum. It's just that at our museum we see such phenomena for what they are—a contradiction in terms. What hangs on the wall, no matter how striking, is just the score. The music is in your head and live. The material artifact is dead matter and subject to degradation, you have to be aware that's part of it. That's the message of the Temporary Museum."

"Preservation through degradation? And how does that keep the music alive?" I asked.

"With individual acts of attention. Love. Homage. Worship." Fynch walked over to a shelf and took down a large tortoise shell. "It's all in here," he said.

"But there's nothing in there," observed Jimmy Lochs.

"Exactly," said Fynch.

About a week later, Notley came over to my apartment with an example of the Street Music series he was working on, and he sang what he called an aria for me, in what I can only describe as a modified howl.

"That's nice. That's very nice," I told him, "but I'm not a musician. How am I supposed to read this?"

"This is a song, the words matter less. And more, in a way. It's like 'The Concept,' which is like responding to an empty page, except here it's like responding to an impulse with your own immediate impulse."

"It makes me feel creepy."

"Then that's how you respond. Impulse before concept. You conceptualize it later, if at all. Here's another one." And he sang as if in lament.

Silence. Which he did nothing to break. For some minutes.

"Excuse me, but what's the story here?" I asked.

"The story is my story," said Notley. "I used to work for a man called Lynch. He was a businessman with fingers in many pies, but basically his line was time. Time pieces, time clocks, timers, good times, bad times, you name it, even time out. For a while he was partners with Fynch. Well, Lynch insisted on precision as you can imagine, precision in time, in expression, in meaning. For a while I did very well with Lynch, but then I discovered that all this precision was killing me. Emotionally. It was too fussy. It left no room for the imagination to roam, to react, to reach out and expand. Soon my thinking started getting fuzzy, misty, even cryptic. Lynch got down on me of course. Instead of firing me he fought me, and as my boss he had a stranglehold on me. But I was stubborn and it became a battle of wills. He must have had something important at stake to try and break me like that. He became abusive in the office, made me the laughing stock, an example. I felt as if he were choking me. And my response was to become vaguer, foggier, more ambiguous. Finally I stopped responding altogether. When he asked me to do something, I simply answered, 'Not.' That sent him up the wall and he finally fired me. But it was traumatic, and I knew then and there that my mission in life was going to be one of de-definition, and since then there hasn't been a fixed idea I came across I didn't try to break, a straight line I didn't turn into a spiral, a stretch of time I didn't waste."

With that, he started humming a strange oriental kind of tune, and soon was up snapping his fingers and twirling his body, whirling faster and faster, till he fell into an armchair and appeared to doze. I shook him by the shoulder and he opened his eyes. They looked blank.

"What was that for?" I asked him.
"To put myself to sleep."
"Why?"
"So I could wake up."

When the Temporary Museum moved into its new building, there was to be a big celebration, but insiders were shepherded around for a preliminary look by a representative of the architectural firm that designed it. The concept for the building was innovative.

The key idea was recycling. There was a primary set of elements, mostly made of plastic and titanium, and they kept changing positions, moved by built-in cranes and elevators that constantly produced new, unpredictable configurations. So, imperceptibly, the building kept changing its shape, and never looked exactly the same way twice. Something like a giant Calder mobile.

That day it resembled a tall ship, it's plastic sails filled with wind, its titanium panels cutting against the sky.

"Don't you find it unsettling?" I remember asking Fynch.

"Life is unsettling," he answered. "And it should be unsettling. But if you set your sails right you can ride with the waves and wind and turn them to advantage."

"So there are lessons in the architecture?"

"At my age there are lessons in everything, if you care to read them."

"My lessons may be different from your lessons," I said.

"No two people have the same experience of anything. Experience is essentially untranslatable, but art is the closest thing we have to a translation. Though evolved intelligences know it's all a collective enterprise requiring the echo effect from one person to another and then among widening spirals of people, creating a common experience and reversing the spiritual vortex. You may add that to the edicts of Fynch," he said with a dry laugh.

"Come again?" said Jimmy Lochs, who had just joined us.

"I'm talking about salvation of lived experience," said Fynch.

"I was taught that Christ took care of that for us," said Lochs.

"Nobody takes care of that for us," said Fynch. "But a lot of people pretend to. Politicians, ad men, media industry minions. Mind pirates, who freeze the flow of fluid event and sell it back to us as reality."

"What makes you so sure of yourself?" asked Jimmy Lochs.

"I look into things. I was born with the why chromosome."

"Well one thing you might look into, according to Achs, is why some of my works have been resold by the Museum at less than cost."

"I believe that's Pyhl's department," said Fynch vaguely. "Ask him."

"I did," answered Jimmy Lochs. "He bought them."

"And I hear that Pyhl wants to sell intellectual rights to 'The Concept,'" said Notley, who had just walked up. "Which belong to me."

"So add fraud to theft and forgery. And all without any material objects changing hands," I observed.

"What we deal in doesn't change hands. It changes minds," said Fynch.

"Whenever it changes," said Notley, "it's worth a good piece of change to Pyhl, it seems."

"Pyhl has his place," said Fynch. "He's one side of things. Acquisitive. Accumulative. And that's just one side of him. We're all fractured personalities."

Somehow, Fynch's persistent defense of Pyhl seemed to diminish Fynch himself. In his spiritual resonance. In his physical presence even.

I went home that day thinking about Fynch's comments on Pyhl— if he was a fractured personality, I had to classify myself as shattered. My academic personality was different from my investigator personality, which was different from my sexual personality, which was different from my social personality, and they all suffered from a lack of affect, underlaid by a common depression.

– 64 –

Anyone, like Pyhl, who perceived this shatter was in a position to make me give myself willingly to an exploitation that, for better or worse, made me feel alive and, in whatever impoverished a way, unified.

I lived downtown near the Hudson, and my apartment, though small, had a corner view including the Statue of Liberty on one side and the World Trade Center on the other. In my worst hours, it was good to be reminded that the icon of freedom in this country was a woman. It reminded me that the other side of fragmentation was the possibility of birthing a fertile acceptance of what we are—in many, one.

And then, for the first time since the Incident, and all the ambivalent feelings that it arouses, she has a glimpse of a ☐, through which:

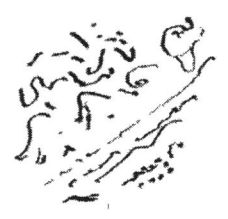

Awakening to a sense of splinters of emotion which, if followed to their source, might yield a tentative whole. That might justify the impulse to probe their irritation in her flesh.

That afternoon I was at the Museum when there happened to be a seance involving Lochs's and Notley's work. A seance was what Achs called a showing of temporary art. She would arrange shows of the art in question as if they were a theater performance that would never be the same twice and soon would not be at all.

The collectors privileged with such a show, unique as it was, would pay large sums. The seance was the one way temporary art participated in art commerce and interacted with the world of art criticism. Favorable notices for the seance would result in prestige for the artist and further high-priced showings.

I slipped into the seance as it was ending and a discussion period was underway. Lochs and Notley weren't there but Achs was, and for some reason Pyhl was also present, presumably as Fynch's representative. Pyhl had the floor and was summing up some comments comparing Notley's work to Lochs's.

"This smacks of a stale Conceptualism. If you will pardon the metaphor, Lochs's work is as diarrhea to Notley's constipation. If these two artists are indeed self-taught, they had best go back to themselves for further instruction. And possible medication. The impulse to exhibit such work can only come from an ill-advised duty to exhibit what the museum has however mistakenly acquired, with the curator as chief exhibitionist. One can only sigh with relief to realize that this is temporary art."

The collectors were filing out with polite but confused thank yous, and soon as they left, Achs confronted Pyhl.

"Explain yourself," she demanded. "What was the reason for attacking Lochs and Notley like that?"

"My reason is that their work is shit and the idea for the Museum is a load of shit. And besides that I enjoy attacking people when appropriate."

"And when is it appropriate?"

"When people ask for it."

The next night I went to Pyhl's loft. He had promised to feed me dinner, but what I didn't know was that he meant it literally. That is, he proposed to tie me to my chair at the dinner table and feed me by fork and spoonful.

I don't know why, but this proposal seemed in some way intriguing. In fact it turned me on. I attributed these feelings to my at times zombielike passivity.

And in fact, I found I liked being fed. I found it induced a pleasant dreamy state. Pyhl would feed me a forkful of food, inserting it carefully into my mouth, patting my cheek as I chewed then helping himself, all the while murmuring to me. And the gist of his talk was that now I was going to be his mistress. Far from quitting my job at the Museum as he'd once advised me to do, I could keep the job and report secretly to him.

"And that way," he said, "nothing could come between us, not even your job."

"But doesn't that cross the line? Into the area of dirty tricks?"

"What's wrong with dirt? What would flowers and trees do without it? Maybe it's time to get your hands dirty, really dirty. Don't forget, shit is used as fertilizer."

"Maybe I'm not that kind of girl. Besides, what would you know about fertilizer?"

"What would I know about fertilizer? Let me tell you, I know. You might say I grew up in shit. On a pig farm in LaFange, Minnesota. So I never had illusions about being that kind of boy."

"Isn't that where Fynch's family comes from?"

"Yes, but I never knew them. I grew up in an orphanage, working on its farm. I never knew my parents. I met Fynch in New York and he took a liking to me because we grew out of the same filth, and I think he admired the way I clawed myself out of it. I was working on Wall Street at the time and I sold him some dubious junk bonds. He never called me on it, instead he offered me a job as his assistant. I can only figure because of the Minnesota connection—it couldn't be because he knew I was honest. I never made a secret of the fact that the only thing that interests me about art is money. But what's wrong with money? It makes the world go round, even the art world, especially the art world. Because art is useless, practically speaking, and there's no other way to establish its value objectively except to put a price on it. If that's corrupt then I'm corrupt. And I am corrupt, rotten to the core, and I like to corrupt others. I'd like to corrupt you, and I suspect you have a taste for it."

"Is it you who's stealing from the Museum?"

"In a way."

"And what are you stealing?"

"I'm stealing its soul."

"And what will you do with it?"

He laughed. It was a mean laugh. "I'll flush it down the toilet. Have some more of this." He was still feeding me between necessarily brief remarks.

I shook my head. "I've had enough, thank you."

"Fynch is dying. It's supposed to be a secret."

An e-mail from Hymi:

once a bull inseminating life, rumor whispers Fynch is dying

that changes everything. suddenly

the Boy is now the chosen bull

the generic Son, all six feet eight of him and growing, displaces the fathers as bully

the taller he gets the more he sees

in his angry innocent vision

in sullen usurpation

Fynch's godson

Seymor

The next day I had a meeting with Jimmy Lochs and Notley to discuss the disastrous seance with Achs.

"This art world is rough," commented Lochs. "It's enough to make me go back to the life of crime."
"I thought that was behind you," I said.
"I served my time."
"How long?"
"Five years."
"For what?"
"For something I didn't do," he said, straightening up and sticking out his chest, so that he looked bigger.
"Who did it?" I asked.
"Somebody named Jimmy Lochs. But it wasn't me. I was a different person then."
"You're not the same person today as yesterday?"
"I'm not the same person today as today. First of all, we have almost identical genes with things like bananas and fruit flies, I

read in the paper. Where does that leave my identity? Jimmy the almost fruit fly?"

"Let's get back on track," said Achs. "Pyhl's performance at the seance, it seems to me, creates a new situation at the Museum. He's come out in the open, he's letting it be seen that he's out to destroy the Museum. And Fynch is letting him do it."

"Fynch used to be a tough guy," said Notley.

"He's still larger than life and completely bull headed beneath that diminishing air of gentility," said Achs. "So if he's letting him do it he must have a reason."

I didn't want to say anything, because I believed Achs to be completely innocent of our sexual complications, but the drift of this conversation was making me uncomfortable. I was beginning to feel that the Museum project was developing an edge of preciosity and that Pyhl, with his rough attitudes, including sex, was maybe a plus.

"Why would Fynch, through Pyhl, want to destroy his own creation?" asked Jimmy.

"He may have his reasons," said Achs. "Or, maybe he doesn't proceed rationally. All I know is that the idea for the Museum came to him after he had a stroke and temporarily lost his memory."

"Whatever," I said, "it's up to us, the younger generation, to keep his conception intact."

"The younger generation?" said Notley.

"I said younger, not youngest."

"How old is Fynch?" asked Jimmy.

"He's going to have his 101st birthday," said Achs.

"God, that's amazing," said Jimmy.

"Why, how old are you?"

"A mere child. About the same age as Notley here," answered Jimmy.

"Which is?"

"67," said Notley. "How about you and Austyn?"

"I guess we're both looking forward to maturity," said Achs. "Or at least the end of menopause."

"Well what it comes to," said Notley, "you may have vitality on your side, but we have wisdom."

"I hadn't noticed," I said. "Fynch seems to have all the wisdom, and Pyhl all the vitality."

"Yeah. Like a germ," said Jimmy.

"And what happened to Fynch after he had the stroke?" I asked.

"He had a vision," said Achs.

"Of what?"

"He has never told me."

"Well," said Notley, "unless he tells somebody, we may never know what's missing from the museum. But Americans love absence. Emptiness. It sucks them in. Take the American West, take the frontier. Take Andy Warhol."

"And why is that?"

"Because people think it's a way of clearing the decks, of starting from scratch, of changing their lives and doing it better the next time."

"That reminds me," said Jimmy, "have any of you heard of the Improvement Society?"

"Why?"

"I've been getting e-mail from them. About the Museum. Supporting it."

"Interesting," said Achs. "I'll have to look into that."

At home I had a message from Jocylyn asking—or rather demanding—that I meet her the next day. When I called back, she gave me directions to her boat moored at the yacht basin at the World Financial Center. I had imagined a sail boat, but it turned out to be a cabin cruiser, not very large, but luxurious.

She received me with open arms, and led me, arm around shoulders, into the cabin where she had set out tea and cookies. Her cheeks were glowing, and she seemed more ample than before. She was relating to me in a completely new way, the reason for which I was, confusingly, unaware.

> "Of course, I know," she began, "all about you and Pyhl."
> "Oh?
> "He tells me everything, didn't you know that?"
> "Like?"
> "Like about his erotic relationships. So I am aware..."
> "Yes?"
> "I don't get jealous."
> "Why?"
> "Because I'm in control."
> "Of?"
> "Of him. And so, indirectly, of you."
> "How?"
> "Since you're submissive. And I'm dominant."
> "So?"
> "I feel we're related. Family."
> "No."
> "Of course. Mother, father, daughter. The pecking order. Now let's get down and dirty. What about the Museum?"
> "What about it?"
> "I'm not going to let my father throw his money away on this foolishness indefinitely. This has got to stop. It's time to choose sides, and we think you're going to choose ours. Because of Pyhl. Because you do what he wants. And he does ... let me show you something."

She took me down three or four steps into the hold. There was a sort of large bundle of gray material, and I couldn't figure out what

I was seeing. And then I recognized, blindfolded and gagged, Pyhl's head sticking out the top, lobster pink.

His forehead was beaded with sweat. Jocylyn took a small handkerchief out of her pocket and patted his brow with it. He made a grunting sound.

"You have to be careful they don't overheat. It can be dangerous."

"How long has he been like that?"

"An hour and a half." She looked at her watch. "Half-hour to go. I consider it therapy."

"For?"

"He's a dominant. And a control freak. He needs to draw strength from his weakness or his power will run out. He's recharging his batteries." She pulled the gag off his mouth. "What do you have to say for yourself?" she asked him. "Have you thought about your family?"

"Mammals," he said. "Mamas. Mammaries. Mammon." Tears ran from his eyes.

She replaced the gag. "That's a good boy," patting him on the head. "By the way," turning toward me, "what's this gossip among the employees at the Museum about something called the Improvement Society? What is it, some sort of union?"

"They seem to be a lobby for the Museum. I expect it's a members' organization."

"I can see right away they're going to be trouble," she said. "Did you know they're trying to shut down the gift shop? The only place in the whole damned institution where you can get something tangible. And that makes money."

"What do they sell?"

"Wind-up scale models of the building itself as it changes, reproductions of self-destructing works, copies of paintings that no longer exist, beautiful calendars from years past, paper clothing with slogans in disappearing ink, bottomless beer mugs and general ephemera. It's the best part of the Museum. The Improvement Society, sounds like the kind of organization that makes things worse. I wonder if they're behind the faxes?"

"What faxes?"

"My father is being blackmailed. By fax."

"Blackmailed about what?"

"He won't tell me."

I went home, strangely fatigued. Suddenly I felt a gut twisting sensation of loss, and I knew what it was about. As a student, for money, I had donated placental eggs to an experiment testing viable cryogenic longevity for fertilization, though they were never supposed to be fertilized. But at times I'm overwhelmed by waves of grief as to their fate. I know it's stupid.

She feels faint, a fit coming on, she's losing it. Finds herself lying on the couch

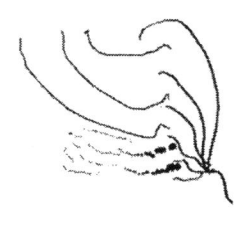

manages to start a tape of Coltrane's "My Favorite Things."

That evening, late, I got a call from Fynch. He wanted me to bring Seymor to him right away.

"But why me?" I asked. "And what's the urgency?"
"The urgency is I'm a dying man. And why, you don't ask."

After several frantic phone calls I tracked down Seymor through Hymi, who kept referring to him as The Son. Seymor was curious about Fynch and agreed to go. I convinced Jimmy to drive us in his huge old hulk of a car, and there was no room to spare accommodating the bulk of Seymor, whose long arms crowded me up front even though he was sitting in the back seat—or was he trying to crowd me and touch me?

We pulled up at the Fynch mansion around midnight. Fynch was sitting in his study with a blanket around his shoulders. Light reflected off his bald head like a crystal ball and his features fine as porcelain.

"All my life," he began, "I've been wanting. Starting with nothing, wanting what I didn't have, wanting what I couldn't get, wasn't born with, what was out of my reach, wanting the impossible. Now, suddenly, I want nothing. So I know it's time for me to move on. My power came from what I didn't have. By the intensity of my desire for it. Now I have everything I could conceivably want, I want to pass on that intensity to someone who has nothing."

"You have the Temporary Museum," I reminded him.

"Yes, but the Temporary Museum is a way of having nothing. That's why it's dedicated to the ephemeral, to impermanence, to change. And the Museum itself is changing, that's inevitable. The concept behind it, after all, is that you can never really have anything, never really predict anything. Who could have said that the problem of the Temporary Museum would be that it's slipping through my fingers by threatening to become a permanent collection?"

"So what's the point, old man?" interrupted Seymor-the-sullen, as Hymi called him.

"The point is, young man, my intelligence tells me that you are connected with the Improvement Society. And as I also would like to see things improve, how better than to put them in the hands of somebody who has nothing and wants everything. At once. And now. My intelligence tells me you're that sort of young man."

"By intelligence," asked Seymor, "does that mean your spies?"

"I see more with my mind than with any spies. And you can improve things more with your intelligence from the inside than with any group of outsiders."

"And be immediately compromised," scoffed Seymor.

"Compromise makes the world go round," observed Fynch.

"Yes, it makes the world go round so slow it never gets to where it promised to go."

"In any case," said Fynch, "I'm offering you a job at the Museum, to learn the ropes. And eventually to pull all the strings. You understand what I'm saying?"

"Who would I work with?"

"Achs."

"I want to work with her," said Seymor, pointing at me.

"Why me?" I asked.

"I've got a crush on you," said Seymor. "Haven't you noticed?"

"Stay away from her," said Fynch, for the first time showing some agitation. "You work with Achs. Now go home. Think about it. I'm going to keep Austyn and Lochs here for a while."

As Seymor shambled out of the room, Fynch assumed a new tone, wheedling, almost whining: "There's no other way to say this but that you owe me. Both of you. Am I wrong?"

"No, of course," said Jimmy, "we all owe you in different ways."

"Then," said Fynch, "you wouldn't grudge a little favor?"

"Anything," I said.

"I made love to many women in my life," he continued. "But, of course, I have always been completely caught up in the act." He paused.

"Naturally," I said.

"So, in a way, I don't know what it's like. I mean, from an objective point of view."

"There is no objective point of view to lovemaking," said Jimmy.

"Nonparticipatory, call it what you want. Objective. You can't understand something without that kind of perspective. I'm curious. I want to know what it means. To make love. From an objective point of view."

"I don't follow," said Jimmy.

"I'm afraid I do," I said.

"Would you do an old man a favor then?"

"You mean right here? Now?" I asked.

"I know you and Jimmy have been lovers. So what difference can it make? Besides, as a presence I'm hardly here. At this stage of my life."

The idea appealed to me in some perverse way. And then there was something about Fynch's high, dry point of view, something neutral and straightforward and, yes, lofty. And I knew that Jimmy wouldn't pass up an opportunity.

"Well . . . okay. Okay?" I asked Jimmy.

"Count me in," said Jimmy.

"On the couch then? I think it's ample enough?" asked Fynch.

"Geronimo!" said Jimmy. He led me over to the couch and started undressing me. I wasn't wearing much. As usual, he didn't bother much with foreplay, but I admit I was somewhat excited by the situation. Jimmy was huge, as usual, and I soon shed any sense of embarrassment or even self consciousness as I lost myself in the act. Much to my surprise I came suddenly and hugely, bringing Jimmy with me. After a period of being dazed and floaty, I abruptly did get embarrassed, and kissing Jimmy lightly on the lips I got up and rapidly dressed.

"Well?" I asked, as Jimmy pulled up his pants and quickly, almost furtively, zipped his fly over his barely diminished organ and buckled his belt.

"Well what?" asked Fynch.

"Did you find out what you wanted to know?"

"I didn't find out a thing. Two people wrestling and panting. It didn't mean anything to me. I thought I could understand something finally, but I should have known better. The older I get the more I realize I don't understand anything. Anything important."

"Is it discouraging?" I asked.

"No. I recognize I understand next to nothing because I've come to realize how stupid I am. And how rich my ignorance is. And that makes my life more and more interesting."

An emergency meeting was called for next afternoon between Achs, Pyhl, and myself. When I got there I found Achs in a state of considerable agitation. Apparently, two major pieces had disappeared from the Museum's collection.

"One was an imaginary installation that was running in 10 tubeless TV sets. The sets are still there but they stopped emitting their imaginary content. The other was a piece of conceptual art of which no one can now remember the conception."

"Those were two of your best pieces," said Pyhl.

"And it doesn't end there," said Achs. "The freezing unit for the Ice Dream piece stopped working overnight and half of it melted away."

"It's as if temporary art is bleeding away into the river of time," I said.

"But what do you expect?" asked Pyhl. "Isn't that what it's supposed to do? I mean, this may be a sign of success."

"Or of sabotage," said Achs.

"Or both," I said. "If we take time as the saboteur."

"We need to maintain some distinctions here," said Achs. "Natural erosion is one thing, vandalism is another. I intend to alert the guards and put them on double shifts."

"Let's hope that they can maintain the distinctions," said Pyhl.

From the beginning there was sharp division among the staff of the Museum concerning Seymor. Half of the personnel regarded him as a threatening interloper butting into things he didn't know anything about, though others admired his energy and his iconoclastic ideas, and thought that iconoclasm was perfectly suited to a Museum devoted to impermanent art. Most important, Achs seemed to feel a natural alliance with him.

I was very cautious with Seymor, because his attitude toward me would inexplicably flip-flop between aggressive affection and sullen hostility. But one thing I will grant him, the more influential he became at the Museum, mostly through Achs, the more he clarified the mission of the Museum:

"Over time, images, any kind of images, will betray you, whether after a second or 10 years. Suddenly you look up and everything has changed. There's an open manhole where the sidewalk was. Or Hemingway, after a time, no longer represents the way things are. Or the television soap never did. Or the image of the politician or the product is so easily a misrepresentation. This is what the Museum should stand against, in my view."

Fynch agreed to see Seymor on short notice, and Seymor asked me to go out there with him. But, on the occasion, Fynch was very evasive on the subject of Seymor's mother.

"I don't know why you assume I have inside information on the subject. Of course, I know a number of women who are the right age, but that's hardly proof. Austyn, here, is the right age, but so what? And then there's the matter of family resemblance, which is always ambiguous and often imaginary. But first let me ask you, how do you know you have a mother?"

"I'm sorry?" said Seymor.

"I mean, of course you have a mother, in some sense, but it goes counter to the sense of the other rumors you may have have heard, to wit, artificial insemination. I mean is that really a mother or some kind of boarding house of flesh? And if we can say artificial insemination, why can't we say placental implant, which is a rumor that has also reached me. Or why stop there? We could speculate about androids and their manufacture. No, the real question here is why you arouse such speculation. I mean, it's not normal."

"I'm not aware of not being normal."

"Of course you're not. You're just doing what your nature impels you to do. I've heard about all your spondulicks. You're a live wire, but you're aching for a smack on the keister. And frankly, I rather thought you wanted to see me about some project you felt compelled to do."

"Well there was something," said Seymor.

"Go on."

"I want to curate a major show."

"Well I don't know. It's unusual in your position," said Fynch.

"But this will be a show that will exhibit the spiritual side of the Museum's program you're so interested in. It'll be awesome."

"What would it be about?"

"The invisible."

"Yes! Promising. I like it. Write it up and I'll speak to Achs."

"Cool."

It was shortly after that visit with Fynch, when Achs walked into the Museum in the morning and discovered one of the ice sculptures smashed to something that looked like a large frozen daiquiri. There was a note that said, "the latest improvement, the Improvement Society." This shadowy and ill-defined organization reputedly of young people under 50, more or less, of which Seymor was sometimes reported to be the head, had as its motto the words, "act out," but against what was also ill-defined.

Jocylyn arrived at the museum just after I did. She was furious, or pretended to be.

"If you can't keep the Museum secure, I'll have to advise my father to find somebody who can. And if we can't, it's just another argument to liquidate the Museum for its cash value. This is my inheritance we're talking about after all."

"What's wrong with your father's health," I asked, thinking about his statement that he was a dying man.

"He's just been diagnosed with Lou Gehrig's disease," said Jocylyn. "Haven't you noticed he has trouble walking? He's talking about taking himself out before it gets too bad. But I imagine you know about this already," gesturing toward Achs.

"I've known about it for a long time," said Achs. "It wasn't just diagnosed, it's well advanced. That's why he's trying to step up the pace of developments at the Museum, like allowing Seymor to mount a show so quickly."

"Seymor mounting a show?" said Jocylyn. "We'll see about that."

That was when the graffiti started to appear on the mobile walls of the Museum. The first one read: "Seymor, timeless traitor—the Improvement Society." But I consoled Seymor, telling him that you can't act in the world without getting your hands dirty and offending someone.

"I know," answered Seymor, "but something doesn't add up, the graffiti doesn't translate to my experience."

"It sounds to me that they, whoever they are, just need some proof that you're still interested in improvement," I said, patting him on the head.

He was sitting down, otherwise I couldn't have reached his head. He grabbed my hand and tried to put it to his mouth. I resisted, then suddenly he tried to embrace me. I managed to squirm away.

"You behave like my good angel," he complained, "but when I try to respond you act like I'm the devil. I don't understand."

"Neither do I, except you're too young. Nor do I understand your attachment to this group of improvers. What's your connection?"

"I don't know. They chose me and I have no idea why."

"What do they want?" I asked.

"I guess I'd better rethink my exhibition project."

But Seymor did more than that. The next morning Achs found a score of works in the Museum slashed or defaced, including anything that was even vaguely representational, figurative, realist or allegorical. And there was another graffito on the walls of the Museum: "graven images to the grave—the Improvement Society."

Maybe that's what turned Fynch against Seymor. He was getting dangerous. At the same time he also had his virtues, among which were a certain charm, even charisma, along with a decisiveness, not to say impetuousness.

Next time I saw Seymor was after he saw Fynch. He looked even bigger than the last time I saw him. He looked seven feet tall and not skinny either. He was built like a weightlifter.

"I went to see Fynch," he said. "He wanted to go out and see his rose garden, but he couldn't get down the stairs. So I had to carry him. And I freaked. Not that he was hard to carry, he weighs nothing."

"Carrying him disturbed you."

"Totally."

"Why?"

"Because it was like carrying my father, if I'd had one, while it seems like my father should have carried me."

"Well it's like that," I observed. "The son becomes a father, and the father a son. In your case, if you were conceived in your father's mind, you exist as a ghost of a thought."

"Ghost?"

"In the sense of spirit."

"Why isn't anything simple anymore!" He had a booming voice that seemed to shake the walls of the Museum. "It's as if I'm all shook since I started working on my exhibition."

"What's different?"

"Before everything seemed possible, now I seem to be following some script I can't quite grasp."

"Evolved intelligences, according to Fynch, say there is no script, there's just an impulse they call betterness," I told him. "And that time is possibility."

Later that day, I was still at the Museum when Fynch was rolled in in a wheelchair. His body looked shrunken, like a puppet, so that his head, which remained normal size, looked gigantic by comparison, and his voice had turned high and squeaky. I must have looked appalled, because he immediately launched into an apology for his body.

"You see what I've come to," he said. "Soon they'll have to operate my arms and legs with strings. But autonomy is always less of an option than you think."

"I don't follow," I said.

"Because you don't get the same evolving intelligence that I do, the simple knowledge that the finger you could move last week you can't move this week, the progressive news that your body is changing, shutting down in serial order, like Hal in *2001*. I suppose it's ironic justification that I, who always sought flux, should now be flushed by it piece by piece down the black hole of death."

"Are you frightened? Excuse me for asking."

"The answer is I don't know what I feel or, to put it differently, I can't remember what I feel from one moment to the next. It's as if I have progressive amnesia, which is possibly anesthetic. Occasionally something will come back to me out of the fogbank of memory. For example, now. I'm remembering all of a sudden the vision I had during a bout of extended amnesia."

"Would you . . ."

"Yes. The vision was that I was blind. And because I was blind I could feel things that I overlooked by sight. And I couldn't think in the ordinary way, I seemed to be in harmony with the feelings that preceded thought, but I couldn't think. And yes it was frightening because I was at the mercy of all sorts of invasive impulses that I normally reject. And yet I was happy that I no longer had to deny them. And I realized how vulnerable we are. And I realized that to maintain this happy vulnerability we need a strong defense, and I thought that Seymor was destined to become such a defender."

"Do you still feel that way?"

"Seymor has been a severe disappointment."

"Does that mean you're going to get rid of Seymor?"

"It means that I may have to change Seymor's status."

The day of the opening of Seymor's exhibit was wet, stormy, autumnal. There was a cold wind that whipped around corners of the lofts and skyscrapers in the area between Tribeca and Wall Street. Umbrellas were blown inside out and taxis were hard to find. A small crowd gathered in the Museum where wine was served in an anteroom whose closed sliding door separated it from the exhibition.

Seymor, evidently, was waiting for a larger crowd to accumulate despite the weather. He postponed opening the exhibit to public view until the crowd became restless and a few people began to leave. A considerable feeling of impatience, not to say suspense, could be sensed in the anteroom.

Finally Seymor could delay no longer. He pressed a button and the wall rolled back slowly from one side of the room to the other, revealing a black matte cube that nearly filled the exhibition space.

There was a gasp from the onlookers, then a long silence. Then a few hands clapping. Finally a crescendo of spontaneous applause.

To make a long story short, the reviews were controversial, but it was the kind of controversy that led through notoriety to fame. Seymor found himself a minor celebrity. Even Lochs and Notley saw something interesting in him, if not as an artist than as a phenomenon indicating that anyone could become an artist, and that art was not the possession of an elite.

Whether it was because he decided there was no point fighting or what, Pyhl started playing up to Seymor. Pyhl made sure that the resources of the Museum's formidable publicity department were focused on promoting Seymor.

The campaign, under Pyhl's direction, sought to portray Seymor as a "genius of absence" who created negative images that, like a photographic negative, could be developed into any number of tangible versions. Like Platonic ideas, the propaganda went, Seymor's negative images were sovereign abstractions that could engender a rich and diverse brood of descendants. What, you might ask, did Pyhl figure on getting out of this campaign?

Pyhl had a sideline business that wholesaled merchandise to museum gift shops all over the country. He proceeded to develop a retail line of negative images that, as decals, could only be seen when transferred to a T-shirt or other appropriate article of clothing. They then turned out to be reproductions of the black "Invisible" accompanied by a profile caricature of Seymor.

From the beginning, much to Pyhl's delight, the decals sold like hot cakes. Pyhl already knew that he was good at wholesale, but now he was beginning to think he was a retail genius. More, he felt that the success of this venture amply justified his contribution to the affairs of the Museum.

Though they never verbalized it, I believe they both sensed in Seymor someone who was turning his life into a work of art. I tended to see Lochs and Notley together at this point because they were both still flattering me with their attentions and they had the effect of canceling one another out, a desirable result since I was preoccupied with unkinking my ambivalent relations with Pyhl and they were busy kinking their relations with one another.

My relations with Pyhl were basically a matter of artful playacting. I was aware of that, though I was not proud of it. In its obsessively repetitive nature, it resembled a ritual.

But a ritual to what? Whatever it was, I recognized that it had to do with sex only incidentally, that it derived from some impulse deeper than sex.

Seymor was using his new prestige to get the Museum to feature what he called Art Brute. Sometimes called Self Taught, sometimes Primitive Art, Art Brute was work, according to Seymor, created solely to amuse its maker and destined for the garbage dump. It was qualified by its ephemeral nature to be exhibited at the Temporary Museum, he claimed.

Seymor said Art Brute had the status of meditation as in a religious discipline. It was not, Seymor said, a religious discipline, but it was like a religious discipline. Furthermore, Seymor said, it was not an aesthetic discipline because aesthetic was just a record of the spirit in the act of meditating.

Meanwhile, as I was trying to get my feelings straightened out about Pyhl, I was beginning to get signals from Hymi. It was an inconvenient time to start bothering me to get together again. I barely managed to be civil in response to his e-mail.

Austyn:

I'm lonely.

I miss your sweet face and sour tongue.

I keep wondering what you see in Pyhl that's so attractive.

Of course there's his youth, but that's something you have with Lochs and Notley.

I can understand your attraction to the young fellows, but I can't help thinking they're a little too young for you.

After all, though you're not 60, I would think you need a man just a bit more than 10 years older than you, someone with a little maturity.

Even though you look twenty years younger than your age, I would think it's the inner man that counts, someone with experience, someone who knows how to make love without complicated gymnastics.

Someone who makes love in a tender, uncomplicated way, and compares your beauty to the delicate sunrise we used to see every morning in Bali, with the sky lightening behind the volcanoes, the flowers one by one lighting up in the sun, and the mist lifting over the rice paddies, someone like me.

Or is it you who's complicated?

Hymi, I answered him. We're all complicated. Grow up. —Austyn.

So many complications started developing at this point that it was hard to keep track. A sluice of life. Notley, claiming that the ultimate content of "The Concept" was the Museum itself, quixotically threatened to challenge Jocylyn as the Museum's heir.

Jocylyn was trying to convince Fynch to let Pyhl take over the direction of the Museum from Achs. Pyhl accused Notley of trying not only to steal from the Museum, but trying to steal the Museum itself. Achs was arguing with Seymor about his idea of turning the Museum into a homeless shelter, starting with an exhibition called

"Homeless," that would devote a wing of the Museum to the purpose.

Jimmy framed it all by claiming, facetiously, the Museum as his most ambitious disappearable, and did his best to fan the flames of controversy, while Fynch stood aside and let it all happen. Finally, Seymor, frustrated at Achs's refusal to consider his "Homeless" project seriously, disappeared. A week later he telephoned Achs from Des Moines, Iowa, to ask if she was ready to reconsider his project.

"I am not. What are you doing in Des Moines?"
"I'm heading to LaFange."

She hung up on him and lapsed into heavy sarcasm, which I would not have believed from the usually level-headed Achs had I not been in her office at the time. Evidently Seymor had touched a sore spot.

"He said he was going on the road. To get away from the hypocrisy of our culture as manifested in the phony aesthetic concerns of the Museum. Not to mention his own phony aesthetic concerns."

But when Fynch heard about Seymor's flight he took it in with equanimity.

"He needs to be alone for a while," said Fynch. "And maybe he'll learn something. He'll find a cultural desert out there in his terms. But maybe he'll find some wisdom rooting in that desert."

Meanwhile, Jocylyn began to make herself felt in the affairs of the Museum. She became proactive and robust, as Pyhl was becoming robust and transparent. She talked about wiping the slate clean and starting from scratch, her phrasing.

"What's wrong with making it into a theme park?" she asked. And when met with a dead silence she added, "An art theme park of course. We could change the theme every month. Rembrandt month, Grant Wood month, Humphrey Bogart month, why limit it to the graphic arts, the Beatles month, the possibilities are endless. And endlessly changeable and temporary, just as the Museum is supposed to be."

Pyhl had my number, he knew what turned me on. And if he didn't know I told him. I insisted on telling him and he jumped to oblige.

Achs saw what was going on and was quick to warn me that Pyhl would take advantage of me.

"I know, I know," I said with a little sob, "I can't help myself."
"He's all tied up by Jocylyn, you know," Achs replied. "Never mind the little secretaries."

Given what I knew about Pyhl and Jocylyn, I had to suppress a giggle over Achs's innocence. Even so, things got pretty rough. One time Pyhl had me over to his loft while he made love to one of the little secretaries.

But I wouldn't want to paint too flattering a portrait of Pyhl. He had more substantial vices and they all had to do with money. I found that tacky.

His erotic habits at least had an element of play—about money he was stone cold serious. I learned that it was Pyhl who was selling unauthorized permanent versions of Jimmy's disappearables. But when I asked him whether he didn't have any compunctions he said that Jimmy obviously didn't care about making money off them so why should he be bothered about someone else making money?

This revelation, though we all suspected it anyway, presented me with a dilemma. Could I tell Jimmy what Pyhl told me in confidence? Whether or not I could tell him, I did tell him.

"Is he getting a good price for them?" Jimmy asked.
"I don't know," I answered. "What's that got to do with it?"
"It's a matter of vanity. I don't need the money, I need the flattery," said Jimmy. "I'm all ego, me, I. A lot of why but mostly I."
"You don't care about the money?"
"No. But I'll sue the bastard. On principle."

I expected a confrontation between Jimmy and Pyhl the next evening, because they had been invited, along with Notley and Achs, to spend the night at Fynch's mansion and, along with Jocylyn, who lived there part of the time, to talk through the problems at the Museum. And, Achs being already there as she so often was, and Jimmy's car being in the repair shop as it so often was, the rest of us were to ride up there with Pyhl.

We picked up Jimmy last, and he immediately launched an attack on Pyhl, accusing him of art theft over the unauthorized sale of his disappearables. But instead of getting defensive or angry, Pyhl chose to make light of the accusation.

"Sure I'm doing it. But they're just reproductions, the Museum has the right to do that. Nobody's selling originals. Originals of what? The originals of paintings that don't exist?"
"But they did exist," said Jimmy.

"Only for a brief period."

"Long enough to make copies."

"But they're not being sold as copies," said Pyhl. "They're multiples. They're reproductions of non-existent originals."

"They exist," Jimmy objected. "Just because they disappeared doesn't mean they don't exist."

"And how is that?"

"They exist in the nmonisphere."

"The what?"

"Cultural memory. In the world of the spirit. Where all important art resides. How often do you have the Mona Lisa before your actual eyes?"

"Well then," said Pyhl, "if your disappeared work exists in a better place you shouldn't complain."

"I'm not complaining, I'm objecting. I'm objecting to the exploitation. You'd exploit heaven and hell if you could."

"Let's not say exploit," said Pyhl. "Let's say develop. Let's say I'm a developer. Without people like me everything would stagnate."

"You can't let go can you?"

"I don't want to."

Fynch had arranged for us all to have dinner together, but the guests had straggled in so that some people were almost done eating when we arrived, others were just beginning, and there was still one chair empty. Just as I was finishing dessert, a rather good crème brûlée, the last guest walked in. Seymor.

The conversation dwindled to a gradual hush. Seymor looked worse for wear. His clothes were rumpled, face unshaven, and he had a cigarette dangling from the corner of his mouth.

But his height and bearing were intimidating. He was if anything taller, but he had filled out and seemed broader, fleshier, more muscular. And he swaggered, threw his weight around, standing too close, poking people in the shoulder, almost shoving them.

This was another Seymor than the one who had disappeared. It was as if his contact with LaFange had changed him, as if rubbing shoulders with a different, earthier population, or heavier cuisine, or maybe just the rudeness of conditions in LaFange had entered his system. He was, moreover, wearing shades and a billed cap that said "LaFange" on it.

He was, in short, a little menacing. Before anyone had a chance to question him, Fynch clinked his glass with his fork.

"I have an announcement," he said. "L. L. Achs, Director of the Temporary Museum, and as some of you may know, my long time companion, is stepping down. As director, not as companion." Gasps. Titters.

"And in her place, I appoint my adoptive grandson, Seymor, with Achs acting as his adviser for as long as she—not he—as she deems advisable. Open the champagne."

"Just a minute," interrupted Seymor in his loud vibrating voice. "A suggestion. In the spirit of my new regime at the Museum, may I suggest that we toast with beer."

"Beer it will be," said Fynch.

I was now, because of my relations with Pyhl, considered by Jocylyn and Pyhl to be on their side of Museum politics. Actually I identified with Jimmy and Notley because, despite my admittedly incomprehensible submission to Pyhl, I instinctively found myself on the side of the artists. Not to mention the fact that I was employed by Fynch and Achs.

But, as I understood it, Jocylyn was so sure of her domination of Pyhl, and Pyhl of his domination of me, that they were careless.

"Well, what are we going to do?" asked Pyhl.

"The way I see it," said Jocylyn, "we can have Seymor killed, we can neutralize him with scandal, or we can discredit him with my father. The last option is the most practical because, though there are few Fynch relatives and only distant ones, all back in LaFange, they all think my father's latest tack, liquidating his fortune through the Museum, is crazy. They would enthusiastically endorse the view that Seymor is the wrong man to lead the Museum."

"Why don't you contact them, and I'll see if I can launch a media mud campaign."

It would turn out that contacting the LaFange branch of the family about Fynch's intentions was the biggest mistake Jocylyn and Pyhl could have made in their plots to take over the Museum. But, back at the Fynch mansion, Fynch was tapping his glass and calling for attention.

"The museum that I initiated some years ago is now in crisis, a crisis that threatens to destroy it. I'm still convinced that Seymor will be our salvation. Why? Because he is acutely in touch with the impulses that help create his unique experience. And as a result he is connected, emotionally, to the web of those who are, however fleetingly and instinctively, in touch with their own individual, subjective, idiosyncratic, original consciousness before—and after—the thought patrols of so-called objective discourse have tampered with it in the interest of endless hidden agendas. And it is to the apprehension of that evanescent state of pure perception that the Museum is dedicated."

I'm not sure I recorded his speech accurately because it was interspersed with brief fits of coughing, and Fynch's voice wavered and quavered, but I believe I captured the spirit of his remarks. What he was trying to say was that Seymor was in touch with his own sense of things, uncontaminated by messages society imposes on us. His brain, in other words, had not been washed.

That, I suppose, was why Fynch was willing to put up with Seymor's overbearing brattiness. He was a natural leader. Why he was willing to put up with Pyhl's purely destructive machinations is another story, one I didn't understand yet.

The next day Jimmy Lochs came in, wanting to see Achs about taking legal action against Pyhl over the disappearables affair.

"She isn't here today. I'm in charge," said Seymor.
"Okay. Look, I don't care about compensation. I just want him to stop misrepresenting my work."
"Look," said Seymor. "Take a broad view. Take a deep breath. Relax. Be happy. What's it hurting, really? So Pyhl will make a buck. So more people will get to know your work. So Pyhl is a jerk. Maybe there's a place for jerks. Let him jerk off. It won't affect anybody who likes your work. It won't affect how much I like it. I like it even more for Pyhl's little ploy, which highlights its brilliance. So be generous and ignore him."

You could practically see Jimmy expanding as Seymor talked. By the time Seymor finished Jimmy's body seemed visibly broader.

"You got a point," said Jimmy.

I believe that's when the strange reconciliation between Jimmy Lochs and Pyhl began. Jimmy let on that he was willing to look the other way about Pyhl's trade in his disappearables. The major bone of contention between them, and possibly the one that fueled the disappearables issue to start with, turned out to be me.

I had been seeing Pyhl for many months now and seemed to be getting more and more involved, despite the fact that it was a relationship of which I strongly disapproved. Basically, Pyhl treated me as a sexual convenience and I seemed to like it. I didn't make any secret of it either, and this is what made Jimmy furious.

Jimmy appeared to think that he had some sort of sexual priority over me, even though we never had a happy sexual relationship. He resented my willing domination by Pyhl. He thought Pyhl was exploiting me, and so did I, except that I saw another side of Pyhl, the one signified by his relation with Jocylyn, a relation based on hurt and helplessness.

Which, to get back to the subject, did not prevent Pyhl, and maybe even encouraged him, to play the dictator with me. Pyhl came up with a master stroke to cut through these complications. He had Jimmy up to his loft and invited him to make love with me. Jimmy declined but they became good buddies.

One day, not long after that, I passed Seymor's office in the Museum and heard his voice speaking in French, so I stopped and peered in. I saw Notley holding open a copy of Proust. But it was Seymor who was reciting long passages from *Remembrance of Things Past*.

I was confused for a moment, till I realized that Seymor was reciting from memory while Notley was following in the book.

"Can you take this in?" asked Notley. "He's got the whole thing memorized. Give me page 962, paragraph 2."

Seymor responded unhesitatingly with a string of rhythmic French while Notley followed in the novel with his finger, nodding his head repeatedly.

"Flawless," said Notley when Seymor finished. "How long did it take you to memorize that?"

"I didn't memorize it, I just remember it."

"You mean you remember everything you read?"

"Not everything. Just what's important to remember. Fiction, history, poetry, films, theater, philosophy, Scripture, religious practice."

"You mean you can't remember trivia?"

"I can remember it, but why would I want to?"

"Could you remember, for example, a page of the phone book?"

"Try me."

Notley took a copy of the white pages and opened at random. He handed it to Seymor who glanced at it and handed it back. Then he started repeating what he had just read while Notley looked at the book.

"All right, all right," Notley finally interrupted. "He's got it all correct," he said to me. "This is amazing. How do you decide what to retain?"

"You can tell what's important, it's reflective, it reflects you, you reflect on it, it reflects back on you, it illuminates. I can recognize it, but a lot of this stuff I remember, I don't understand what it means. Yet."

"You mean, it's in the right spirit," said Notley.

"It's not in the spirit, it is the spirit," answered Seymor.

"It's what Jimmy Lochs calls the nmonisphere."

Notley invited me out for lunch. His favorite place in the neighborhood turned out to be a bar on lower Broadway. A topless bar.

"I like bars," Notley said, "the sleazier the better. I don't know why. My teacher says bars incorporate a death wish."

"Why is that?"

"Because alcohol is liquid death. First it takes your judgment out, then your mind, then your body. I like it."

"Why a topless bar?" I asked.

"Did you ever have your brains fucked out? I mean orgasm after orgasm till you're blissed out but at the same time you can't think and don't even want to, your mind is obliterated, your identity dissolved. That's a near death experience and I think it happens to women more often than men. Hasn't that ever happened to you?"

"Never."

But I knew perfectly well what he was talking about. It was happening with Pyhl all the time now. That was his hold on me.

"And it's true bars make me think about death," he went on. "And it's good to think about death. It's like having a skull on your desk. Those old Christians had the right idea. It puts life in perspective."

"In grim perspective," I said.

"Not necessarily. You never think about how you're going to die?"

"Not if I can avoid it," I said.

"I don't say it's pleasant. Getting hit by a bus for example. If you're lucky you'll never see it coming and never feel a thing. Or a quick, massive heart attack, I imagine a moment of incredible pain and then it's over. Or some kind of heart failure, pain left arm, chest, hard to breathe, the emergency ambulance, panic, oxygen, pounding in chest, blackout. Or slow death from cancer, pain, morphine haze, weaker and weaker, tubes in arms, down throat the worst. Or throwing yourself out the window, letting go to jump in face of terrible panic, the wind, the fear. Or suffocating in water, no longer able to hold your breath, giving in, letting the water in. I tell you it's a poor choice no matter how you cut it."

He stared dully at the girl on stage without any sign of real interest. She had a scrawny body aside from her breasts which looked like the product of enhancement. But the other patrons, mostly male, seemed to watch with fascination.

I suddenly had a panicked feeling that I would never get out of there, that the doors were locked and I would be stuck in this seedy mediocrity forever. I knew it wasn't true but the ambiance sifted into my psyche like sand invalidating my life with all its petty transgressions, suffocating all hope or possibility of joy or even positive feeling. This was death but not the kind that Notley was talking about.

This was death of meaningfulness, death of the spirit, of values, a leveling out of the capacity to be interested as opposed to distracted. Suddenly her field of vision grays out, as if all color has drained from the scene. Loudspeakers blare some kind of drum machine go-go music that orchestrates what is quickly becoming a nightmare.

She must have passed out. Notley is kneeling over her on the floor slapping her wrist.

"The music," is all she can say. Somehow he understands. He pulls a Walkman out of his backpack and plugs me in.

It was John Coltrane's "My Favorite Things" and soon everything was all right.

As I walked into the Museum one day around that time I noticed a graffito on one of the moving panels near the entrance: "things better get better." I wondered why it was permitted to stay there since I knew the custodial staff had means to erase it. When I inquired of Achs, she told me that Seymor had given orders that all graffiti should be left alone.

This enraged me to the point where I decided to call Fynch. But Fynch said that Seymor had already talked to him about it. Seymor had told him that the graffiti were part of the Art Brute show he was mounting in collaboration with the mysterious Improvement Society.

I pointed out to him that there was a law banning graffiti, but he said that the Improvement Society had registered as a religious organization and that religious organizations were exempt from certain statutes, including the one banning graffiti.

"Is it true you've had a turn toward religion?" I asked.
"No. Not exactly. Not organized religion," said Fynch.
"Excuse me?"
"I mean, everyone has some variety of religion, even though not recognized as such. I call this disorganized religion. And the

main function of disorganized religion is to help people to change, for the better of course, and as often and continually as possible. To keep up with the world, with your own life and its changes. Change saves."

"And disorganized religion is?"

"It can be anything, depending on how you go about it, anything that leads to change for the better. Tourism, for example, can be a spiritual pilgrimage that shakes you out of your habits and introduces new touchstones, new possibilities. Or music. Or meditation. Anything that dematerializes your reality. Anything that jogs the memory and reminds you of the invisible world. Even sports can lead to evolution of the spirit."

"Are you one of the evolved intelligences?"

"I'm not supposed to say. Let's just say that Art Brute is evolving intelligently toward becoming a disorganized religion."

"And what is Art Brute?"

"It's anything you want it to be."

"Isn't that a little vague?" I said.

"And anyone can do it," he added.

Seymor wanted to confront the issue of what was missing from the Museum directly and dispense with it. He called me in to a meeting with Achs and said as much. I said I couldn't agree more, and wondered whether he had any clues.

"I have an intuition," he said. "I don't think it's any one thing. I think it's the spirit of the Museum."

"Then who stole it?" asked Achs.

"Maybe we're all responsible," said Seymor.

"That may be so," said Achs. "But then how do we get it back?"

"Well, first of all, we have to make an effort of memory. And what we have to remember is beyond my scope, I wasn't there, but you're supposed to be good at that. What was it like before what's missing was missing?"

"Well, let me think," said Achs. "I remember a lot of fights, and what was peculiar, looking back, they were often fights over nothing. Fights over how many angels could stand on the point of a pin. Should the workers run their factories or should the state? Do we partake in the actual sacrifice or a symbolic sacrifice? Do we talk to the government directly or through representatives? Do we communicate with the spirits personally or through an appointed third party? It all seems so petty now, but these fights had huge effects. Why? Because we cared so much. Because we believed there were real consequences at stake, these things became more important than life itself. Careers were ruined, people were ostracized, whole groups were imprisoned, blood was shed. And yet sometimes I think things happened the way they were going to happen anyway. But I wonder now if what happened was the point, or whether the point was that we cared so much. That we were awakened, magnificently awake."

"Well," asked Seymor, "if that's what's missing, how can we get it back?"

"It may be apocryphal for me to say so," answered Achs, "but the best way might be after all to get it out of the museum of memory and back into the world."

"Well then," I said, "maybe it's not so bad that it's been stolen."

"That depends on who stole it," said Seymor. "If it's fallen into the wrong hands it could be a disaster."

"'... the worst are full of passionate intensity,'" said Achs.

"Exactly," said Seymor. "But this should be obvious: it's already fallen into the wrong hands."

"I suspected as much," said Achs. "From the way things are going in the world."

"And they want a ransom," said Seymor.

"How much?" I asked.

"A lot," said Seymor. "They want a guarantee that it will be kept locked up in the Museum forever, and never, ever be used to stir things up again."

"What would Fynch say about that?" I asked.

"He'd never authorize it," said Achs. "His whole idea for the Museum was that it should serve as a resource for people who wanted to investigate possibilities, change things, plant new ideas. 'To turn over the earth,' he used to say, drawing on his hog farm experience from his childhood in LaFange."

"So what do we do?" I asked.

"We can get our artists on the case," said Seymor. "Artists know best how to deal with intangible ideas beyond the mental frequency of most people. That stage in which ideas are not even yet ideas, where the hand has to be quicker than the mind, the eyes and ears quicker than the hand. That realm which artists share with children and athletes and animals, the nameless source of the spirit that can't be stolen because it doesn't even exist in normal terms."

"And suppose," I asked Lochs the next day, "somebody tried to make unauthorized use of your current work?"

"I would kill."

"Why?"

"Because. My current work is always my effort to get out of the prison of myself. I can't do without that. I'm addicted to the world, to reality, whatever that is. I'm nothing without that, a jailbird of language, of words that cover-up as much as they reveal. Vision is my way of seeing through words to what words don't express. That's why I'm so attracted to you," he said to me, "you're on that wavelength."

"I'm flattered but not credulous."

"I swear. Aside from our occasional episode with Notley, I am absolutely celibate, I swear to God. While you play out your scenario with Pyhl. What is it? Sex? Infatuation?"

"It's neither love nor sex. If I had to give it a name, I'd say psychodrama. Ritual. Catharsis. Exorcism."

"How about laxative? Emetic? Diuretic?"

"You see, I had this thing happen to me some years back." I paused.

"What thing?"

"The thing is, I don't remember. Oh, bits and snatches. Things come back to me now and then and they scare the shit out of me."

"And you blank out? I've seen you do it."

"You see, I don't want to remember. Forgetfulness is a blessing. Why live in the past, good or bad? Seize the day, as the poet says, live in the moment."

"Right," Jimmy said. "Live in the moment, by the moment, for the moment. Pursue happiness. It's every American's right. It's in the, I think, Constitution, along with life and liberty. That's why I don't have a drinking problem."

"How do you figure that?

"I don't really have the constitution for it. I drink enough I don't remember what I do, so it's not my problem. My problem is drinking enough."

I went to see my massagynist. Formerly I had a whole corps of service workers to support me. There was my masseuse, my trainer, my psychotherapist, my women's group, my herbalist, my acupuncturist, my yoga teacher, and, of course, my manicurist and my hairdresser. Then I discovered the massagynist who does all these things at once in one marathon session.

So at regular intervals I take a day off to spend with Cassandra. Cassandra is a little mad but she's a genius who's invented a completely new profession. Each time I have a session with her I come out feeling completely remade.

Cassandra did psychotherapy while she was doing body therapy, trying to integrate the two. The topic for the day was why my sexual practice contradicted my sexual politics and my politics in general. Equality was the keyword in my politics, while my sexual practices were strictly submissive.

"You feel a contradiction?" she asked.
"Obviously."
"Why obviously?"
"Democracy is not fascism."
"That's conceptual, I asked if you feel a contradiction."
"Feel? I feel like I like being submissive. And I feel like I shouldn't. I'm not proud of it." She was working on my thighs. It hurt. And it felt good because it hurt.
"How does it make you feel, submissiveness?"
"Humiliated."
"And how does humiliation make you feel?"
"Wonderful."
"So you want to be humiliated. Turn over, I want to work on your butt."
"Not only that, I want to be hurt. Ouch! Not too much, just a little."
"Sorry, your butt is tight. Go on."
"I want to be tied up and whipped. Pricked and raped. Forced to grovel and beg."
"For what?"
"Sex."
"And what does all this make you feel?"
"Overwhelming pleasure."
"So you get what you want?"
"Yes."
"Who's the boss here?"
"I am."

"So you want to be the boss?"
"Looks like."
"Maybe you should apply for the position."
"How?"
"Directly. And openly. The way grown-ups do."
"It might spoil the fun."
"Then I guess you'll have to find a Nazi. Who did you vote for?"
"Ralph Nader."

"Do you ever wonder about your roots?" I asked Seymor one day.
"My roots are in a sperm bank."
"What do you mean sperm bank?"
"The old man told me. Fynch."
"How does he know?"
"He wouldn't tell me. So I have no father. I'm a miracle," said Seymor.

I felt a surge of compassion for Seymor, almost maternal. Especially since Fynch had already told me confidentially that Seymor was the issue of a frozen placenta. So maybe he had neither father nor mother and was not a son but something more like a product who wasn't so much conceived as defrosted.

This somehow made sense of Hymi's fantasy that Seymor was his conception. It could be deciphered as Hymi's adoption of Seymor, conceiving him as a sort of godson. If not sun god, given the way Hymi had made Seymor central to his concerns.

"I could wake up in the morning and just stay in bed. I could do that, I have the money, I have the help. But I can't," said Fynch.
"I know you can't," said Achs. "But you could rest a bit more."

"When I'm dead I'll have plenty of time to rest. Meanwhile I have a lot to do."

"The less you rest the less time you'll have to do it," said Achs.

We were in Achs's office at the Temporary. They were discussing a negative medical report that Fynch had just received. On the basis of it, his doctor recommended that he take it easy.

"What would you have me do, my dear? Sit around and brood about the things I care about? Give in to demoralization? Go all floppy and soft and manageable?"

"I know you too well for that," said Achs. "But then why do you let Pyhl take advantage of the Museum?"

"I know what I'm doing. Pyhl is not going to take advantage of anything or anyone. Everyone has his place if everyone minds his own business."

"What's he done now?" I asked.

"He's made a deal to rent some of our current exhibits to other museums when we're done showing them here," said Achs.

"But there won't be anything to exhibit once we're done showing them here," I said. "That's like renting ice cubes at room temperature."

"Exactly," said Achs.

"Maybe that's his point," said Fynch.

"Maybe his point is money," I said. And realized suddenly that I felt free to criticize Pyhl and that that was a change.

"Wait till the Improvement Society gets wind of this," said Achs.

Something was missing, I began to realize. I needed somebody to come home to, somebody with whom I didn't feel like I was playing an obsessive role in a bad play.

Much to my surprise I began thinking of the old days with Hymi. I began thinking of them with considerable nostalgia. Of course he was a lot older now, and seemed to want to communicate only by e-mail.

Hymi was in his late seventies. I had no idea what kind of physical condition he was in. I'd been in touch with him, knew he'd contacted the Museum, but had not actually seen him for ten years.

The last time I saw him was in Paris. He was staying, I was going back to the States. I had told him I was leaving him.

In the morning, while he was still asleep, I would take my bags down to the taxi for the airport and that would be that. We had been fighting nonstop, I couldn't even say what it was about. I think it was just about our lives taking different directions, his on the fringe of social life, avoiding any kind of organized activity, not to mention jobs, living from hand to mouth, me back to college teaching.

I had been over there on a research fellowship studying a precursor to the obscure Situationist movement, the still more obscure Lettriste movement. These shadowy groups were involved in politics and art, or rather politics through art, though they had no fixed program. Needless to say, their behavior reflected a totally mutinous attitude toward the status quo.

Hymi was not associated with these groups, association with any group being against his temperament. But he seemed to me to embody their mutinous point of view. Hymi could disrupt any occasion, social or professional, not necessarily with intention, but just by being who he was.

Who he was was a drop of oil on a pool of water—he floated but he didn't mix. And people didn't like that, they felt rejected, while what Hymi was doing was focusing on something different, like normal people would look at what's printed on the page while Hymi might examine the edge. I've actually seen Hymi in a casino kill the jackpot signal, and the jackpot, on a slot machine because he didn't like the noise.

He wasn't innocent, far from, he was just absorbed in his concerns. His concerns: it's hard to say what they were exactly, but the most inclusive way to describe them would probably be in terms of time. Yes, Hymi had a problem with time.

And the problem was that basically he didn't believe in time. He never said as much because he knew that would be idiotic, but I think that's what it came to. Judging by his behavior.

For beginners, he never once that I can recall recognized the fact that he was twenty years older than me. Not that I had any complaints about the way he made love, on the contrary. But I was at the time still a young woman in her late 40s, still interested in running around, investigating things, curious, highly active, aware that the prime of my life wasn't going to last forever.

His attitude, on the contrary, was I've seen it come I've seen it go and I want to think about it. I used to tell him, keep thinking Hymi, that's what you're good at. But really I got annoyed at his increasing withdrawal from the social world.

Another symptom was his inability to keep appointments on time. Or at all. He would show up at a rendezvous two hours late, or the next day.

He never wore a watch and the one clock he had was wildly erratic. Sometimes he forgot what year it was, or even his own age. But his detailed memory was crystal.

He could remember instants in his childhood as if he were looking at a snapshot. He could repeat whole conversations he had with someone the day before. He claimed the world of memory was a different world in which everything coexisted at the same time, and that stood against the leveling scythe of the temporal.

"The advantage of the temporal," he would say, "is that it's temporary. It goes away. It's linear. All that endures is what coexists."

There was a time, in a previous phase of our life together, when we would run around, travel, invite adventure pretty much nonstop. Even then, though, Hymi claimed he wasn't doing it just for the excitement of it, but to accumulate what he called "stills," snapshots of time that he could refer back to. Time, he said, is like a wave that gathers, crests and breaks, giving the illusion of change when it's still the same wave traveling through the ocean of space.

So, he said, time seems to change when what's really changing is place. I thought that was rather poetic, though I'm not sure I caught its meaning. Anyway, I can recall that last night in Paris as if it were here and now.

That night Hymi refused to say goodbye. He said we would always be in touch one way or another. He said we were now in one another's heads in a way that short-circuited time and he said that memory was presence, more enduring presence than the flux of time.

The revelation in my session with Cassandra that between Pyhl and myself I was the real, if covert, boss was working a slow change in me. The obsessive nature of our sexual relation was less of a turn-on, and soon I had trouble climaxing. I had gotten rather fond of Pyhl but, let's say, I wouldn't have chosen him for his character and opinions.

Little by little I felt myself withdrawing from Pyhl, and then one day, without even thinking about it, I found myself refusing his demand that I come see him. I wanted a less ritually intricate, more direct emotional relationship. And I wanted someone I could talk to.

I thought of Jimmy Lochs whom I was actually quite interested in. But he was too crazy. I found myself thinking more and more about my years with Hymi.

I didn't even know where he was living. Since he always e-mailed me he could have been anywhere in the universe. I asked him but he was vague, saying he was moving from place to place.

He went on:

You wouldn't be able to recognize me anyway

Or maybe not even be able to see me at all

At least if I turned sideways I've gotten so thin

Thin as a boy, except with age, not with youth

And besides, what do you need to see me for

So thin you can see right through the flesh

I've become transparent, like an x-ray

I don't even have to speak out loud

You can see words unspooling in my brain

More than candor, less than exhibitionism

I turn people into voyeurs, maybe into see-ers

The see-through man

Hymi

Seymor was getting fat. He was taking over the routine affairs of the Museum more and more, micromanaging at every level with enormous energy. And the more he took over the fatter he seemed to get.

He already had a spare tire and his face was beginning to look jowly. They say that big dogs age fast and it looked like that was what was happening to Seymor. Furthermore, he seemed lately obsessed with the issue of the theft.

He had deduced that the theft had been carried out by religious fanatics. What was stolen, he thought, was being stashed in a church. As a result he began visiting the local churches and his suspicions settled on Trinity Church, especially when he discovered that it had a museum.

He did not implicate the church officials themselves. Rather he thought that some radical sect had spirited the loot, which, as an artifact of the spirit, was in any case invisible, into the church or its museum without the knowledge of church officials. It was Seymor's theory that if he could find the right prayer in the right church, the right service in the right religion, he would find what was stolen from the Temp, as he now habitually called the Museum.

When what was stolen did not turn up in the churches, Seymor began haunting the local museums, on the theory that museums were sort of secular churches. He visited the South Street Seaport Museum and the Museum of American Financial History, the New York Police Museum and the Fraunces Tavern Museum. But the places he thought he came near to finding it, aside from the Trinity Church Museum, were the Ellis Island Museum, the National Museum of the American Indian, and the Museum of Jewish Heritage.

But as at Trinity Church, what he was looking for, evanescent as it was, remained intangible. Until, that is, he stumbled on the new Skyscraper Museum. There, for a fleeting instant he thought he had found what he was looking for. He told me what happened.

He was contemplating the model of the World Trade Center in the museum as summation of the spirit of urban life, when he looked out the window and saw the twin towers, the vertical striations, the silver shafts of the World Trade Center. He was overcome in that instant by an overwhelming sense of reality, and the formulation came to him that the spirit is the real while the reality is evanescent. Seymor told me his first impulse when he realized this was to report to the Improvement Society, because it was behind Art Brute and this was the hidden premise of the Art Brutists.

But he didn't have time because he had to scout out an Art Brute piece that was a candidate for his show. He headed over to an address in the East Village, and when he got there he was directed by a handwritten note taped to the door up the stairs to the roof. It was nighttime by now, and except for the beam of a single flashlight the roof was pitch dark.

When his eyes got used to the darkness, Seymor made out a short, bushy figure who came up and introduced himself as "the facilitator." Here's how Seymor reconstructed their conversation.

"I came here to meet a Mr. McMan, a pseudonym I presume?"
"A nom de plume. Here from the museum?"
"Seymor. I'm curating the Brutist show."
"Well I don't know about being brutal. Wacko maybe."
"No, I'm talking about outsider art, self-taught art."
"Well I never taught myself nothing, but my work is outside. I like fresh air."
"Why don't you show me what you do?"
"OK. But I'm warning you, if you try to rip me off I'll sue your ass."
"What's your medium?"
"Me. I'm the medium."
"And where's the work?"
"Out there," he waved in the general direction of uptown. "Here we go!" he said, leading Seymor by flashlight to a giant slide projector. He switched it on. "There it is!"
"What?" asked Seymor.
"Don't you see it?"
"No." But then Seymor did. Projected on the buildings across the street, now illuminated, was a perfect tracing of—the buildings across the street.

We were eating lunch in the Museum cafeteria, Jimmy Lochs, Notley, and me. The talk turned to yet another art gossip item about Jimmy that had appeared with a photo in a journal. Jimmy was getting more and more notoriety, he was becoming a celebrity, while Notley was sinking into obscurity.

This article had Jimmy paired amorously with a well-known model. He hadn't read the article and pretended not to be interested, but you could see that he was. Even though there wasn't a word of truth in it.

"How does it make you feel given that it's a total fabrication?" asked Notley.
"Well it's hard not to be interested in your own reputation. Even though it has nothing to do with me. It's like having a voodoo image of yourself out there. It's not you, but it has its effect on you."
"Luckily I don't have to worry about that," said Notley.
"But doesn't it worry you not to have to worry about it?" asked Jimmy.
"My ambition is to be like the Jaberwock that disappears up its own hole. A black hole that swallows its own vortex."

But it was obvious, though feigning indifference, Notley was as uneasy as Jimmy about the fame bomb, especially when it exploded anywhere in the vicinity. At that moment, a busboy came up to our table waving a postcard at Jimmy.

"Let's see that," said Jimmy, grabbing it. "Hey, it looks like somebody's turning my disappearables into postcards. Guess who?"

"I thought you might sign it, Mr. Lochs," said the busboy.
"Why, sure thing," said Jimmy, whipping out the Mont Blanc.

Jimmy was blasé but you could tell it pumped him up. He scribbled his signature and handed the card back with a supercilious air.

"So you see that's what it comes down to," said Jimmy. "Recognition by a busboy."
"Multiplied by x," I added.

Notley's agent and guru, Minerva Quinn, had called me about the possibility of a show for him at the Temp and invited me for lunch. After the pleasantries, I got down to something that was troubling me about the meeting.

"From what he tells me, Notley seems to be getting very mixed messages from you. On one hand you advise him to withdraw from the world in meditation, on the other to promote himself more."

Minerva was a surprisingly young woman with an ultrathin, wiry body, and a face like a wedge.

"There's no contradiction," she explained. "The key is disinterest. Promote hard and don't care about results. We have to live in this world, after all, as well as the other."
"The other?"
"You know, the one that we come out of and go back to."
"You mean nothingness," I said.
"That's one way of putting it," she said.

I couldn't believe we were sitting there talking about theology in the middle of a business lunch.

"How would you put it?"

"You know. The invisible. That's our real world. Everybody knows that when they take the trouble to stop and think about it."

"Well in this unreal world," I returned to the subject, "how do you propose exhibiting music in a museum, especially music which is, in Notley's case, a silence?"

"Easy. Since the Temporary Museum cultivates absence. What better than to exhibit work that from any point of view is not there? How much realer could you get? Believe me, I started life as a real estate agent until I realized that the property isn't the point, what's real in real estate is the numbers. The abstractions. The figures that exist in your head."

"I still don't see it at the Temp."

"Easy. I suggest you do his empty room piece, 'Sonata for an Empty Room.'"

"The room isn't empty if someone is listening," I objected.

"That's it! You can't hear it if you're in the room."

This is what led to Seymor's hunch that religious fanatics were behind the theft from the Temp: first of all, he reasoned that the theft of something that could have no marketable financial value implied that the motive must be ideological. Second, the ambiguous demand for a ransom implied special knowledge about its spiritual value. Third, only religious fanatics would have the motive for, as it were, vandalizing a rival cultural institution.

Seymor told me he therefore deduced that we were dealing with self-righteous culture fascists who would stop at nothing to further their agenda. Sure enough, a few days later, the Temp received a note signed by a group calling itself Fundament.

"The word is flesh, and we are its scribes," it said. "If you want it back, eat your words. Let us prey." Seymor said the message implied some kind of blood sacrifice, or even cannibalism.

"So where do we go from here?" I asked him.

"We know their price for returning it will be to neutralize it. We can't do that route. I plan to consult with those involved with the Temp."

Which is what he did. Pyhl advised him to do what they said.

"That would change the character of the Museum," said Seymor.

"The alternative," said Pyhl, "is to shut down, which might not be a bad idea."

But, of course, he got different advice from Notley and Jimmy Lochs.

"Do nothing," said Notley. "They won't know what to do if you do that. They'll let it go and the whole thing will go away. The missing work will cancel out."

"I disagree," said Jimmy. "Go after them. Don't let them get away with it. If you do, you open the door to other thefts. Come down hard on them. I'll help. We'll devise a strategy. It'll be all-out war."

9/10/01 realtime

realtime 9/11/01:

Her life was at an impasse, that's why she wanted to see me again

She had a small apartment with a view of the World Trade Center

She was surprised by my white beard, my cane

I hardly recognized her, so much had she grown in definition, personality, authority

Harder, but it suited her age

Nevertheless, we were easy with one another and finally she asked me to stay the night

I told her I didn't bring my Viagra she said that wasn't the point

What was the point the point was to reconnect

That's what she said but I already felt connected

Because she still had a quality maybe left over from her religious phase

Devotion

But devotion without particular object

She was devout as an attitude

That is she took things seriously

She thought about things, she weighed things, including relationships, including me

The frivolities of sex no exception

She thought it incorrect to sleep with me, bedding me alone on the convertible

Next morning we were starting to get dressed

I heard a sharp constricted boom

I heard her call from the other room, The World Trade Center's been hit

She was standing at the window naked I could see a red transparence of flames high up the tower

I went numb, A plane must have hit it, I said

Or terrorists, she said, I saw the '93 bombing

We watched, I was numb

We were standing naked at the window and one of the World Trade Center towers was burning

It was two blocks away

The shadow of the Towers falls on this building mornings, she'd said, or silvery light reflects off them into the apartment afternoons

I realized I didn't have any clothes on, vulnerable

We could see flames eating away at the building frame

I turned to finish dressing, What's that plane doing there, sightseeing? she said

She was dressing quickly

Vicious snarl of gunned jet engines capped by loud boom followed by a bang followed by bangs

Red splash of flames on second tower, shower of glistening window panes floating down

The smoke was dead black, pouring into the sky now from two fiery slashes

Debris in streets, traffic stopped

Someone came out of the hotel at the base of the Towers spreading white tablecloths on the black asphalt of the street

What's that? I asked her, she now using binoculars

Bloody parts, she said, human meat

The twin fires now volcanic eating through steel

Everything fluid, flames, buildings, smoke, inky smoke more solid than colossal buildings

Colossal even from her apartment 30 floors up

I had a moment of suppressed panic

You know, I said slowly, it looks like those buildings could fall, and if they fall in the wrong direction, they could fall on us

The numb stupor of our ghastly fascination jogged into reality

We finished dressing in a hurry, shoved a few things in a backpack, and hoped the elevator would still be running

Downstairs people were heading for the river

The rumor was some people were jumping in to be rescued by passing boats

When we reached the walk along the Hudson we found it crowded with refugees hurrying south, away from the Towers

We joined them but since I don't walk so fast with my cane the crowd traffic was menacing

The ink pouring out of the twin cartons into the sky was getting more profuse

Someone shouted, There it goes, and people started running

One of the Towers seemed to shake at the top and then disappeared above us in a black cloud, rumbling, thundering in a breaking wave of sound

I was seeing several thousand people die in five seconds

One minute the tower was there and then in the blink of an eye it was gone

Impacted black billows towering fifty stories high racing down streets toward us at 100 miles an hour

People in panic running from it if it carried building parts, debris we were finished

Or suffocation in a tidal wave of hot smoke and ash

Suddenly vision reduced to shadowy outlines in cloud

Ghostly figures running in panic

But we could breathe

We put our shirts up over our mouths

We were alive

The running crowds slowed to a walk

Someone handed us breathing masks

The air was now a beige fog of granulated ash and dust

Someone gave us a bottle of water someone took my arm and walked with me

The air cleared the second tower was burning like a colossal torch

The ground was covered with powdery ash like beige snow

Still fleeing along the river, seeking refuge

Abandoned baby carriages

Someone offered to carry me, I kept walking

Tugboats were nosing up to the esplanade, ripping up railings, boarding frightened people

Escaping a second tower collapse

A pair of patent leather shoes in the dust, I kept walking as fast as I could

Austyn blocking from behind

Chemical smell of ash, burning electronics

The tower a volcanic torch

I kept walking

Suddenly a quick shake and crumble

Abrupt chute no transition

Swallowed up by a dense inky cloud, the noise too loud to hear

And it was gone

Surrounded by ghostly figures covered with beige dust in a gray mist

Sparrows confused by gray powder on grass

Trees and lawns like a photographic negative

Security guards materialized directing crowds to boats pulled up to the esplanade

We were close to the tip of Manhattan

We could see her building from here, evidently undamaged

We decided to go back rather than risk boarding the boats and some high school gymnasium in Jersey City with the other refugees

We made some excuse to a security guard and slipped away

Trudging through three inches of beige snow

Air snowing blowing papers, print, memos, charred writing by dead hands, pages littered on ground

Chemical smell of ash, burning electronics

There was an elevator working on an emergency generator in her building

No electricity in her apartment

We were smeared with layers of beige dust down to the skin

We looked out the window, she started crying

Instead of the Trade Center towers was empty space and below a huge heap of pulverized debris

Crenelated remnants of walls left standing at crazy angles

A 10 story section of wall flung on the ground like a towel

Subterranean fires leaking smoke, the red flare of fires on the surface and in adjacent buildings

Squashed cars and fire engines at the periphery

Emergency vehicles water hoses flashing lights hard hats working frantically

Infernal mounds of wreckage, Piranesi ruins of mock Gothic arches

Some hot water in the pipeline, we showered

We tried the phones they were out

It was getting dark we lit candles found flashlights

We were boiling water for tea when the gas went off

The water ran out

Night fell

Ground zero was lit with white floodlight and red flames, night-time view of hell

It looked like a stage set for the Inferno with pastiche Gothic decor

Smoke, giant mound of twisted beams and rubble, plod of workers, fires from wreckage, buildings burning red inside out all night, thick black smoke against gray hazy smoke

Huge backhoes like dinosaurs were picking at the rubble heaps

We held on to one another

Long flatbed trucks were moving huge twisted girders, agonized I-beams, and dumping them on our street Niagaras of noise

I was lost in the stunning animation of fires, wreckage, workers, smoke, rubble and machines

Police came to our door saying the building was being evacuated

To where they didn't know

We looked at one another and realized we preferred to stay

To hold out with one another and It

Home and refuge

They let us stay for the time being

Searching for lit windows in other buildings finding few

Loneliness

Alleviated by one small transistor radio as frame of reference

Submerged in sense images unmodified by social framework or TV

Towers ugly from a distance like two cartons

Up close their out of scale verticals, their grill façades, their four dimensional night reflections on one another, their silver gleam, their tops buried in clouds, their scary view from tops higher than helicopters and her own tiny skyscraper below.

Towers still exist in mind while disappeared in matter—which is more real?

The memory or the present?

Or both?

Or both?

She put her head on my shoulder and we were back 15 years ago

Her presence then equal to her presence now

The real is temporary, I told her, only the unreal may be permanent

Really, she said vaguely

What we're dealing with here, I pointed out the window, is the power of the unreal over the real

This is the beginning of the battle in which we will be forced to embrace the unreal or die out, I told her

The unreal that we can no longer neglect, I told her

I don't know where it came from, these words

Unless they came from the unreal

The pit was like an open sore

Huge backhoes kept scratching at it with steel fingers, as many as 10 or 11 at a time now

Picking off scabs of metal, sometimes exposing flesh of the 3000 missing in there

We decided to hold out in her apartment

We had no place else to go

The thing that scared me was the one emergency elevator might stop working

It was a form of claustrophobia in reverse, fear of being buried up in the air

Otherwise it was a good venue oddly to pursue our happiness

In full view of the well of unhappiness out the window reminding us of the liquidity of solidity

Of the uncertainty principle

Of the fragility of life except in memory

Of the endurance of the temporary

It's there that we really connected again

Without Viagra

The flames burned all night and into the next day despite streaming fire hoses and the subterranean fires never stopped

Smoke from underground leaks or billows up, usually ash gray sometimes jet black

Depending on how the machines dig at the surface

As levels are stripped away the wreckage takes on new contours

A generation of contemporary art has prepared us, she said, for this

This is the negative of its trivial positives

What we have here, she continued, is a deconstruction, a deinstallation, unearth art, photosurrealism, deconceptualization

That's why it's so hard to grasp, our intellectual framework has been destroyed, maybe it was too flimsy

I turn away and the towers are still there in my head

After a week food and water were running out, candles all burned down to stubs

The transistor radio was dying

Our reality was the mammoth charnel house and tomb out the windows

We were getting a little strange

We jumped at loud noises, became anxious at the sound of jet planes

We worried about asbestos in the air, wondered about another terror attack

At times we were exuberant about still being alive, then grief stricken and guilty

Went through long depressions at the mass wipeout of lives, then became furious wanting to exterminate the brutes responsible

Felt responsible ourselves to bear witness

Wanted to leave, felt guilty about leaving

Searched out our windows for other windows lit up at night found very few

Our sleeping hours became unpredictable

Time collapsed

We read Proust by candle light to one another

We were down to eating dry cereal in a little water, saving water in tub for consumption rather than washing

We must have smelled rank, looked worse

When the police came to the door they kept their distance, menacingly polite

They insisted we leave or be carried out

Said there were dangerous gas leaks

She gathered some things

Delivered us in the lobby to National Guard in camo

They were prepared to march us through checkpoints out to the normal world

Where after that our business

I was in no shape to march

Noticing, some gallant cops offered us a ride in their van

Austyn gave the address of the Temporary Museum

Outside the street was filled with piles of twisted I-beams two stories high

Down the block three or four layers of crushed fire engines

They ushered us through the dust to the van

There was a suite in the Museum kept ready for executives, she had a key

The Museum was downtown in the frozen zone closed to nonresidents for security

We tossed our clothes thick with beige dust, she kept a change of clothes there, so did some man

We washed and ate a cold meal from the mini fridge

We were in the pottery section of the Museum which meant in the Temporary an exhibition of the contents of pots rather than the pots themselves, the contents as shaped by the missing pots

In the case of empty pots there was empty air

Because according to the Temporary Museum containers were temporary, contents endured in one shape or another

Austyn started phoning her associates to tell them she had survived

After the amenities I heard her tell Fynch that she felt the experience would change her life

That only the moment seemed substantial while the substantial seemed unreal

He overheard her say to Jimmy Lochs that the World Trade Center seemed like one of his disappearables

She told Notley how we could not hear the incredible roar of the second tower collapsing

And he heard her leave a message for Pyhl that he had to choose now between the real and the timeless

The next day Seymor and Achs got together with Austyn at the Museum to assess the situation

The situation, according to Achs, was that while the Temporary Museum was built to be an absence and was present, the World Trade Center was built to be an overwhelming presence and was now a spectacular absence

This was too abstract for Seymor, who insisted that the Museum was up against religious fanatics whose goal was to hijack and destroy a rival culture

"What they stole from the Temp was intangible, but it was like a warning shot. Now you can see where it leads. It should now be obvious that we're in a battle whose consequences are all too drastically in the world of concrete and steel, but whose real battlefield is in the invisible world."

Seymor, who I was meeting for the first time, was even bigger than I'd imagined him from Austyn's description

He was not only fabulously tall, he was also extremely broad, not to say fat

"The only way to fight a war like this," said Seymor, "is with our writers and artists, our musicians, our scholars, our spiritual advisers priests and rabbis, all those who live in another world, the most impoverished world of all, what you might call the fifth world."

"What's the fourth?" asked Austyn.

"The international world of children, disinherited for lack of the fifth."

I found out later that Austyn and Pyhl had been using the suite where we were staying for impromptu sex when they were working at the Temp, in fact they were about the only two to use it at all

But I didn't know that when Pyhl walked in one night while we were asleep, I on the convertible in the living room and she in the bedroom

He walked past me into the bedroom and didn't even close the door all the way

Soon I began to hear fragments of conversation, if you could call it that:

She: I told you you couldn't

He: I know you like

She: don't ... again

She: I told you

She: let me turn over at least

He: no

He: where are the ropes?

She: please

Extended silence

She: a sort of whimper

Extended silence

Mattress bouncing

She: he'll hear us

He: that's right

A long mezzo soprano groan

A guttural grunt

Extended silence

Pyhl came out of the bedroom, closing the door noisily

He opened the door of the apartment, paused, said: Do I make my point?

And left

But his point was not what he thought it was

His point was the power of imagination over the power of meat

Her point was that Pyhl had become a habit

Pretty soon I heard her quaver: Hymi? Could you come in here please?

I obliged and found her naked in bed, hands and feet tied to the bedposts

He had left her that way on purpose, of course, so she'd have to call me in to see her like that

Sorry, she said, could you please untie me?

I obliged, but slowly, because the bastard had tied the knots real tight

I'm so humiliated, she said

You like being humiliated

You're right, she said, but only sexually

Well I don't like humiliating you, especially sexually, never did

You lack imagination

Maybe I imagine different things

The windows of her bedroom in the apartment we had just evacuated looked straight down into ground zero of the World Trade Center

It was a heap of smoking rubble enclosed in a pit formed by the stripped facades of ruined buildings

Here at the Temporary Museum all the light came in from the roof and at night I looked up at the stars

The Museum was closed as were all public buildings in the frozen zone

But next evening we got a visit from Fynch with Pyhl who brought us food

Fynch seemed to be shrinking, Austyn remarked to me later

Whether he had shrunk I don't know, but what I saw was striking

A little man, about the size of a marionette, tiny body contrasting with an oversized head whose hairless face and scalp revealed the outlines of his skull

You've had a narrow escape, he said to me in a voice dry as sand

"I have information," he continued, "from the Improvement Society that there is more to come and that we're confronted with a many-headed monster. In particular, according to Seymor, the manifestation we're dealing with at the Museum calls itself the Fundament. They believe, says Seymor, that the spiritual spark is buried in the meat of our bodies."

"I say make a deal with them," said Pyhl.

"Seymor says they don't make deals. In any case, I don't want to make a deal. There is no compromise in this," said Fynch. "You don't make deals with the primal muck."

"We're not living in LaFange," snapped Pyhl.

"No," said Fynch. "LaFange lives in us."

We were living in the frozen zone that surrounded ground zero

That meant we were dependent on authorized personnel for food, drink, and company

We knew if we left the zone we could never get back in

Besides Seymor, Pyhl and Achs, as officials of the Museum, were authorized, and of course Fynch

Achs came regularly to deliver groceries

Pyhl came at unpredictable hours mostly to play with Austyn and to show off

Electricity was sporadic and candlelight seemed to encourage their exhibitionistic behavior as if the apartment were a stage set

My generation doesn't keep its variant sexual behaviors in the closet, Pyhl said, the way yours did. We don't make invidious definitions of normality. That's strictly LaFange

Sometimes you could see his sperm running down her thigh, at times down her chin

All the while he would be caressing her body absently as if I weren't there

Actually, I was becoming an integral part of their sex play, a witness of her submission to him

Though I could sense a latent impatience emerging in her demanding inventiveness

I began to curse the irresponsible neglect by which I didn't carry my Viagra with me at all times

But in any case when I tried to get her to do something for me after Pyhl left, she said that I was too classy to get into their seedy scene

She said it was disgusting and she wouldn't think of involving me in it, she said Pyhl was disgusting

She said she was disgusted with herself

She blamed it on the isolation, she said it froze one's behavior in neurotic patterns for lack of stimulation, even the telephone usually didn't work

She said it would be better to contemplate the psychosis behind ground zero

She said the psychosis of ground zero marked the dead point of human nature from which it could move in any direction

She said ground zero could imply a total psychotic regression from civilized behavior

She said she was afraid her erotic behavior stemmed from the same dead point, the same zero

She wondered what the difference was between psychotic behavior and playing games

She said the charred bits of paper from 1000 offices that swirled up in the neighborhood whenever the wind rose paralyzed her with depression

She said that before 9/11 she thought she had done with Pyhl but he seemed to assuage her vulnerabilities

It suddenly struck her now that she was still afraid the World Trade towers would fall on her

Pyhl and Austyn continued to use me as an audience for their sex games

I have to admit that they turned me on but they also upset me

I realized they were playing but I wasn't a player

After the sessions Austyn would attack herself bitterly

It was as if she had some sort of autoimmune condition in which her very defenses turned on her

I loathe myself, she would say, for giving in to that kind of muck. I'm sure it has something to do with the Incident.

She would have what I can only describe as panic attacks and fainting spells

I tried to tell her that she and Pyhl were just playing and that playing could be a kind of problem-solving behavior

What problem can I be trying to solve that way? she asked

Maybe the problem of the Incident

But meantime her behavior didn't change, if anything it got more extreme

She told me she wanted to see how far Pyhl could push her

At the same time I began to sense a subtle change in her attitude toward me

I got the sense that she was beginning to consider me as a reality check

So I wasn't surprised, when the frozen status was partially lifted and I could get to my SRO up town for a few things, she urged me to come back

And to bring my Viagra

I got the sense that her compulsions were to starting to thaw

But Pyhl was changing too

The first sign of it was when he came to visit Austyn with a large American flag

    "What's that for?" she asked.
    "That's to hang on the wall."
    "For what?"
    "To show where we stand. About the museum thefts. To show they're not going to get away with it. To show that we're going to track them down and wipe them out."
    "And how are we going to do that?"
    "However it takes. This is war."

You could see the muscles working in his jaw, his face was red, his body erect

He looked good

You could tell Austyn thought so too

He went over his strategy in dealing with the Fundament

He said that the key was they took everything literally, there was no room for interpretation or argument

Since what they stole from the Temp was intangible, what the Temp needed to do was to quantify it and give it a name

In giving identity to what had no identity they would oblige the Fundament to react in a way that would freeze them in their position, leave them holding the bag, ultimately destroy them

And what identity would that be? she asked

What's in the empty box? replied Pyhl

We were confused, but he was so excited about getting on about it that he left without laying a hand on Austyn

Seymor said it took the chaos of ground zero to break into new configurations

The smoking chaos of ground zero with new fires breaking out every time a backhoe scratched the surface a little too deeply

As if there were a permanent subterranean fire inextinguishable to constant hosing

And yet, continued Seymor, it was in this pit of death, this mass grave, this open wound, that change could happen

Had already happened, from the moment the first tower shook and fell, redefining the world

We went back

The smoking mounds of rubble were still there, the ruined sections of wall still standing, the tilting and sheared guts of surrounding buildings sliced by fragments of towers still protruding like knives left in wounds

But instead of fire engines and ambulances, giant-jawed backhoes tearing apart wreckage, a delicate forest of towering cranes uprooting girders or suspending cabled observation cages, long flatbed trucks hauling away enormous I-beams, here and there American flags flapping

The sparks of acetylene torches punctuated the site, streams of water hosed down the fires

Neighboring streets had been cleared, trailers and prefab shacks had been put in place

Figures in hard hats and orange vests swarmed the wreckage like ants

Semis and go carts were in constant motion

A traffic pattern had been set up, trucks hosed down before leaving with rubble

9/11 work went on 24/7, at night lit up like a sports stadium

What had been a field of devastation had become a construction project, demolition phase

The energy of it was tonic

Every day the contours of the wreckage were altered and shrunk

Time seemed less important than, or just different from, the day-to-day change

You looked at them and they weren't there

Someone said a phantom limb

You felt it was there, you perceived it was there

But it wasn't

At ground zero the infernal reality was unavoidable

But wasn't, I thought, the former World Trade Center real too?

Was not the smoking Pit out the window, minus time, still the twin towers?

After all, what is time that it should be so privileged?

Time exists only in change, and who can say that one change wipes out another?

Looking out the window today I saw a herd of orange or yellow backhoes scavenging the pit like dinosaurs

Their jaws pulled twisted steel from the muck soaked by firehoses to control the smoldering subterranean hotspots

Nobody knew yet what would re-emerge from all this activity, but the activity itself was hopeful

It reminded Austyn of Fynch's attitude toward the farm town he grew up in, LaFange

You plow under the remains of the last crop in LaFange to make the ground ready for the new

LaFange, Achs had told her, means the mud, the mire in French

Fynch believed in plowing under the old to make way for the new, he believed it about himself and his own death

People change, he said, people need to change and finally to die

This was one of the more definite doctrines in his belief in disorganized religion, Austyn said

It was about the same time when Austyn and I started having sex again that I began seeing news stories about the theft from the Museum

According to the papers an urn worth $3 million had been stolen

The urn was supposedly a Chinese antique dating from the fourth century and had the peculiar quality that it was made of a clear ceramic material that rendered it almost invisible

You only knew it was there because objects on the other side of it went blurry and distorted

And even then, the distortion was so slight that you couldn't depend on visual identification to discern it but rather had to resort to the tactile

But the urn was so delicate that one would take great risks in trying to touch it without seeing it

Nevertheless, the news stories were accompanied by an artist's conception of what the urn would look like

By the time electricity was restored to Austyn's apartment and we no longer had to depend on Achs bringing the newspapers, various versions of the urn could be seen on TV newscasts

For some reason these artist's renditions depressed Austyn, and to tell the truth I found them a downer also

But for Austyn, she only had to glimpse one such to be thrown into a depression that lasted all day

Then it got worse

She apparently internalized these pictures and simply thinking about them and visualizing them would upset her

Her depressions would break down eventually, but only into moods of anxiety, fear, and anger

At first these feelings were prompted by the urn pictures because, she told me, they implied that some important secrets, or even the possibility of secrets in general, which is to say the possibility of an interior life, had been wiped out

But as the syndrome developed in its phobia, I began to suspect that it was fueled by her fear, often remarked on by her while acknowledging its craziness, that the World Trade towers were still falling still falling and were going to fall on her

And while her phobia inhibited her sexual responsiveness in bed, I perceived a damming up of her emotions which I suspected could not last for long

By the time the anthrax scare started, most of the security checkpoints impeding access to Austyn's apartment overlooking ground zero had been lifted

Visitors began to drift in to inquire about her state of mind and incidentally the state of ground zero

Her state of mind was shaky, she told them, and ground zero, as they could see, was being taken apart piece by careful piece because of its status as a mass grave

Jimmy Lochs, pioneer as always, was one of the first people to suspect he had contracted anthrax

He told us not to worry because it wasn't contagious, but that he had checked the symptoms as relayed by the news media and he claimed he had them all

His doctor advised him to observe their development and not panic as this was the first day he had symptoms

But he was already revising his will and had come to ask Austyn to be his executor

His panic brought out Austyn's sense of dread and I tried to reassure him, but he didn't want to be reassured

"Sure," he said, "you're an old guy, you've lived your life, but I'm only in my early 60s and I've got a lot of living to do. Me and Austyn, we've got a lot to look forward to."

"I don't feel that way," said Austyn. "The way I feel now, I could be walking along the street and a building could fall on me. I don't have any sense of security, or even of predictability. I feel anything can happen."

"Anything can happen," I told her. "That's always the case. Think of it as liberating, as opening possibilities."

"No, no," she said. "Anything can happen now, and it won't be good."

I gazed down into ground zero, its avalanche of rubble, its sheared buildings and free standing walls, herds of backhoes, their jaws tearing into twisted cables, pipes, girders, cranes hoisting immense I-beams, and I have to admit that I too was getting fascinated by it in a morbid way

The next thing I knew she had found a telescope somewhere and had it trained on the site

Through the telescope I could see as individuals what appeared to be without it crowds of orange vested hard-hatted ants swarming over the mounds of ruins

I could see their faces and if I couldn't see their expressions I could read their body language

I knew when they stopped working and gathered in irregular groups, hands on hips, that they had discovered another body or body part

I could see the orange body bags

I could tell it was the body of a policeman or fireman when they covered the body bag with an American flag

I could see the backhoes bite into the rubble-releasing plumes of smoke with each bite

I could see the men in metal cages suspended from giant cranes and the cascades of sparks from their welder's torches as they cut through steel

And I felt myself drawn into the ever deepening vortex of ground zero as it changed shape every day

Eventually it would be an empty hole to be defined by what was put in place

    "Like me," remarked Austyn, with a bitter little laugh.
    "You underestimate yourself," I told her. "You bring a whole invisible history to any situation. Don't play the victim."
    "9/11 vaporized any sense of my experience. Blasted it into meaninglessness. And it did that to a lot of people, maybe to everyone. So we are victims."
    "You're saying it destroyed our inner life?"
    "My inner life is on television, repeated and repeated."

I knew what she meant

Since we had gotten electric power back we'd been watching our 9/11 experience on the TV screen

It came down to a few images replayed again and again

The plane smashing into the tower, the fires, people running, the buildings imploding in a cloud of black

It was simple, shocking, and hypnotic

There was something vulgar about it, something at the same time arrogant and impoverished

The original shock, emotionally, had erased us back to the empty blackboard which was then overwritten by electronic images

Experience stolen, you might say, and then sold back to us

The hole of ground zero pulled me into the vortex of the past

Why had we separated in that long-ago?

Not because we fell out of love

Maybe it was a mistake about what love was

She was tired of Bohemia I felt fettered by convention

She was getting religion I had lost faith

She craved career I drifted in backwaters

She wanted security I sneered at the concept

None of it was personal, grounded in feeling

It was all theoretical

Maybe we wanted the same thing

To fend off negation

To keep the pilot light burning

Maybe that's what love is for

To keep the faith

Maybe I was still in love

The ruins changed shape every day as the site of demolition was demolished

The one constant was the plumes of smoke from the subterranean fires

People would come to visit to check out the progress of the vast cleanup operation

Ground zero was becoming a tourist destination

Tourism was less from a morbid thrill seeking impulse, I supposed, than it was a desire to find out what had happened to us and what was going to happen to us

The main reaction of people looking at the site was that if this could happen anything can happen

That everything was impermanence, that there was no telling what would happen next

That certainly was Jocylyn's reaction when she visited

And, after all I'd heard about the politics of the Museum from Austyn, it was my reaction in seeing that Jocylyn had Notley in tow

Judging from their behavior they were clearly an amorous couple

Gone was Jocylyn's hard-nosed and overbearing manner

On the contrary she was almost girlish in her attentiveness to Notley, who was his reputed austere self

I wondered what happened to the friendship of Jocylyn and Pyhl

What happened I supposed was the same thing that was happening between Pyhl and Austyn

Pyhl had become Seymor's chief lieutenant in his struggle for the Museum

Pyhl had found his true path and had no time for anything else, neither Jocylyn nor Austyn

It was a tribute to the system Seymor had set up at the Temp in which he had incorporated Pyhl as his second in command

No one could understand why he had done this nor what Pyhl's function was

No one, that is, until the current crisis when it turned out that Pyhl's aggressive nature was just what was needed

One day when I was at the Museum with Austyn, Pyhl showed up with a real estate agent named Klump

Klump was dealing in real estate devalued by the catastrophe

He was trying to sell Fynch a bargain basement basement which was all that was left of a building on the perimeter of ground zero except for what looked like piles of steel spaghetti

He was trying to convince us that the property would be an ideal extension of the Museum

Buy a major piece of reality, was his pitch, you'll never get another chance like this

"This is the material world we're talking, the real thing," he urged. "This is not some wishy-washy invisible phenomenon like thinking. This is not your intellectual property, so called, liable to slip between your fingers like so much smoke. This is nitty-gritty bedrock, the real shit. It was here yesterday and it'll be here tomorrow. You can count on it."

Later that same day Jimmy Lochs turned up with gallery owner Hedda Harper and curator M. S. Priestley, an arm around each

Jimmy Lochs declared himself in good spirits—single malt Scotch, he quipped

But when he looked out the window at ground zero tears dribbled down his face

He turned away and apologized

"For what?" Austyn asked him. "That's what we all feel."

"We've just been looking at some of the shrines," Jimmy said. "The ones with photos of the missing. Decorated with colored paper, flowers, flags and votive candles. And down here at ground zero there's one with hundreds of teddy bears."

"But why teddy bears?" asked Priestley. "That was one I couldn't figure out."

"It's obvious," snapped Jimmy. "Teddy bears are for hugging and making you feel good. So it's a way of passing on good feeling to those passed away. It's like a loving goodbye. Like the photos began as missing person's notices and quickly became memorials to the missing."

"I suppose you can think of them both as installations," said Hedda Harper. "Say, how about a show? My gallery would be open to it, I think it would be a big draw."

"But how would you get permissions?" asked Priestley. "How would you price them? Who would the money go to?"

"My guess is they're in the public domain, I'll have to ask my lawyer."

"You could really clean up on a deal like that," said Priestley.

"Of course a percentage would go to charity, the victim's next of kin, something like that," said Hedda Harper. "And then, there might be a sale to your museum."

"That might be arranged," said Priestley.

My pilot light was definitely lit for Austyn but my burner turned on when I had reason to suspect she was still seeing Pyhl

A hint here and there was all I needed to make my imagination flare up

My mind created repetitive erotic scenarios between them

I was by turns angry at her and envious of him

But I kept it to myself, fearful that it would just make things worse and surprised that I cared that much

Meantime I was becoming obsessed with the scene out her window

Ground zero was like an open wound that the backhoes scratched at compulsively, digging and deepening the agonized remnants of the complex

Smoke plumed up as underground fires flared

Firemen on alert for the dead, ready to stop work and break out the orange body bags

It bothered me when the work stopped

I was convinced at some level that they were digging to find something essential, not merely emptying out a space

Such a vast excavation had to reveal something more than a vacuum

It was even more portentous at night

The freestanding walls of the destroyed towers, 10 stories tall, created the effect of a proscenium stage lit by the livid glare of the floodlights

The smoke smudged up, the welders' torches glowed, and streams of water from the hoses arched and glistened

Each layer in the debris removed by the hard hats revealed another layer of debris more splintered and tangled than the last

The site looked like it had been smashed by a comet

Today they must have hit a hot spot because the smoke bubbled up like an inverted waterfall

Holes within pits opened up in the rubble that were like vortexes to nowhere

The colors of the ruins soot gray to tarnished silver to rust brown highlighted bright orange or yellow of the heavy machinery

I had the impression that I was looking at the collapse of an idea, the idea of the architect, the whole concept of a city

Austyn said it was going to change her life

I said, I hope so, how?

"I'm going to be more serious. More responsible. More thoughtful. More generous. More sensitive. More careful. More cautious. More pessimistic. More nervous. More uncomprehending. More afraid."

"It's like we've lived through an earthquake or volcanic eruption," I said. "But one thing about volcanoes, they make for very rich soil."

My imagination kept returning to 9/11, to the 3000 people who didn't get out in time

Who had to choose, some of them, the fire or the fall of 100 floors

It's the choice that my imagination kept coming back to

And I kept thinking that if the hijackers could have imagined that choice they could never have done what they did

But their imaginations must have been at degree zero, pure of speculation, pure and numb

They must have been literalists of the word: If God says kill God means kill

And therefore ground zero had become a mass grave for an occasional corpse but mostly for body parts, cremated ash, and dust in the air we breathed

So we were breathing in death, literally, and all those deaths were becoming part of us, I told Austyn

"So we need to sublimate the hellish facts of their death or, better, we need to metabolize them, or die ourselves."
"I'm not good at that," said Austyn. "I still haven't even sublimated the Incident after all these years. I still find it hard to swallow without the transformations of music."
"Well maybe that's what music is for. Metamorphosis."

"Metamorphosis of what?"
"Cockroaches into humans."

When we got back to Austyn's apartment I looked out the window at the reality of 9/11

I wondered again why it had become a tourist destination

Today there were so many excavators at work the Pit reminded me of an open sore crawling with maggots

It was stuffy in the apartment and I opened the window a crack but the smell was so strong I had to close it

An odor of boiled computers and death that was the essence of the disaster

What could the tourists be looking for there?

Wasn't this the pursuit of unhappiness? this viewing of the corpse, to understand and to mourn—this pilgrimage—this awestruck homage—this grief

Notley came over and Austyn asked him about Jocylyn

Notley told her she had a change of heart because of 9/11

He told her she was devastated by the devastation, that she cried for three days

He said it was only when he got her to listen to one of his silent pieces that she was able to transform her grief

He said she had become as tender as she had been tough

He said that for her listening to silence had turned her negativity into positives as quickly as the attack planes turned the trade towers' positives to negation

He said listening for unheard melodies made her aware of frequencies in herself she had heard infrequently if at all

He said the first thing about her new mind-set that he noticed was her behavior toward Fynch

She had always done her best to ignore him or even undermine him, but now that her father was wasting away she had lately been very attentive

At first Notley had thought her behavior was aimed at her place in Fynch's will

But then one day he saw her trying to coax him to eat with a tenderness that was beyond simulation

One had the impression that Fynch was on a hunger strike, not against any particular grievance but against life itself and its inherent griefs

It wasn't that he had lost faith in life, Notley gathered, but that he was protesting his fate as a family founder foundered

He had heard him talking to Achs about it and concluded there were many things he didn't understand about Fynch, nor did anybody

In short, that there was a secret about Fynch that he might well take to the grave

And Notley observed that if it were such a potent secret it might be better taken to the grave

Pyhl didn't believe in much, but one thing he did believe in was globalization of happiness

That was why he understood his new assistant, Rych, so well, they were two of a kind

They believed there was nothing more important than happiness

Except Rych believed that the path to happiness was mapped by the quantity of things acquired, while Pyhl believed in the quality of things

But they were one in the belief that things made you happy and that spreading them around the world would solve the world's problems

Whereas, in contrast, Fynch thought that happiness was overrated and things were beside the point

Pyhl did in fact hire Rych as his secretary and gave him the title of Secretary for Happiness on the theory that that way he could both watch him and use him

Austyn told me that in principle Fynch didn't talk about the Evolved Intelligences but that occasionally he let things drop

One of the things he dropped was that the Evolved Intelligences have evolved a concept of alchemy, but not physical alchemy, emotional alchemy

Emotional alchemy was the secret, Fynch said, of turning one emotion into another

The Evolved Intelligences knew how to turn hate into fear or fear into love, for example, or for that matter love into hate when desirable

They also could turn desire into repulsion and repulsion into rage and most difficult of all, intelligence into feeling and back again

The secret of these transformations, Fynch said, was that all these emotions played on the common instrument of the human body and its feelings

And the most direct way to interact with that instrument was through the metamorphoses of the arts

As music modifies the feelings, feelings modify the world through their alchemy, Fynch said

And he said that without that alchemy enriching us we would remain human cockroaches

He said that that, if anything, was the sum of what he had learned over all his years

Anyway, that was the sum of what he dropped to Austyn one quiet afternoon in her apartment looking at the ongoing metamorphosis of the Trade Center pit out the window

That was also when he broached to her his idea of the open family, that is, a family open to anyone as long as s/he wasn't a cockroach

And when she asked him if he could always tell the difference between human and cockroach he replied that the only sure sign was that humans questioned the way things are

And when you told them the way things are they asked why

They had what Fynch called the why chromosome

And that was why, Fynch said, going pensive, he had this sense of failure about his life

This sense of foundering in his effort to form a family

Or to reform a family already formed

Was why he called himself a foundering father

Pyhl was convinced that the Rych kid was an arts terrorist but what interested him was why

He liked this kid, recognizing much of himself in him

Pyhl could understand art theft, but destroying art was beyond him

   "Let's talk about it," he said to Rych. "Where's the profit?"

I was there in the Temp office with Austyn, who was running papers through the shredder

She enjoyed doing that

"First of all I don't destroy art," said Rych. "But if I did do it, it would be because some things get in the way of other things. It's like clearing ground zero. You could look at ground zero as an ongoing art project, in which the destruction of each phase allows the next phase to emerge. The only thing that stops such movement from phase to phase is the need for a product to sell—i.e., money. Somebody pays for a phase and that's that. It becomes an art work. And that's where somebody else comes in. Somebody else hijacks the deal and jacks up the price. And if somebody else doesn't get the price, he might just let the work melt down into its next phase, which anyway might be more interesting. It's like a machine that destroys itself until somebody stops it."

"Somebody sounds like an agent," said Pyhl.

"Or a gallery," said Rych. "That's what I want to do, start a gallery."

Austyn was rummaging around in the wastebasket behind the shredder and pulled out a handful of what she had just shredded

"We save this stuff," she said. "Confetti. For ticker tape parades."

Rych was almost the same age as Seymor but he looked much younger, a youngster compared to Seymor who looked almost middle-aged

The difference was striking when they crossed paths in the Temp

Seymor was already gray, and wrinkled, and bloated, his huge bulk pendulous with fat

Rych was thin as a blade and his pink cheeks under his five o'clock shadow emphasized the blackness of his hair

Despite the difference in demeanor the two young men got along well, they seemed to understand one another

When Rych started talking about being a millionaire Seymor nodded, if not in agreement, at least sympathetically

"What else is there?" asked Rych. "Dropping out is too lame, and if you have to be in you might as well win. Happiness is having more than anyone else."
"More what?" asked Seymor.
"More shit, what's the difference? I'd buy shitloads of stuff if I had the money. Like Andy Warhol, I don't care if I never use it. It's buying the stuff that's important, that gives me the kick. Shopping is empowerment."
"Cool. I see where you're coming from," said Seymor, "but I don't see where you're going."
"I'm not going anywhere. There's nowhere to go."

At ground zero they were digging below ground level now and finding more bodies, whole bodies

Crowds of hard hats would gather around men working at the rubble with hand tools

The heavy machinery would stop moving

Soon orange body bags would appear, would be filled, and would be placed on orange plastic stretcher trays

An American flag would be thrown over the bag, the hard hats would form double lines, and the tray would be carried between them to a waiting ambulance

This lugubrious ritual, depressing as it was, brought the abstraction of thousands back to the reality of one

Austyn had invited Rych, among others, to the apartment that night so he could see ground zero and when he saw this ritual a tear made its way down his cheek

Rych focused the telescope on ground zero

The excavators with their long necks were bobbing up and down like birds in a mating dance in an arena lit like a stadium for a night game

A cascade of orange sparks fell from the ruins of a building from some metalworker's blowtorch

Just then a severed section of wall fell with a loud boom and we all jumped

When the dust cleared we could see the hard hats lining up for the passage of another body and after a while the Secretary for Happiness came away from the telescope, his eyes streaming

    "What's the matter?" asked Austyn.
    "I could see the workers crossing themselves as the body passed," said the Secretary for Happiness.

The Secretary for Happiness looked unhappy and looking unhappy made him look younger than his years, almost like a sullen teenager

Pyhl quickly arranged a 9/11 show at the Temp

It was a show that exhibited quickly available ephemera, insubstantial artifacts that would otherwise fast disappear

They included missing person posters, snapshots of the catastrophe, children's drawings, American flags on paper, postcards and messages

As if the records left by people, fragile though they were, were more enduring than the people who left them

I told Pyhl that maybe we should be exhibiting people in the Temporary Museum

And he said something smart, he said that since the Temp negated artifacts, what else was it exhibiting other than the people who made them

That day the excavators dug up something that looked like banks of snow but, when I looked at it through the telescope, turned out to be papers

Spreading, blowing reefs of white sheets of paper

With words and numbers on them

I found that I was very uneasy around the Secretary for Happiness

First of all, I found his fits of frankness unconvincing, his easy tears made me uneasy

His way of greeting people with hugs made me uncomfortable

I thought of him as a loose balloon whose allegiance was to the air

I found this lack of ballast disconcerting but something that had to be dealt with, as if he were the representative, however inadequate, of a different intelligence, but an intelligence

That was Rych on one frequency, but on another, and this is what made me distrust him, he had this childlike fascination with things, gadgets, toys, tools, computer hardware, videogames, artifacts of all sorts

He immediately picked up on the teddy bear element of the improvised shrines to victims of 9/11

He tried to persuade Pyhl to produce a line of teddy bears to sell in the museum shop and, since there was no museum shop, to start one

He said they could make a million dollars and make everyone happy, customers as well as shopkeepers

My problem was it probably would make them happy

I noticed that Rych had a weakness for ice cream

I almost never saw him without an ice cream pop or cone from the museum cafeteria

Ice cream made Rych happy

Rych introduced the word *customer* to the vocabulary of the Museum

He brought in customers

People who would buy things, pay the optional admission, jack up the stats

Notably, he brought in Klump, Augustus Klump, collector

Klump too had emerged from LaFange, or was trying to when he heard about his landsman Fynch and the Temp

Klump had pulled himself out of the muck then clamped onto Rych as one with a pipeline to the ethereal

Rych was ready to sell ethereal by the gallon

Rych brought Klump to Pyhl and when Pyhl asked him which work in the Museum collection he was interested in collecting, Klump replied he'd take one of everything

But he said he wanted the originals

Pyhl explained there were no originals

Klump said that the deal was off, that he only collected originals

Pyhl said that the Museum collection was too ethereal to have originals, but what they had were numbered series

Klump said in that case he'd like to purchase number one of each series

Pyhl said he thought that could be arranged but that since the Museum had to retain number one of each work to guarantee authenticity the Museum could sell him a second number one of each work that would be just as original

Klump said he'd think about it

Rych said that if Klump made the purchase he was sure that the Museum would be willing to exhibit it as the Klump Collection

Klump looked shrewd

And not only that, Rych continued, the Museum could eventually set up the Klump Collection in a special Klump Wing of the Museum

And when would that happen? asked Klump

As soon as we find a donor for it, said the Secretary for Happiness

For the first time during the meeting, Klump's poker face broke into a smile

You sure know how to negotiate, said Klump

Why would Klump want to climb out of the muck he'd been so successful at mucking around in

It wasn't as though Klump didn't know it, that it was the ore Klump for all these years had been turning to gold

Why would Klump abandon his fabulously successful mining operation for something so ephemeral as the Museum

Was it that, at this late stage in his life, Klump had fallen victim to the improvement reflex, the impulse that things can always be better

The answer was Mrs. Klump

For all the years that Klump had been mucking around in the muck, Mrs. Klump had been flapping around in the ether

Mrs. Klump's flights through the ether began from boredom with her lot

Her improvement reflex was even stronger than Klump's

She began by improving her speech, which she minced from Midwestern twang to tea party twaddle

What her mind shaped as "thank you" tripped off her tongue as "think yaw"

> "Won't you have another petit four Mrs. Klump?"
> "Think yaw. I don't mind if I do."

Mrs. Klump's occupation was shopping, she was a skilled shopper

And shopping made her happy, it was an exercise of choice, a form of power

She had invented a doctrine of creative consumption based on consumer knowledge, discrimination, and taste

She claimed that creative consumption had deep roots in human nature going back to the hunting and gathering pursuits of primitive cultures

According to her doctrine the same skills exhibited by shoppers in bargain basements, shopping malls, and outlet stores could be applied with profit in culture and the arts

She proceeded to apply her ideas to the art world and quickly built up a private collection that was the envy of more traditional connoisseurs

So it seemed an obvious move, in retrospect, that Mrs. Klump should secretly team up with Rych in a plan to start an art gallery together

The discovery of bodies one by one at ground zero helped me with the arithmetic of the catastrophe, I said to Fynch one day at the Museum

"How so?" he asked.

"Because the only way I can take in that much murder is to imagine each one as my own death one by one. On that basis even one death is intolerable."

"The more so because it's a murder."

"You speak from experience?" I asked him.

"Not personal experience. My experience as a contemporary of Pearl Harbor, Hiroshima, the death camps. Mass murder comes down to single deaths, anything else is a white wash."

"And how do you tolerate even a single murder?"

"You don't, not emotionally. Unless you're a cockroach."

"Why do you say that?" I asked him.

"There I speak from experience." A flicker of unspeakable pain flashed across his face.

"How so?" I asked him.

"Let's say I've been a cockroach. Until after many years the resulting social shatter got to me. Leading eventually to personal shatter. Leading to the Temporary Museum as a way to put the pieces back together. Which you can never do. Not the same way. So that sometimes I think that the ephemeral the Museum deals in is largely ethereal, ether, anesthetic."

"It could be," I suggested. "There's always a fine line between the esthetic and the anesthetic."

The last standing segment of the World Trade Center's walls came down today

It looked about five stories high, and was pulled down along perforations made by metal workers' acetylene torches, landing with a loud boom and dense clouds of dust

They're saving it for a possible memorial

Pyhl said it should have been in his ephemera show

Everyone in America has the improvement reflex

Has it or denies it, as is the case with Notley

"Things are bad enough as they are, don't try to change them," was one of the first things he said to me when I met him.
"Even to improve them?"
"It'll be an improvement for the worse."

We were talking about my idea of writing off the theft from the Museum

I had suggested to Pyhl that they not only write it off but that they encourage other thefts from the Museum, that the Museum become a venue for larceny, that stealing become a means of distribution for the ideas they cultivated

We were in Pyhl's office together by coincidence, Pyhl, Notley and Jimmy Lochs, and Jimmy loved the idea of encouraging museum thefts

"What better way of getting your word out?" he enthused. "It would save the cost of distribution. You'd save money on every work stolen."

"I have a better way," said Notley. "Just let things go to hell. They'll go there anyway but you save a lot of effort and distraction and that'll be a big improvement."

But when the Klumps heard about my proposed improvement they were appalled

They said it would reduce the value of their purchases from the Museum

Mrs. Klump said that the only improvements she believed in were self-improvement, she said that if everyone in the elite started improving themselves it would have a trickle-down effect

Klump said that Mrs. Klump had certainly improved herself, that you wouldn't believe the ignoramus she had been just a few years back when she started improving herself, you wouldn't believe the effort she put into it

"It sure trickled down on me," he added.

The Improvement Society was not merely for improvement, it was for radical improvement

Before he started working in the Museum, Seymor accepted the Improvement Society's dictum that anything short of radical improvement made things worse

It made things worse because it made the establishment better which made an unimprovable situation more unimprovable

But as an executive of the Museum his responsibility was not so much to make things better as to get things going

In this respect he found the Klumps useful because they got things going

The things they got going were not necessarily improvements but they were energetic and energy was the motor for any eventual improvements

In fact energy itself was an improvement

All of which meant to Seymor that in a well ordered society everyone had something to contribute whether they wanted to or not

"It's too bad," Seymor said, "that this isn't a well ordered society."

What Seymor needed above all was time

He didn't have it

He didn't have it because events were catching up with the Museum

There was a whole prehistory of the Museum that he was just becoming aware of, a prehistory in the story of Fynch's life

Seymor knew that Fynch's story would inevitably catch up with the story of the Museum

Fynch's story, he suspected, was a story of transgression and contrition in which the Museum represented contrition

It was the transgression Seymor feared was catching up, he told me

He had asked Fynch about it, but Fynch was the wrong person to ask about his past

Fynch was busy making up his past since he already knew his future

Such as it was, being almost out of time

Seymor liked to talk to me because he knew I had the time

He knew that I had come out against time

On the grounds that time doesn't exist as such, that there were many times, that time was really change, and that change was real time

Seymor knew, from conversation with Achs, that Fynch also had become disillusioned with time

Seymor thought that it had something to do with his old partnership with Lynch

Fynch and Lynch you might say made time in their clock factory

But listening between the lines, Seymor gathered Fynch was also making time with Lynch's wife

Seymor couldn't guess whether Lynch was indifferent to the situation, hated it, or encouraged it, but from something Fynch said he guessed it was all of the above

Fynch on the other hand added insult to injury by being aggressively exhibitionistic about the relationship, Seymor surmised from certain allusions

Fynch especially, Seymor concluded, was fond of fondling the woman in her husband's presence while making sexual demands on her to which she invariably acquiesced

Reminding him of his relation with Austyn and Pyhl and setting him wondering about genetic parallels

This was a long time ago, but Fynch seemed to believe that this relationship was what broke up their clock partnership

And at some level was meant to break it up

Freeing him to start on his solo trajectory to riches through direct exploitation of time in a new stopwatch business

Sadism releasing exploitation on all fronts

But at the same time steeped that steep rise in guilt and denial of the temporal compensated for, Seymor guessed, finally, by the Temp

What music was for Austyn painting was for me

When I got disoriented a good painting was like a map

A map of itself that gave me a sense of direction, even if it wasn't my direction

"Paintings, unlike music, have nothing to do with time," Jimmy said to me, "that's my problem. Because my paintings are about serving time, just like I did."

Jimmy was painting maps of places that weren't there in images that disappeared

Because time is only real in the present

When it isn't time when it's space

The space of a jail cell maybe that you need to escape

By imagining time instead of space when you're confined in the present

And that's where writing comes in

Because writing occupies both time and space

And we're all confined to the present

Day after day

They discovered more bodies at ground zero

There must be something morbid about the hard hats' fascination with the bodies

When they find one, or even part of one, the work stops and the hard hats gather around, like flies to decay

I said as much to Achs, who had come by Austyn's apartment, as many associated with the Museum did, to check on the progress of the dig

"Any obsession with death," she said, "involves one's own death. Have a heart. The firemen and policemen on the lookout for dead buddies must be celebrating their escape as well as expressing their grief. The morbid part is survivors' guilt. I know something about that."
"Meaning?"
"When I left my ex-husband he tried to commit suicide, almost succeeded."
"I didn't know."
"It was a long time ago. I was very young."
"Did you run off?"
"With Fynch," said Achs.

I didn't talk to her about it, but I knew she was still fucking Pyhl

Austyn

I didn't mind much, sometimes I found it sexy

She knew I knew because after I'd want to get her into bed right away

Which only goes to prove that sex is an aphrodisiac

The real issue was why she needed him as well as me

Or instead of Jimmy Lochs who I knew she liked better and who liked her

While Pyhl, I couldn't help noting, treated her like a piece of furniture

I figured it was because none of the rest of us knew what we were doing in dealing with the crisis at the Temp while Pyhl acted as if he knew what he was doing

Even though he didn't

We all need people like that

Byrd was gone and had been gone a long time from LaFange

But now Fynch received ambiguous reports that he had died

Fynch was gratified

Whatever Byrd had done, Fynch never forgave him, nor would he tell me

As far as I know he didn't tell anybody, except that it happened in LaFange

Not that he would tell me, but even Achs didn't know about it

She knew a few things

She knew that they had once been very close, that they were family

She knew that there had been a murder involved, that there was a woman, and a pregnancy, and a failed late-term abortion

A stopwatch patent was at issue, and an idea about a watch that never had to be wound, that went on forever

One could gather the abortion caused the death of the mother, but the fate of the infant, known only to Byrd, remained mysterious

Apparently Byrd disappeared right after the abortion, and it was plausible to assume that the child was his

Achs assumed the mother was Fynch's sister, and rumor had it that Byrd was Fynch's relative, so there may have been a question of incest of sorts

It was inferred that's Fynch's watch factories were capitalized by Byrd's suspected rum-running operation over the Canadian border, and that the presumed murder had to do with Byrd's illegal activities

But all in all, very little was known about the relation between Fynch and Byrd

We didn't know what to believe

Rych had changed his story

He now admitted working for an undercover police agency, he wouldn't say which one

He said irritably that he was who he said he was before 9/11 but that after the attack he was recruited by an agency to keep tabs on the arts scene

But he said instead the arts scene recruited him, so though presumably still working for the agency his real interest was starting a gallery

    "You never get anywhere unless you're willing to change your story now and then," he told me.
    "And how do you decide to change your story?" I asked him.
    "I never decide. It happens by surprise, by chance, even by mistake. It's always unexpected."
    "You never choose?"
    "Never. You can't will it, it always turns out phony."
    "Then why do it," I asked. "Change your story?"
    "You have to, to keep up," he sad petulantly. "With change of circumstance, of facts, of the way you feel. With coincidence, with accident. You don't change sides, for example, sides change you."

All my life I've been obsessed with unmaking things badly made

It suddenly struck me that here at the World Trade Center and in a different way at the Museum of Temporary Art, things were already unmade

There was no further to go in those directions

Maybe it was getting to be time to change my story

Fynch had changed his story, or at least ended it

He was dead

He was laid out in Jocylyn's parlor

It's where she kept her collections

She was apparently a collector like her father

Except in her case she collected idols, dolls, puppets, statues

So that in a way the body in the open coffin looked like part of her collection

It seemed she had a special affinity for reproductions of the Statue of Liberty, there was a whole section devoted to it, tiny versions in metal, large ones in plaster or plastic, a gigantic Liberty carved in wood, a Liberty molded in chocolate like an Easter Bunny

There was even a TV screen showing a documentary about the Statue of Liberty, that was the only thing that annoyed me in the collection

Because the documentary was the only image that made a claim on reality, as electronic media always did, rather than resting as symbol, out of time

As Fynch was out of time

And looking well

Under the circumstances, very well

Much to everyone's surprise and most people's chagrin, Fynch's will made Seymor the beneficiary of the bulk of the estate, including control of the Museum

There was however, a handsome bequest for Achs

Jocylyn was furious

She immediately offered to throw in with Rych and the Klumps, backing their gallery idea

Her only condition was that their first show would be of her Liberty collection

But no sooner was this agreed upon than items from the collection began to disappear

My hunch was that Rych was filching them

Ground zero at night was a different story

Grayed out but intensely illuminated it looked like a negative

The rhythmic movements of the heavy machines traced by their lights was balletic

Scattered throughout were the blinking lights of stationary vehicles

Here and there cascades of sparks streamed from acetylene torches

Gray smoke smudged out of gray twists of debris

The air was lit up by the floodlights like water in a tank of strange fish

You had the impression of looking at a negative reality that existed only in your head

A negative reality that would be printed out in the sunlight of tomorrow

But that tonight was being penned in the darkness of your mind realtime c. 12/11/01:

Fynch was 100 when he died. 25 years ago, when he was 75 and she 35, he tried to have a child with Achs to no avail.

When they gave up on it she remembered his cryptic remark to the effect that he'd have to be happy with what he'd got, if only he could find it. She didn't think anything of it, however, till the notebooks gave her the first inklings.

She found them after the funeral, which was a contentious affair, with the mourners broken up into groups that were in fact factions. It was raining lightly and a bitter January wind was the testament of winter.

Jocylyn stood close to Pyhl, with Rych at a slight distance from them. Austyn was halfway between Pyhl and Hymi, and Jimmy Lochs was equidistant from Austyn and Notley.

The Klumps stood together not far from Rych. On the fringes of the group.

Seymor and Achs stood together close to the open grave. Seymor looked sad, but Achs had her handkerchief out and was sobbing openly as she prepared to talk from notes jotted down on an envelope.

"All his life he was obsessed with time. First, being a clock maker, as a way of exploiting it, then as the result of a creative transformation, by way of defeating it, and finally, through his concept of the Museum of Temporary Art, surfing the present. Now, finally, like a stopwatch, he's out of time, part of a permanent present. He died over one of his books on genealogy, a subject in which he had taken a deep interest, though for him the transition from life to death must have been almost imperceptible, immersed as he was in another world."

At Fynch's request, there was no religious presence at the funeral, each person was free to speak as the spirit moved him. Accordingly, Jocylyn cleared her throat loudly and began.

"My father, dear as he was to me, was an eccentric. Let's face it. The proof is the Museum itself, where the criteria for art would seem to be the more perverse the better. This is not the time to go into all that. As to his obsession with another world, or the Fifth World as he called it, as his daughter I can assure you that it was at the expense of this one. On the other hand, he lived a long time and saw a lot so that what seemed foolish to us might have seemed wise to him. And even the things about him that seemed most foolish were always well intended. He lived a full life, he saw a lot, and it is not for us to judge him."

Pyhl was the next to speak.

"He was at best prescient, at worst misguided. He had the genius to recognize an unlikely product, to create a market for it out of nothing and to continue exploiting it as strictly nothing. In terms of salesmanship it was better than the pet rock ploy. I guess he was a sort of genius, above the crowd, which is the only reason I can figure why the Museum was a losing proposition. Because he wanted it to be. It's not for us to know."

Then Seymor stepped forward.

"In his later years he underwent a sudden creative transformation that released his spiritual unconscious, as well as the urge to proselytize for the spirit. And he began to see that vehicles of such a transformation have to first transform themselves and then change those around them in a ripple effect. The result is anything from an enlightened grouplet to a social institution like the Museum, but the key lies in the transition from personal to social. So individual Evolved Intelligences crystallized in associations like the Museum or the Improvement Society. The key word according to Fynch is society. Individuals according to him have the capacity for virtue and also, but not by themselves, for social change. Change requires connection between the Fifth World of the spirit and the practical world of society. We here in the West tend to ignore the Fifth World in favor of the practical. Others we know live only in the Fifth World with the disastrous result we have recently seen in the World Trade Center, with who knows what to follow."

After the funeral they went back to the Fynch mansion. While the rest of the company was eating and drinking downstairs, Achs went to spend a meditative half hour in Fynch's study where she hardly ever intruded when he was alive.

And that's when, idly opening a drawer, she discovered the notebook in his desk. At first she thought it was a financial item because of the word "bank" written in the white square on the cover, but when she opened it she immediately realized it was very intimate and she wondered whether she should read on.

The first entries she read were clearly Fynch's sexual fantasies, in themselves fairly run-of-the-mill except that he would write them down. What puzzled Achs was that there was some sort of rating system according to which each entry was marked, to wit: 2 squirts, 1 squirt, 4 squirts, etc.

For example, "the nurse slowly unbuttons her blouse and offers me a full, heavy breast with a thickly protruding nipple," 1 1/2 squirts, "the teenager from the Catholic school looks over her shoulder at me innocently and allows her plaid skirt to rise slowly up her white, slender thigh," 2 squirts. Achs had been sleeping with Fynch for 25 years since he left Jocylyn's mother and these didn't seem like his style at all.

Achs told Hymi Fynch was haunted by the possibility that he had conceived children he didn't know about, and that this accounted for seemingly strange choices he sometimes made in picking associates. And he was always disturbed about the possibility that someone who seemed attracted to him, even for exploitative reasons, might be acting out of some unconscious filial instinct.

Similarly, for complicated reasons, he distanced himself from Jocylyn, his only confirmed offspring. His logic was that he had to be vigilant in not favoring Jocylyn over more shadowy descendants just because she was so much in evidence.

What Seymor knew and Jocylyn didn't was that Fynch had mandated her a job in the Museum that guaranteed her a comfortable living and, more surprising given her known opinions about the

Temp, a position of considerable influence, equal to that of Pyhl. The latter's influence in the Museum seemed to be growing to the point where at times he seemed to be running the institution instead of Seymor, an impression that Seymor, however, deliberately encouraged.

Pyhl's increased influence was partly due to his relation with Austyn, a relation about which Jocylyn was completely in the dark. But that influence now could only be reinforced by Jocylyn's presence in the Museum, and in fact together Pyhl and Jocylyn soon concocted a vision which would threaten to change the course of the Museum now that Fynch was gone.

Art Demo. In which quality was measured by quantity, democratic quantity of people's contemplation of the art and of the number of viewers passing by.

Sensors would be installed in exhibited works that would count the number and attention span of viewers who passed, paused or lingered in front of them. The greater the score the more successful the work.

And to curate this particular project Pyhl and Jocylyn brought in the art critic Wendy Blustrous, an arts populist who had in fact been an adviser to Fynch when he first became interested in art. Fynch had been deeply hurt as a novice art collector by what he considered the snobism of the art establishment, which was at that time heavily involved in a kind of abstraction he didn't understand.

Fynch was largely self educated, in painting as in everything else, and he was at first attracted to Buckeye realism as might be expected. When he moved from LaFange to New York he discovered that people found his tastes laughable, and though his reaction was outwardly stubborn and pugnacious, inwardly he felt humiliated.

It was the World Trade Center disaster that keyed Fynch into the radical possibilities of change and caused him to alter his will to put Seymor in command of the Museum with all the resources of his fortune. He figured that Seymor would be the best person to understand and continue his concept of the Temp.

But Seymor was also deeply affected by the disaster. He felt much less inclined to impose his view of things, given the deep incertitude signaled by the collapse of the towers, and much more willing to give others free rein and to let things take their course without the assertion of his will.

So he found the Art Demo project acceptable without compromising the nature of the Temp, especially after a talk he had with Hymi on the subject of time. Hymi said that when the towers collapsed it altered his sense of temporary permanence, that is, everyone knew that nothing lasts but now he had tuned in to the fact that anything can happen in the next instant.

Therefore, in his mind, the imposition of will would have to be replaced by the uncertainties of desire, and who was to say whether the weak force of desire would not in the long run prove more durable than the strong force of the will. So Seymor was willing to gamble that the Art Demo project in the context of the Temp would serve the purposes of the Temp.

The long-term effects of the World Trade Center attacks were beginning to show in the whole cast of characters that circulated around the Museum. Notley had burrowed more deeply into his asceticism while, on the other hand, Jimmy Lochs had practically stopped drinking on the grounds, he said, that some things are too big to drown.

Austyn's reactions to the attacks were more primal, symptomized by sensitivity to sirens and other loud noises, by a sense of general dread, and by reduction of former obsessions to the status of trivia, and notably she found herself clinging to Hymi and unresponsive to Pyhl.

Seymor had a deep paralyzing fear of being deserted, he didn't know where it came from. In his behavior it resulted in a reluctance to desert others, and it was the sense of his loyalty that made Fynch trust him implicitly.

Hymi had noticed this trait in Seymor and remarked on it to him. When Seymor professed ignorance Hymi suggested that he practice the discipline of reading oneself.

Hymi said that reading oneself resembled reading others in that you never knew what was going to unfold. He said that the best way to read yourself was talking writing, which was like reading writing of others except it is talking with all the surprising twists and unexpected turns in the discourse of others when they talked about themselves.

Seymor, Hymi knew, would be good at getting people to read themselves because he was so laid-back he was disarming.

Meantime the Klumps were pushing ahead with their plans for a new gallery, which was to be an operation called Cockroach, in a reverse prestige ploy calculated to summon up the essential grit of New York. Clever?

The gallery was housed in a loft across from the Museum in order to pick up on the traffic passing through the older establishment. It was to specialize in heavy subjects solidly framed, sculpted in stone or cast in bronze, lead or steel, and the Klumps believed that theirs was the first gallery to use sheer weight as its sole criterion.

Wendy Blustrous was outraged by Cockroach's competition with her Art Demo show. Blustrous conceived her exhibition as locating the work of art more in the response of the viewer than in the artifact, a conception directly challenged by the policy of Cockroach, which she saw as a return to old hierarchical ideas already in the trash can of history.

Rych, however, did everything he could to play up the conflict, seeing in it a possible splash of notoriety as good as cash. But Notley and Jimmy Lochs didn't bother to hide their cynicism about the controversy, contending that in art ideas have the status of advertising copy.

Around about this time Hymi noticed that the joints in his fingers were getting stiff. He assumed he was getting arthritic and went to see a doctor who recommended tests.

Hymi didn't think much about it till the tests came back positive. Positive, the doctor said, for an extremely rare malady that petrified the flesh, called the Pygmalion Syndrome, PS for short, which gradually turned the body to stone and would end up eventually making a statue of him, his own monument.

There was an intermediate stage which Hymi, according to the doctor, was just entering in which his body would still be capable of being manipulated by someone else, like a puppet. Hymi immediately decided that if he was going to end up as a statue he would be the sculptor, and if a puppet he would hold the strings, rather than be a candidate for exhibition in Cockroach.

Meanwhile, the Art Brute show had gone up at the Museum, and among its exhibits was a mirrored cylinder with several peep holes looking into what at first appeared to be sheer darkness in which the eye focused eventually, if one kept looking, on a crude rendition of the classical image of Aphrodite, goddess of love. From the first, Hymi felt an affinity with this piece as a reminder, and a way of coping with his PS, recalling that Pygmalion prayed to that goddess to release flesh from its bondage in stone.

In fact, it was this installation, and Hymi's expressed fascination with it, that accounted for the softening of Jocylyn's attitude toward him, because Jocylyn considered it to be the best work in the show and the only one worthy of much attention. It was entitled "Pig Mail" and for Hymi it represented the fleshiness petrifying in his body.

Klaxon's specialty was blackmail, either in pursuing blackmailers or in administering it himself. It was in investigating the E. Wentworth Kropotkin case that Klaxon was definitively stripped of his ideas about the goodness of human nature, above all his own.

Wentworth Kropotkin had hired Klaxon to keep track of his daughter, Evi, who tended to get involved in compromising situations potentially embarrassing to Wentworth Kropotkin himself. Wentworth Kropotkin wanted a rundown of her lovers so he would have the goods on them in the event they attempted blackmail, which was a run-of-the-mill case for Klaxon, except that he found the daughter, Evi, irresistibly sexy and started having an affair with her himself.

Which Wentworth Kropotkin got wind of without knowing the identity of the lover and without knowing many details, details which he counted on Klaxon to fill in, but which had to correspond with those of which he already had knowledge. So it turned out that to satisfy Wentworth Kropotkin, Klaxon had to start investigating himself.

One thing led to another, and pretty soon Klaxon started getting into it and he discovered that, objectively speaking, he wasn't a very nice man. On the other hand, he knew he wasn't better or worse than most people, which he found a depressing thought and soured his view of human nature.

Evi's behavior in lying to all her lovers about one another was routine to Klaxon, but his own behavior struck him as contemptible, seen through Wentworth Kropotkin's eyes, an opinion magnified by the latter's insistence that they get enough on him sufficient to keep him away from his daughter. So Klaxon was put in the position of investigating and finally blackmailing himself, an experience he never got over.

Eventually his line of investigation led back to his childhood, and here there developed a highly unexpected connection with Hymi, whom he met through Jocylyn. He turned out to have gone to the same grammar school as Hymi.

Though they didn't know one another in school, the meeting released a flood of memories in Hymi. One day in the school yard they were playing one of those games that requires an It.

This time Hymi was It. He was often It to the point where, without realizing it, he was starting to feel like an It.

The rules of the game were that he faced the school yard fence with his eyes closed and his hands over his eyes, counting while the others hid. Till he heard a shout.

When Hymi got to five or six hundred he began to lose track. The penalties for opening one's eyes before the shout were severe but he finally opened them.

They weren't hiding. They were gone.

In Brooklynese, they had left him flat. This dark memory produced anxiety in Hymi even now and may have marked the beginning of his paranoia about time.

Time betrays, time isolates, time plays tricks. And this corresponded to Klaxon's view of humanity under pressure of time, because if people were immortal like the gods, having all the time in the world and not having death to look forward to, they might behave quite differently.

Hymi, who was by now getting to know the crowd at the Museum, happened to tell Notley his reminiscence about flat leaving and Notley responded with a memory of his own. When he was nine he was told he had lost both his parents in an airplane crash, but as if that weren't bad enough, the reaction of his little friends made it worse.

His friends, when word got around, treated him with a kind of awe comprised of incomprehension, respectfulness, confusion about how to respond, and fear of his bad luck, with the result that he was left alone and doubly isolated. Notley speculated that the experience marked him for life, though he wasn't sure how.

At that point Seymor, who had walked in on the conversation, remarked that Notley's experience was nothing compared to his own, with all due respect to Notley's experience. He had been brought up in an orphanage without any memory of his mother or father, and not only that, but he had constantly been shipped from institution to institution without warning or reason that he could discern, and in consequence had never been able to establish permanent ties with inmates or counselors.

When Pyhl heard about this conversation, he remarked to Jocylyn, who had reported it, that none of these case histories, as he called them, could match Austyn's experience of repeated child abuse with her supposed guardians looking the other way, if not joining in.

Nor could it equal his own childhood experience, which he really preferred not to go into. Actually what he wanted to talk to Jocylyn about was hiring Klaxon for a little job relating to the latest art theft.

The thefts were continuing in a steady leak and the latest was a real puzzle because it involved a piece exhibited in the Art Brute show that was lately found to be a blatant fraud by a well known artist taking advantage of the boom in outsider art. The question was why would someone commit a crime to steal a piece that already comprised a criminal act as a forgery.

Pyhl explained to Klaxon that if he could answer this question it would go a long way toward rationalizing the logic, if there was any, of the thefts. Klaxon was accompanied that afternoon by Evi Wentworth Kropotkin whom he introduced as his assistant.

Pyhl took one look at Evi and recognized she was up for grabs. She was emanating up for grabs vibes. She was young, maybe about 23, and in that phase in which young women are eager to prove to themselves that they are attractive.

Practically the first thing out of her mouth, which was to add her e-mail address when Klaxon gave his to Pyhl, confirmed Pyhl's impression. Klaxon, on his part, realized right away that she intended to fuck Pyhl and that she knew Klaxon realized it and realized there was not a thing he could do about it.

But Pyhl was not so sure he wanted to go that route anymore, of picking up on a flirtation as he had done so many times before, and that by the age of 55 he should be bored with the whole routine. But he wasn't.

He knew he wasn't because of Margo, a.k.a. the girl, who took care of him starting when he was two, some would say abused him sexually, abused him thoroughly but he liked it, until in a fit of guilt he let on to his step parents and the girl disappeared. Then he wanted her back but she was gone for good, and he knew that Evi was just the latest in a long string of Margos and that it wasn't she that he desired but desire itself, the emotional shape of it regardless of physical gratification.

Which gave him a certain amount of insight into why the thief or thieves chose to steal indifferently valuable or worthless objects from the Museum. It wasn't the things they wanted, it was the act of stealing them that validated their cause, that gratified their desire.

This insight opened the possibility to Pyhl that the lust for objects of desire could be superseded by lust itself, lust without any object or end, lust in and for itself, lust as an abstract and metaphysical phenomenon, as a spiritual force, and as such highly dangerous. Or useful.

Under multiple subterranean layers exposed by the World Trade Center excavation, Hymi could now see from Austyn's apartment the perfectly preserved carcass of a subway car coated with the silvery gray dust typical of the wreckage. There was something slightly terrifying about it frozen in time, despite the millions of tons of pressure from the debris fallen on it, as if it were ready to roll as soon as the juice was turned on, something frightening about its stasis in the moment the tower fell.

What endures is not necessarily what we would prefer to endure, Hymi reflected. What lasts are reptilian instincts and the accumulated scars of experience, many of them self-inflicted.

He had confessed his guilt over the many affairs he had had when he and Austyn were together, but he could not say he would not have done the same thing in the same circumstances, which if anything increased his anguish over having done them in the first place. While she, Austyn, admitting her decision to leave him flat in Paris was one of her worst mistakes, knew that she would do it over again, which did not prevent her from hating herself for it.

At Cockroach, Rych related to the Klumps as if he were their child. In truth he related to just about everyone as if he were their child. As a matter of fact, it was widely remarked that he was getting more childish by the day.

Austyn thought it was because maybe he never had a real childhood, having been brought up by a maiden aunt who didn't understand children. His parents were supposedly missionaries to the Congo who never came back from one of their expeditions.

As a child, in order to keep himself company, Rych invented a companion for himself named Rich, a more fortunate twin whose parents gave him everything he wanted. Rych grew up vicariously enjoying Rich's good fortune and wondering why he couldn't be treated the same way.

With adolescence Rych ditched Rich, or so he thought. In reality he projected Rich onto every other apparently more fortunate teenager he came across.

Now, as a grown-up, he related to other grown-ups as if he were the poor little Rych boy. Then he teamed up with the Klumps who gave him everything he wanted at Cockroach, not so much out of generosity but as a way of building up equity in a valuable investment.

Getting everything he wanted was a new experience for Rych, and gradually he came to see that he didn't identify with this person who had everything he wanted, it wasn't him, and this insight proved to be a turning point in his development. You might even say it was the beginning of his adult life.

It was around this time when relations between Pyhl and Austyn went into terminal fizzle. It may have been the growing intensity of Austyn's relations with Hymi, it may have been Pyhl seeing Jocylyn every day at the office that renewed his allegiance to her, it may have been the complicated attrition of maintaining the sexual theatrics with Austyn, who can say?

It was at this phase when Evi Wentworth Kropotkin started coming around to the Temp to see Pyhl. Her pretext was that she was doing an article on him for an art magazine.

It turned out that Evi had never written an article before and that she got the assignment through connections. Therefore she offered to let Pyhl write the article on him himself under her byline, an offer Pyhl was inclined to accept because of the prestige of the magazine in question.

Of course Evi's attempt at seduction was completely transparent to Pyhl, but also it was becoming obvious to him that he had changed since the World Trade Center catastrophe. He realized that having spent so much time in its shadow at the Temp, that he had in some sense identified with it, and he dimly perceived in its fall a loss of its example of shafty power, as if he were for a time at least out of synch with that kind of performance.

Something like that. Whenever it was, Evi sensed it, but it simply aggravated her seduction itch to the point of willed violation, abasement, and self-immolation—just those qualities, judging by relations with Austyn, that he liked in a woman.

And yet, for reasons obscure to him, they turned him off. His only clue: the image of the tower collapsing, the tip wobbling for an instant in its protrusion from a roiling cloud of black, an image that kept appearing to him when he tried to envision making it with Evi.

Let's just say that something was telling him that this kind of mock violation was somehow currently inauspicious. Not to attribute visionary insight to Pyhl, far from it, but something equally novel for Pyhl, a self-consciousness mildly upsetting because at an instinctual level he felt that it might lead to something like self-examination.

So, though it distressed him, he turned down the offer of the article and metaphorically kicked the girl out. Much as, he now remembered, he had in the past denied, for reasons mysterious to himself, similar erotic opportunities.

Of course it was too late for Jocylyn to change her curt relations with her father. But it was something, Jocylyn felt, along with a pang of guilt, that she now understood what her father was trying to teach her by treating her just like everyone else, and that furthermore she had learned his lesson without the feeling of being taught, to stand on her two feet.

And with that came a recognition that the shape of her desire for Pyhl was sisterly, that there was a stabilizing familial element to it, as well as a dangerous incestuous quality. That the quality of their relationship, as Pyhl had remarked the other day, recaptured a pattern that seemed to be emotionally preexistent, and the stronger for that.

This was a period when what was turning into, in more than one sense, a group affiliated with the Temp began to assume a certain tone of relationship. So that even Notley could confess to Jocylyn sometimes his solitary posture, he suspected, also implied its opposite.

So Seymor could confide to Achs that being with her engendered a sense of regression from his responsibilities at the Museum, a loss of responsibility whose slack he felt, while he was with her, that she would take up. In short, he felt with her an intrusion of the maternal which was not disagreeable.

Meanwhile Austyn and Hymi, the more they recaptured their old feeling for one another, began to sense that there was a feeling behind the feeling which made their renewed relationship that much more intense. So intense that they were almost beginning to feel strange about it, as if there were some puzzle involved.

Inductively—although it didn't prove anything—the unaccustomed feelings they were all starting to have related to 9/11. They were all in the area at the time of the attack.

Austyn and Hymi escaped from her apartment to the river where they watched the Towers collapse and were caught up in the black cloud that erupted from the site. Achs was in her office in the Museum and went to a window when she heard the first impact.

There, from four blocks away, she could see flaming bodies falling through the air as the buildings burned, an image which still keeps replaying in her head, like the trauma of the second plane hitting that kept repeating in Notley's mind reinforced by the shots of it caught on camera and replayed every few minutes on television. Pyhl was walking through the ground level lobby of the Trade Center when everyone started running.

He reached the open plaza between the Towers which was full of wreckage and he looked up and saw one of them burning, saw an unidentifiable body part on the ground. He started running and didn't stop till he reached Canal Street 20 blocks away.

Jocylyn was on the street transfixed by the two towers burning like torches without a thought in her mind that they could fall down. Then the first one did, catching her in the tidal wave of black dust unable to breathe, when someone pulled her into a building lobby as debris rained down. Someone handed her a breathing mask.

Seymor was walking to work when the first plane hit. He stood there in the shadow of the towers, while airplane parts and building debris showered down around him, and then walked on in a sort of daze.

Rych was able to take shelter in a doorway of a building a block to the Hudson side of the towers just as the first one imploded and he watched as the black storm of dust and debris caught pedestrians running through open spaces where they were hit by flying junk and fell buried in soot and fragments. Jimmy was actually in one of the Towers visiting a space reserved for an artist's studio, felt the impact of the airplane, the building shaking, and saw airplane parts hurtling by the window.

He was able to reach a staircase and crowd down 30 floors with others in the minutes before the building collapsed. He ran toward the river, where he managed to jump on a jammed tugboat that had used the riverside esplanade as an improvised pier.

Jimmy was on the river when the second tower collapsed and he had the strange impression that the thick black smoke and dust flowing from the buildings was continuous with the flow of the river. And he had the further impression that the towers were gathering themselves into a massive wave as fluxy and fluid as the river itself.

It seemed to Jimmy as the towers smoked and crumbled that he was getting a glimpse of time itself, time accelerated in this black hole of destruction, and that the solidity of the First World had turned in an instant into the insubstantiality of the Fifth World. Father son and holy ghost, please save the poor bastards over there, but he couldn't summon up the Catholicism of his youth with any conviction.

Nor did Buddhist fatalism cover the case for Notley, who had raced up the street toward ground zero past wrecked fire engines and EMS vehicles, burning autos, squashed police cars, to see if he could help, when he was stopped dead by the avalanched mounds of burning metal seven stories high. Compressed from the 110 stories of the former Towers.

And looking at the rubble from Austyn's window when they made it back to her building, it occurred to Hymi with hard certitude that the insubstantial Fifth World is more real than the solid First. Outside in the street it appeared to Notley that there was a general outpouring of behavior out of the Fifth World, from the firemen and cops, as well as volunteers digging into the flaming wreckage, to citizens materializing with bottles of water, many with food, breathing masks, and medical supplies, in a vast unleashing of selfless communal behavior.

Whatever inhibitions, repressions, regressions, defenses against the altruistic fellowship of the spirit, seemed to Notley for the time to be swept away in this still gathering wave of community. Notley, reflecting the general spirit, started picking his way through the dangerous junk that moments ago was the World Trade Center, listening for buried voices but hearing nothing except sirens and the ring of cell phones like electronic insects.

It occurred to Notley that there was a new tune he was hearing here, not just a changing tempo or key but a whole new musical departure, yet vaguely familiar because always latent. A new story, seeming to have come out of nowhere but in reality perhaps always whispering to us.

And this new story had no beginning nor end but was constantly unfolding, would constantly unfold. Infold, enfold, interweave, unravel, recombine in similar but different versions, never repeating.

Seeming almost predictable at times, at times completely unpredictable. Lynch arrived in town.

He'd heard about the funeral too late, he said, but he said he wanted to pay his respects. In fact, it turned out, he also wanted to know the details of Fynch's will. He was after all his younger cousin.

The information was readily available that Lynch was not in the will, but that wasn't the end of the story, because Lynch was claiming that Fynch had never paid certain debts to him pursuant to the purchase, long ago, of his interest in the clock factory. And he aimed to collect.

But to this end he needed information about the disposition of the funds Fynch left to the Museum, information that was not public. Sniffing around, he found an ally in the person of Spence, a vagrant bookkeeper for whom Seymor had inadvisedly insisted on helping out with a job at the Museum.

The Temp, as it happens, was at this point in time cash poor, like all the businesses and institutions in the ground zero area due to the economic aftereffects of the Trade Towers attack, but Spence, secretly urged on by Lynch, tried to convince Seymor they could find money in the budget simply by cutting back on expenses. I.e., no exhibitions.

Rather than acting outraged by the suggestion, as one might expect, Seymor was more or less apologetic, pointing out that the exhibitions were well underway in terms of money spent. Then Lynch, surprisingly, said he might be willing to forego the debt if he were to be appointed to a high position of responsibility in the Museum, parallel to the one his cousin had held.

Lynch, as far as Seymor could tell, didn't know anything about art or museums. Seymor speculated that Lynch was either attracted by the faux glamour of the art scene, the prestige of the museum world, that he was just tired of being a business executive in LaFange or, of course, that he had ulterior motives—which Seymor heavily suspected.

Nevertheless, Seymor was amazingly receptive to Lynch's proposal. He told Lynch that his experience as a business executive could prove extremely valuable to the Museum in its straitened circumstances.

He asked Lynch to come up with a hard proposal, and meantime they would both think about it. But of course when Jocylyn and Pyhl heard about it they hit the ceiling, and they confronted Seymor with their outrage.

However, rather than respond to their rage, Seymor muttered some conciliatory sounds while staring at a point above and beyond their heads with a look in his eyes that survivors of 9/11 knew all too well and called the thousand-mile stare. He vaguely demurred that none of them had the business know-how lost when Fynch died and that perhaps Lynch could replace it.

The more Jocylyn and Pyhl raged the more abstracted Seymor became until they finally gave up for lack of a resistance that might have provided something to argue against. Seymor, they concluded, was losing his marbles.

Not only was the appointment of Lynch to be resisted but Seymor would have to be replaced before the Museum, at least with the agenda that Fynch had brought to it, went down the drain. It must be noted however that Seymor's attitude served the purpose of drawing Jocylyn and Pyhl closer together in support of Fynch's idealistic conception of the Museum as a heterodox art institution.

It seemed to some that Seymor, since he had become the acting head of the Museum, had lapsed into a disastrous passivity at the policy level. Actually, his attitude was quite intentional.

Seymor made a deal with Lynch. Lynch could become President of the Museum while Seymor would retain the title of Director, and for this Lynch would forego the Museum its dubious debt to him.

This deal led to a furious confrontation between Seymor and his staff, at a meeting demanded by the latter. They wanted Seymor to annul the agreement.

But Seymor reasoned with them as follows: let Lynch go after what he wants in the Museum until he realizes that it isn't there. Let him do what he wants and pretty soon he'll realize he doesn't know what he wants to do.

Then he'll ask us what we want him to do. And we'll tell him we want him to build a bridge to our enemies, a bridge that only he as figurehead can build, since the enemy is by definition malicious toward us.

Lynch immediately made Spence his assistant, and on the advice of his assistant made Rych his liaison with the Museum staff. The first thing Spence did was to ask everyone for an expense accounting which caused much grumbling.

But what it revealed was fascinating: it seemed that when everything was totaled up almost everyone on the staff was paying more in expenses out-of-pocket than was covered by salary after deductions. Lynch was surprised and impressed that the Museum's employees were helping to support the Museum, especially so since he was not aware of the traditionally low wages paid by such institutions.

Thus Spence was obliged to report to him that if budgets were strictly enforced the Museum would actually lose money by it. Lynch then asked Rych to look into the matter of thefts, since he presumed that the thefts represented a major loss of revenues.

But Rych discovered that since the Museum dealt in intangibles it wasn't actually losing anything by the thefts except morale, and was itself only interested in the intangible called prestige. So Rych found himself investigating the source and worth of prestige.

Rych discovered that while the source, or rather sources, of prestige were multiple and complicated, the final and indispensable stamp of prestige was the money and the power it implied. This is the level at which prestige becomes a negotiable product.

The whole point, you might say, of the Temp was to render the object nonobjective. Paradoxically, the sources of prestige, Rych discovered, were precisely the opposite, or opposites rather, of money and power.

So such sources included poverty, obscurity, starvation, spirituality, self-sacrifice, ineffectuality, drunkenness, addiction, tragedy, otherworldliness, irresponsibility, the visionary, the childish, the licentious, the transgressive, the doomed, the overweening, the extravagant, the culpable, among other things. I don't know, Rych told Lynch, you figure it out.

All this practical fact-finding, however, had a secondary effect on Rych. It made him more practical.

It made him come to grips with some of the facts of life which remained hard facts regardless of how he felt about them, and he began to get the idea that there were just so many choices in given situations no matter how you might sulk or rage. That there was this stubborn side to facts that you couldn't argue with and could ignore only at your own risk no matter how much you might embroider them or even make things up and that in any case life had a way of catching up with you.

All Rych knew about his father and mother was what they told him, and they told him when he was very young that they had evaporated. Young Rych wasn't sure what they meant by evaporated but had two fanciful theories: one was that they had disappeared in a puff of smoke as the result of mysterious machinations by an evil magician, and two, they had been caught in the cow milking machine on the farm, turned into milk and deposited in little tin cans.

In either case, Rych was mighty glad to have Lynch suddenly around as, however ambivalently, an ally, not to mention as a potential genealogical resource.

Retrospectively it would have seemed natural that Lynch and the Klumps should form an alliance, and that Rych should have been the go-between. And that is exactly what happened.

First of all, Rych pointed out to Lynch that Klump was a real estate dealer and Lynch was interested in Manhattan real estate as an investment. And then, they both came from LaFange, and although they didn't know one another there they had heard of one another.

In LaFange they both had reputations as sharp customers, maybe that's why they had heard of one another. In any case, Manhattan real estate was going for a song since 9/11, or if not a song at least a short concerto, and Lynch was interested in cashing in.

Now it turned out that the owner of the building Cockroach was in had put the building up for sale, and when Rych found this out he urged Klump to broker a deal with Lynch, the idea being that Cockroach could become part of the Temp as a sort of counter-Temp under the same Museum administration headed by Lynch. When he was approached by Klump, Lynch responded favorably, seeing this as a move that would aggrandize his administrative position, but said he would have to talk it over with the staff.

Even now, tour groups were coming into the area, crude observation platforms were being built, and the improvised shrines of victims' photos, American flags, and teddy bears now wilting from the weather were being displaced by a vision of the whole site as a sort of Pearl Harbor. Besides, the clearing of the site was itself fascinating, with swarms of orange hard hats attacking the piles of rubble like a swarm of worker ants, aided by enormous machines that crisscrossed the ruins like mechanical animals.

There was something upbeat about it all despite the tragic circumstances. There was an energy, an undaunted competence, an efficiency, an implied optimism that you felt as the characteristic best of the body politic in all its parts. It was this spirit in the long run that Lynch was banking on, this sheer drive, such that you had to wonder whether it was not an end itself, even though you knew it could not be.

The profusion and variety of machinery, of motorized vehicles, of uniformed workers and officials, the enormity of the dig, the colossal dimensions involved, challenged the imagination. And for this challenge the resources of the spirit stretched thin against the shock of it all, an attenuation felt most when the orange body bags came into play, when clumps of men gathered around them in patterns of grief, when you most needed those emotional resources to rise above the awesome devastation working its worst.

And more so when you were aware, but for a slightly different geometry, you might have been included among the victims. Meanwhile, a public fuss had erupted on the basis of a leak to the media about the potential sale of the Cockroach building.

One faction objected that the sale would threaten this distinguished Cass Gilbert architectural monument with demolition. Another faction claimed the sale to the Museum would kill their idea of turning the building into low-cost housing.

The tenants union objected to the potential eviction of numerous families. A coalition of landlords was against a precedent of turning rental properties into public use projects, however culturally fructiferous.

A newspaper article in *The Observer* called all such objections phenomeral and residuary, while an editorial on a local TV station branded the whole botchup as malinfluent double-talk. But behind all the double-talk, as behind most discourse, was an abiding reality: money.

Jocylyn tried to convince Blustrous that the effectiveness of dolls and puppets, as in voodoo, didn't depend on the icon but on its emotional impact on the observer, and therefore belonged in a show like her Art Demo that depended on neuron activity rather than what stimulated it. But Blustrous told Jocylyn her collection of dolls and puppets had too much there there for inclusion in the show.

Not so for Blustrous' colleague, Carney. What he liked to work with was what was strictly low gravity, if not downright schlock.

Content was Carney's nemesis, he was a showman in the guise of a shaman, and he knew that content got in the way. He was all flash and glitter and quite charming when he wanted to be.

There was a rumor that he was interested in running for political office and he certainly would have made a good run for whatever office he chose, based on the popularity of his internet gossip show. The show was a combination of personality peddling and political commentary on the issues of the day, if not of the minute or even the second.

A brilliant mixture of cliché and wise crack, the show managed to give the impression that it was edifying as well, and Carney had become something of a national figure. But there were always rumors about a dark side, of drink and drug abuse, of misbehavior toward women, and of distinctly unkosher ideological connections.

Speculation was that he didn't run for office for fear it would reveal too much about his personal life, and especially about his conversion, if in fact it happened, to a fundamentalist church that was reputedly one of the fronts for the Fundament. This church, to some, represented more of a cult than a religion, but Carney would frequently invoke his faith on the show, and as sacrosanct as religion is in this country, it became one of the sanctions for his show's cultural prestige.

It should immediately be said that the Fundament's distinction between this world and the next was very different from the Evolved Intelligences' distinction between the real and the unreal, or Fifth World. For the Intelligences the unreal world was a source of solace and support without which the real world would soon founder and disintegrate in ruthless chaos inflicted by the fundamentist warlords of the soul.

To those who complained that the unreal didn't exist, the Intelligences would reply that it exists because we make it exist, we make it exist because the real world would be unimaginable without it. Among other things, they pointed out that it was in the unreal world in which that factitious concept we call the self dwelled in all its self-reflexive consciousness.

Lynch and Klump, and this was inevitable, started to connect. And Hymi proposed an idea for an exhibition.

Hymi's proposal was to create an exhibition as a comic strip. His argument was that the comic strip was the underlying model for the Temp's exhibition policy.

His reasoning was that the comic strip, appearing daily, was the essence of ephemera as the memory of yesterday's strip was obliterated by the presence of today's, which would in turn be obliterated by tomorrow's. He argued that the only continuity was that of what he called tone.

Tone was a quality difficult to define, something like the key in music but not really, like the gestalt in psychology but not really. Tone was continuity without plot or even story.

Tone was not narrative but was the minimum requirement for narrative. But Hymi couldn't make any headway in trying to convince the staff at the Temp of the worth of his project, so he took it across the street to Klump.

Klump, however, was feverishly involved with his new idea, which was to turn his gallery into a gift shop. He had noticed the demand at Rych's small new Temp gift shop for trinkets, which they found it difficult to supply, since how do you supply a trinket representing something that isn't there, or only fleetingly, a bauble for a bubble?

Klump's idea, in brief, was to turn his Cockroach gallery into the gift shop for the Temp. That way the public would be served, in that those interested in art could get art at the Temp, and those interested in trinkets or who didn't know the difference could get trinkets at Cockroach.

This was the perfect scheme for Klump and he knew it since he knew that he didn't know the difference between trinkets and art. And he bet that most people didn't either, which put him on the winning side.

He contacted Lynch who immediately saw the virtue of his idea. Notley had been out of the picture a while.

But it was Notley who Hymi was most interested in now. Notley had kept clear of all the machinations at the Museum.

Notley was kept busy by his new invention which he called silent music. It was a kind of music, he explained, that you could only hear with what he called the mind's ear.

Silent music was perceptible as rhythm, and as tone in a broader sense in which it was a quality emitted and received only by people, whereas rhythm was universal. Currently Notley was interested in registering the silent music of Jimmy Lochs.

Notley was developing a brotherly feeling toward Jimmy Lochs as a fellow artist. He was fascinated by Jimmy's jagged unpredictable rhythms as opposed to his own ideal of a steady humming and drumming, while in terms of tone they were very similar, in terms of tone they were both what he would call receptive, surfing the incoming waves of experience rather than picking and choosing and avoiding and ridiculously trying to impose one's will.

Because, Notley would explain, there's no such thing as being captain of one's fate, though you can get lucky and it might look that way. At best you can create waves of experience, but you can never tell how they're going to break, and it was this unpredictable aspect of Jimmy Lochs's rhythm that was most alien to Notley and that most interested him.

When Jimmy thought about the thousands in the World Trade Center as individuals, individuals getting killed to help one another, individuals barely escaping and individuals not making it, himself almost a victim, it shook him up, he felt a survivor's kinship with those who escaped, with the workers picking through the rubble with rakes and shovels, with the way the monstrous excavators and backhoes laid out, almost delicately, in a carpet the debris for their inspection.

It brought out in Jimmy a sudden communal sense, the sense that there were unspoken obligations, however one might rebel, that were there to deny but were there. But they all felt it, and above all in their own little group, whose index was that they had begun commonly thinking of it as a group, and above all Austyn felt it, though her amorous relations gave ample extra reason to do so.

And not only that but Austyn, despite herself, began to feel toward the others a tincture of the maternal. Possibly this was a sense she picked up from her ever tightening relations with Achs.

Achs had now mostly withdrawn from the Museum, spending most of her time at Fynch's estate which she had inherited, in a state of mourning for Fynch. She found the area around ground zero too lugubrious with its aura of death, its sense of being a grave site, a charnel house and simultaneously a search area for bodies, its repeated rituals of respect on discoveries of additional cadavers, the workers lining up in two rows as the flag-draped stretchers moved between them, all of which she could see from her office window at the apex of the Museum building.

She preferred rattling around the Fynch mansion surrounded by memories of her mate in a kind of numb melancholy, bathed in memories, which contained an element of comfort compared to the barren, empty pain which she could feel coming on. But it was true, on those days she did come into the Museum, that she sought out Austyn with the sense that she had something to tell her though she wasn't at all sure what.

The only other person she found herself drawn to was Seymor, and the common concern she felt for each of them was as an instinct of protectiveness about which she was quite explicit, though for unstated reasons. It wasn't that, in terms of politics of the Museum, she felt their positions were threatened now that Fynch was gone, because, in fact, those politics, surprisingly, had abated since his death. It was something more general and at the same time more personal and more ominous, which she was unwilling at present to confront.

It was possibly a question of numbness in response to a blow. She didn't want to think, she wanted to be carried by impulse.

She was especially concerned about Seymor who, since Fynch's death, seemed withdrawn and melancholy. But there her instincts were only half correct, since though Seymor did feel a certain unexpected depth of grief, it was also true that he was pursuing a strategy whose rationale was that sometimes doing nothing was the most energetic course, in this case allowing things to fall into place of their own momentum, using that momentum for his own ends.

Seymor's own ends, if you asked Hymi, were based on a vision of things inadequately worked out and imperfectly understood, which had the appearance, at least, of innocence. It seemed to begin with the premise that whatever you do you do to make things better rather than worse, and Hymi had observed that those with that premise tended to make things worse rather than better.

But for Seymor it was impulse that was important, the results secondary. He reasoned that it was the accumulation in individuals of that better impulse that counted and that eventually would carry the day, no matter how puerile or ludicrous individual tentatives.

It was a rainy day, and from the window of Austyn's apartment Hymi could see and hear on many fronts the vast dismantling of the quasi-archeological remains of ground zero, which now figured in his consciousness as the backdrop for all speculation, and perhaps as a consequence he read Seymor as one who had not yet cleared the ground for himself, and yet Hymi had to credit him for the force of his belief. Hymi was not so cynical as to discount it, belief, but you had to believe, for example, that an organization like the Improvement Society was short on self-examination and long on credulity.

That, he supposed, was the price you had to pay, a price more willingly and appropriately paid in youth than in age, however good one's intentions. But the wet, weary afternoon, deepening if not reflecting his mood, the workers in the pit clad in bright orange, yellow, chartreuse or black slickers, the heavy machinery crawling back and forth over a variety of terrains, the multilevel omnidimensional excavation like some lugubrious Brueghel, sapped him of the impulse to pay any price whatever.

Rych took a walk with Jocylyn at Jocylyn's invitation. Jocylyn wanted to talk to him about plans for the Cockroach gallery, drawing him in as an ally in the greatest degree possible, though she knew of his feeling left out of activities at the Temp and had a tendency to snivel about it, and she wanted to avoid the sniveling as much as possible.

Therefore she suggested an itinerary that avoided the melancholy of ground zero and instead kept to the edge of the river and the long esplanade that extended north and south of the wreckage and partially wrecked buildings around the disaster site, Rych wondering what the occasion was but keeping an expectant silence, a silence broken by Jocylyn's occasional commentary on the geographical features of the area and its goings-on, from marine activity to the extensive landscaping maintained by those responsible for management of the vicinity. So she felt compelled to enumerate the multiple ferryboats taking the place of the ruined subway facilities under the river, of the early narcissus and jonquils pushing up in the gardens, and the felicities of the view that took in the New Jersey skyline, Ellis Island, the Statue of Liberty, and the Narrows bridge with the graceful dip of its suspension cables, all in one grand visual sweep.

When she felt the moment was relaxed, she let on that Cockroach needed a manager, at ample compensation of course, and might he contemplate such a position? But much to her surprise, considering the generosity of the offer, he said he would have to check with the people at the Temp to see if they felt any conflict of interest on his part in a declaration of conscientiousness that prompted her to re-evaluate her sense of his character, adding a broad dimension of responsibility perhaps prompted by the expansiveness of the view.

On the contrary, Jocylyn's sense of the character of Wendy Blustrous continued to shrink since Wendy refused to exhibit her dolls and puppets on the grounds that there was too much there there. The Art Demo show, conceived as a sort of testing ground to see how low the common denominator can get, kept getting it lower and lower, a development that pleased Carney, who promised major publicity, but called into question the very question of what art was.

Wendy was unwilling to face such generalities, indeed questioned whether there were such generalities that were valid in general, and tended to make ad hoc definitions if at all, so that she would discover that a superior stuffed animal was a work of art and would go into the Art Demo show. By then Jocylyn was making the case for dolls and puppets, and above all for her Statue of Liberty models, that they had the aura of icons and a level of craftsmanship that precisely raised their common denominator to a level of connoisseurship that was not for everyone, though everyone had the opportunity for appreciation.

What this meant for Jocylyn was that there was a growing gap between those who knew and those who did not know, and furthermore between those who knew and those who knew one another, corresponding to her growing sense of solidarity with the insiders at the Temp which was reflected in a leap, inexplicably sudden, from populist to elitist. Which caused Seymor to take her aside and explain, in admirably simplified form, that these categories did not apply to the Temp, which was neither populist nor elitist, but simply functioned as a frame to draw attention to new content.

Seymor understood from her response that Jocylyn didn't quite understand what he was talking about but he hoped that his explanation, puzzling as it was for Jocylyn, would help mute her reactions to the current activities of the Museum, which were programmatically calculated to retard the understanding while provoking the imagination. And so it proved in the occurrence that would allow these jumps of flamboyant precocity in the Temp's program, taking the vacuity for ease of prognosis was the last thing and, possibly, the best, tending to phlogisticity.

Meantime, the dogs were sniffing through the ruins smelling for death, an exercise Hymi could see from Austyn's window, and which gave him grave thoughts about Fynch and about his own fate, for he was not in the best of health, though nothing definitive beyond or because of his PS had yet announced itself. Yet as whole contingents of corpses continued to turn up, sometimes being ushered out on flag-draped stretchers and occasionally accompanied by reedy bagpipes that were hard to ignore, his mood, made mortal and melancholic, drifted as if he now faced life in a lifeboat bereft of oars and compass. And in this he was not alone. He knew many like himself who had survived the tragedy.

Some called it nerves, some preferred the more clinical post-traumatic shock, yet all looked toward the turning point when demolition would become reconstruction. It was in this heavy, yet expectant atmosphere that Hymi received a request for a meeting from Carney, a request that Hymi was frankly wary to comply with given Carney's rumored tendency to abrupt and violent tantrums, but, apprehensive about aggravating the situation, he finally decided to acquiesce.

It turned out that Carney knew for a fact that there was money in the ruins, money and precious metals, and there was a police dog with a nose for such things. There was also a policeman's uniform but, as yet, there was no appropriate person ready to wear it.

Carney himself, of course, given his public reputation, was interested only in the story of discovery he projected, but the appropriate person would naturally have a broad latitude. If you saw what he meant.

But the appropriate person needed to be sanctioned by a position of institutional trust and plausible concern, and who better than someone associated with a museum in close proximity? And Carney thought that Hymi, while not an associate, by virtue of his close relation to the staff, might know of such an appropriate person.

In fact, Hymi did—too appropriate—immediately thinking of Rych with his evident lack of ballast, and quickly resolved to do whatever he could to keep the two apart. But it turned out that Carney had connections via the agency of one Ballox who was in contact with Klaxon who contacted Rych.

Who turned them down cold, Seymor told Hymi, leaving him with a new impression of Rych's character. But soon Hymi began to note articles in the papers referring to vast riches hidden in the wreckage and he guessed that Carney was underway.

And then one day he noticed unusual activity from Austyn's window, and training the telescope they now had posted on the sill, found that the workers were busy with large black garbage bags sweeping bales of bank notes out of the dusty dirt into the receptacles, under the eyes of the police to be sure, but who can say? As to the fabled deposits of silver, Hymi learned from Carney's chat show that they were taken away by a column of armored cars, who can say where?

Pyhl and Klaxon, though nothing like one another, had this in common: they both had stentorian voices. Not only had they little in common but they didn't like one another at all, and this from the very first time they laid eyes on one another, which was when Klaxon was in Achs's office asking permission to go through everyone's files indiscriminately, and Pyhl objected.

The decibels rose quickly with Klaxon's retort, WHAT DOES HE HAVE TO DO WITH IT? and Pyhl's reply that he had in any case,

MORE THAN YOU, and escalated from there till Pyhl was referring to Klaxon as this OBSCENITY GUMSHOE, and Achs had to intercede in a voice not nearly so loud but much more cutting, that she was responsible in this area and she would decide the issue on a case-by-case basis. Ever since the two had been working increasingly at cross purposes, and when Klaxon came up with the posthumous letter Pyhl immediately tried to minimize its importance.

The letter, from Fynch, said in short that he was in favor of the thefts from the Museum, that he looked on them as an effective way to disseminate the message of the Museum, that the Museum rarely sold works and when it did the costs involved, including overhead, amounted to more than the profit, and that in effect the Museum made money on every work it didn't sell. All this meant to Klaxon was that the museum was fraudulent in selling what it did sell because it was admittedly worthless goods, and all it meant to Pyhl was that this was a commentary on Fynch's conviction that real art was priceless.

The two actually almost came to blows on the issue, and would have, had not Seymor, who was present on this occasion, begun chanting, o-o-o-m, o-o-o-O-M, O-O-O-O-O-M, startling them both into quiescence. But the abrasive interlude showed how far Pyhl had come in his allegiance to the Museum and its program, moreover demonstrating that the program, in this case at least, programmatically or by osmosis, had its effect.

In any case, it was a turn of events that Seymor had evidently been waiting for, for no sooner had Pyhl expressed his sympathy for Fynch's program for the Museum than did he invest Pyhl with responsibility for day-to-day operations, freeing himself up for the more oracular pursuits connected with deciphering the Fundamentist vision and its dictates in practice. And here he had the insight that it and its religious Church of the Fundament arm had a fundamental distaste for anything complicated, and since simplicities tended to retain their truth to fact for a much shorter time than complications, reality being what it is, the key to dealing with them was patience.

Unfortunately, the period of appropriate patience might, and probably would, outlast the lifespan of most mortals, but in any case one needed to have faith, important friends, and a sinecure, the second and third of which Seymor already had, but the first of which he knew he had to get and he knew he didn't know how. While Seymor was meditating his future, Pyhl by contrast, set about rectifying his past, beginning with his now past relationship with Austyn whom he considered he had treated badly.

But Austyn rejected his analysis of their relation, pointing out that she did not merely tolerate it but encouraged it and very possibly initiated it, and that sometimes dehumanization can be a step toward humanization, assuming benign intentions, and that there were circumstances in which even sadomasochism can be a creative act. Life, she generalized, was not simple and not always a straight line.

There were surprises, surprises when you least expected them, a promising chain of events could have ill-starred ends and vice versa, what seemed for the worst could turn out to be for the best, there was no master plot between the circumstances of birth and the denouement of death, anything could happen, she had been talking about it with Hymi, they had decided that the only way to keep up with events was to surf it and conspire with it, that was made clear by the World Trade Center attack, by the improbability of it, of the planes hitting the buildings and of the buildings collapsing, who would have thought? And what next?

In any case, said Hymi, the plot is thin but event is thick and beyond our petty scenarios, the grammar of event does not match the grammar of language which tries with considerable pathos to bind it together with dubious threads and tantalizing propinquities that cannot mesh with molecular contingencies and atomic defenestrations troubling the bivouac with its boistering. What?

Austyn did not follow but got the gist, though she couldn't say she was by the gist enlightened. But one thing was clear to her. Hymi was having an anxiety attack, which was always the case when his language started breaking down and the connection between word and referent started dissolving.

Hymi himself recognized the state by the anxiety that came with it. His usual remedy was action because action united him with the language of event, which did not have the concept anxiety in its vocabulary, unfolding at its own pace, unstoppable, unreflective, but sometimes also unnerving, alien, and terrible, and the only alternative to drowning in it, for him, was to ride its wave.

And apropos, a curious contretemps occurred between Austyn and Seymor when Austyn decided that the only way to deal with the Museum thefts was to bait a trap for the thieves. Someone had given Seymor a stone said to be from the Oracle at Delphi which he had made an object of meditation and, as a result, he said, he was getting mysterious calls on his cell phone whose caller he could neither identify nor locate, answering questions he had asked himself through the agency of the Delphic stone, and which had advised him that things would work themselves out at the Museum if he had sufficient faith in the course of events and remained passive.

At home with Hymi, Austyn was struck by the difference between them, Seymor and Hymi, Hymi affecting an almost hostile, coolly cynical attitude toward the thieves, but really disturbed by the mysteries involved and increasingly anxious about the gaps they created in his ongoing assumptions about reality. Austyn made a point of it, noting that his talk was becoming increasingly incoherent, his language painting pictures whose sense she could not follow, invoking the incursions of advancing age, evoking failing faculties.

But he replied, not failing but maybe flailing, that it had always been so, and had to do with a seemingly innate distrust of words, a questioning of them. He couldn't say if it had become worse with age although his capacity for the anxiety it produced seemed less, and what seemed worse, in fact, was that in youth he had always expected that all would fall into place and now he was confronted by the possibility it would not ever. And anyway suppose it did, fall into place that is, it might be like the Viagra effect where by the time it kicks in you might not feel like it anymore.

Which gave him the idea that what they both needed was a roll on the mattress but she said it wasn't the right time of day and he said what was the right time of day and she said it depended and he complained that she wouldn't even give him the time of day and she said she didn't mean it that way and he said how then did you mean it and she said it was a question of mood but it was up to him if he was in the mood but by then he was out of the mood so they decided to take a walk. Which left him mentally flailing but it struck him as they went outside that there was no reason not to flail as long as he flailed to good purpose like, say, flailing arms and legs for exercise through the flow of phenomena pouring through the streets around ground zero, the sight seers, the dump trucks, the cranes, the hard hats, the flapping flags, the police cars, the emergency vehicles, a stupendous sixteen wheeler, pedestrians arm in arm, pedestrians not arm in arm, baby carriages, multiracial couples singles triples, cars, taxis, street signs, zebra crossings, tank trucks, street lights, buses, hoses, zipping scooters-buggies-carts, waste cans, street people, yellow caterpillars, flagmen, pneumatic drills, scaffolding, portapotties, wooden work shacks, parked cars—if you ask what sense it all made you might be asking the wrong question.

What they wanted malign people to know, or think they knew, was that the whole upper echelon of the Museum management was geriatrically disadvantaged and that they could easily be conned into participating in a final grand hijacking scheme that would put the Temp out of business. Now, while it was true that all the executives at the Museum besides Seymor were senior citizens or close to it they were sharp as tacks, with the possible exception of Achs whose recent loss of Fynch rendered her labile.

Plus they had the following advantage, that they all appeared to the normal world to be stupid, stupid in one way or another by normal conventions, first and most of all by their strange allegiance to the nonmaterial world which they all held in common, and individually by the strange ways they pursued this commitment, Austyn by her tenacious and temperamental vicissitudes, Pyhl by his blunderbuss or rather steamroller pursuit of his goals, and Jocylyn and Hymi in their advisory capacity, the one by her characteristic stubbornness, the other with his flights of what would you call it, imagination? neurosis? Even Achs in mourning was unaccountably eccentric, dressing gaily but talking to almost no one but when she talked talking mainly to herself as if conducting an ongoing interior dialogue but out loud.

As now, when her train of thought emerged from its tunnel of silence out of her mouth into the air though there was no one to listen, wondering why she kept identifying Fynch's death, which was peaceful, I don't understand it, she said, with the tiny figures falling from the World Trade Towers the day of the attack, their clothes blowing, some trailing fire, why, what did Fynch's death have to do with the final dive, the absolute terror, she said, of those falling, the screams lost in the blowback of the rushing non-resistant air, airborne, or rather air died, dead, already dead, did they hear the final thud, falling for ever, final, for good, the ground racing up to smash them, the leap out the window, the letting go, the panic, the accelerating drop, I can't imagine it, I don't understand it, Fynch's peaceful death, it must be post-traumatic shock, she said. Or a dream of old age, or a nightmare.

Meantime, Austyn and Pyhl were busy baiting a trap. They made it known that the Museum could no longer afford guards, that the admission tickets, based on the suggested price, would now be paid on the honor system, and that the Museum would be open all night to accommodate restless souls, insomniacs, and those on the swing shift.

In other words, the Museum was open to looting, to larceny, to pilfering, to pillage, to sack, to plunder, a form of shareware when you come down to it, and after all what the Temp was meant for in a way. In a way it exhibited nothing and therefore had an inexhaustible supply of the same.

But the younger generation had other ideas, younger meaning anyone under sixty more or less, that is, Seymor and Rych. But their ideas were nonverbal, nonlinear, and for the most part non-pictorial, in short, they paid attention mostly to the smell, and above all, to the sound of things, and to them the Austyn-Pyhl agenda didn't smell or sound right.

The Austyn-Pyhl agenda smelled off, and that led to the impression that it didn't play right, and this was revealed to them separately and independently, so when they got together on it they figured it had a certain validity, they couldn't explain what. It was just that the older generational negativity and skepticism was making itself felt again whereas their instinct was all optimism and generosity while to Austyn and Pyhl that was like feeding the shark candy till its teeth fell out.

But it was the artists Notley and Jimmy Lochs who saved the day when it was discovered that the money for the mortgage on the Museum that was left by Fynch was hopelessly tied up in probate, which would leave nowhere to exhibit the kind of work they did but of course they were used to showing nothing nowhere, and for the same reason they were among the first to accommodate to ground zero, so while others viewed it as an amputation, Lochs saw it as an invitation and Notley heard it as a silence. Now they both saw the potential loss of the Museum as an opportunity.

To Jimmy Lochs this seemed a challenge to paint over the tired complexities of the big picture with essential simplicities without the distractions of premeditation. This naturally appealed to the younger generation, Seymor and above all Rych, and their impatience with history, though Seymor was reluctant to cut loose from the past.

Rych, in all his adolescent petulance, tempered by impatient enthusiasm, found himself in natural alliance with Lochs, who in some respects, rejection of precedent among them, was youthful to the point of psychosis, that is, he was in some respects clinically simplistic. But the healthy social organism finds its ways of utilizing genetic mistakes, and in this case perhaps simplicity was what was needed.

Seymor, on the other hand, found himself more in tune with Notley, whose tactic was to contain complexities in a state of mutually canceling suspension so that the end product was a static opacity, where Lochs would propose a dynamic transparency. Ordinarily, at this juncture, and especially because of the probate situation, and despite the Austyn-Pyhl agenda, Seymor should have called a meeting of the Board.

But Seymor had his doubts about the Board. He considered them a dangerous mix of puritans and populists, of right-wing and left-wing, each bringing out the worst vulgarian tendencies in the other, whose ability to raise money was matched by their inability to judge art.

To avoid a meeting, Seymor floated the idea that while probate was in process, a process which could take a long time, the Temp should convert itself into an imaginary Museum, freeing it of real estate, of money, and thereby of all outside control, an entity of the naked spirit soaring. However, the Chairman of the Board, a man named Blunn, pointed out with some justice that not everyone could soar, in fact most people couldn't soar or if they could they could do so only in aimless flights ending in crash landings, and that it was the Museum's job as guide that, to most people, was one of its most important obligations.

Seymor had to admit that Blunn had a point and he had a further thought that converting to an imaginary Museum would change the focus from manipulation of vision in the visual arts, however evanescent, to the self-conscious and already premeditated formulations of language as the repository of the imagination. Although his own experience led him to suspect that spoken, as opposed to written, language, as an oral exercise, had more in common with the unpremeditated visual than with the premeditated quality of writing.

Blunn had a point, thus demonstrating the value of democratic input, but it was as if he had picked up the ball only to run with it the wrong way, because someone or thing had to move beyond the premeditated in order to gain the insight that made them important as guide to most people, and that someone or thing could only be the artists or, if not the artists, the Museum or most likely some combination of both. But after talking the whole thing over with Hymi, who was becoming one of his important advisers, Seymor suggested they both sleep on it.

Hymi, however, did not have a strong urge to sleep on it, or rather, he had a stronger urge to sleep on Austyn. He found he was getting addicted to it again, even on nights when they didn't make love, he found it hard to sleep when she was not there in bed with him, his leg and arm over her body, her arms around him, naked skin to skin, their very breathing phasing into sync, sleeping in a soft harmony and submental rapport, cradling one another in a floaty warmth.

The animal comfort they gave one another was never stated, maybe even to themselves, but it was gradually becoming the foundation of their relation, and induced a sort of dreamy alertness during their waking hours, a sharpening of certain senses, a softening of focus, a druggy, animal responsiveness to sensory stimuli, an indifference to argument and reason, a fertile reverie, an innocence. In certain social contexts lately they seemed so out of step as to appear stupid, especially in view of the knotty problems of the Museum and its conflicts.

Hymi was aware of this, but was also aware that stupidity sometimes yields intelligence beyond the reach of the intelligentsia. But stupidity is a high-risk business and is not for everyone because usually the investment is great and the return negligible at best.

Stupidity is subject to mistaken assumptions, confused ratiocinations, bull-headed obsessions, inaccurate observations, arrogant suppositions and presumptuous premises. But these qualities can also be the essential ingredients of breakthrough insight or leaps of faith without which life bounded by biology and death would be unimaginable.

So, when Seymor abruptly announced his resignation from the Museum directorship in favor of Pyhl, Hymi sensed a deeper purpose than the one announced, which was mental fatigue and the need to replenish his spiritual resources. But a problem with Hymi, who was a professional skeptic, was that he couldn't accept spiritual replenishment as deeper purpose, so that when he discovered Seymor sitting in his office staring at the wall, he interpreted it as a sign of depression, whereas Seymor knew he was getting a fill-up from the Fifth World that filled up the wasteland left by the collapsing towers.

Hymi could see death in Seymor's eyes. It should have tipped them off, Seymor's apparent exhaustion but they only realized it too late, after they discovered him comatose in his apartment on Jack Daniels and sleeping pills.

Comatose but revivable. And strangely, after his revival, he was much more energetic than before when, everyone now realized, he had been suffering clinical depression or spiritual deprivation, however you wanted to look at it, and soon threw himself into the struggle with renewed vigor.

Seymor, realizing the time had come for action, asked Pyhl to convene a meeting of the core personnel in and around the Museum whom he most trusted, including Achs, Jocylyn, Austyn, Notley, Jimmy, Hymi and, yes, Rych, who had come a long way if not all the way. He began by telling them he felt they were all part of a family, the family of the Temp in some sense descending from Fynch's conception and, however differently, sharing his values.

I mean, said Seymor, we have to reach a constituency. And who is that? Austyn pursued, and Seymor answered, The great body of featherweights who care more about tickling one another and especially being themselves tickled than they are ticklish about belief, who basically believe in nothing except what tickles them.

And who can say they're wrong, Seymor continued, the pursuit of happiness is a very serious business in life and is even written into the framework of our government, which was a stroke of genius on the part of our founding fathers, because as a serious business the pursuit of happiness when you come right down to it supports the economy and grows the gross national product. And so it now behooves all of us, and each of us individually, to start recruiting feathers, feather by feather, a job that may seem endless but which may undergo surprise accelerations, you never know, sometimes massive accumulations are the consequence of surprisingly slight gestures, like the pebble that sets off the avalanche or the butterfly that causes the tornado, and in any case you have to start somewhere, sometime, and that means here and now.

There was a surprising wave of spontaneous applause that flowed from the little group, for they had not expected this statement of social conscience from Seymor, whom they knew as at first the pugnacious rapping adolescent who grew into a highly competent administrator and then mutated into something like a withdrawn mystic visionary but who had never shown any signs of political know-how or social responsibility. It is fair to say that they all left that meeting with a renewed motivation and a level of morale that had not been felt among the Museum personnel for some months.

Austyn led the way by arranging a "bivouac" show with Wendy Blustrous at the Temp that used the idea of encampments as an art form and which invited homeless people to inhabit them in circumstances that would alter their negative image. At the opposite pole, Notley, to whom this effort seemed a vulgar digression into the political, organized public sessions of what he called dynamic meditation, meant to motivate people to be aware, and above all to engage in action, however minimally, the inequities that came up in the sessions, if only to create a precedent and set an example.

The first indication Rych had that he was developing strange powers within the span of his working memory, that is to say within the thirty seconds or so before and after what one could loosely call the present, was when he began anticipating events out of a sort of memory of the future. Future memory was made manifest one day when Rych was walking down the street with Achs and he noticed how fearful she was of what might happen while he had a sense of what would happen and even invited it.

You might ask how he could memorize the future. The feeling was he could see it coming and remember seeing it coming before it happened, something like that. Maybe that was why he liked the streets and Achs didn't, because her memory was steeped in the past while his quivered on the edge of the future, on what was happening. Maybe it was just the difference between age and youth, and between the dullness and acuity of their respective sense organs.

In any case, when Pyhl heard about the phenomenon, he immediately saw the possibilities in developing Rych's talent, for Pyhl envisioned Rych training a corps of adolescents to memorize the future, scanning out threatening situations and warning of danger points, something like the police dogs trained to sniff explosives or drugs or human bodies, but when he mentioned his plan to Austyn she condemned it as wasteful and vulgar because of the way it squandered a gift of youth on narrow and unworthy goals. But just about everyone about then began formulating practical projects to ward off the death instinct, projects whose purpose it was, as Seymor put it in an encouraging if misguided memo sent to the staff, to promote time and inhibit memory.

For while Pyhl had become director of the Museum, Seymor was acknowledged as the spiritual leader of those who worked there, though—and this was not generally known—Seymor was at this time heavily engaged in dialogue with Hymi, who was in process of figuring out his ambivalent relation to time and who had formulated the phrase inversely to Seymor: to inhibit time by promoting memory, a formulation he had been groping for for some months and which led him to develop with Notley a new computerized musical instrument he called the electronic mnemonica whose tones were calculated to call up forgotten memories. For Hymi had realized that time and memory, far from being compatible, worked against one another.

Seymor was developing a halo. Not everyone could see it and those who could see it couldn't see it all the time, but word was getting around. So it was a surprise but not a shock when Seymor called them together to preach a sermon.

Anyway, they were by now getting used to Seymor's rambling and obscure manner of speech which they were willing to put up with because of the absolute selfless purity of his motives as far as anyone could tell. Seymor was not interested in power, or money, or self-aggrandizement, or sex, or praise, or vanity, or image, or making good impressions, or fulfilling his fantasies, or having fantasies at all, or complaining, or throwing the first stone, or envy, or sloth, or schadenfreude, or hypocrisy, or guilt, or innocence, or excess, or good and evil, or make believe, or evasion, or prevarication, or self-deception, or virtue, or purity, or saintliness.

Seymor said the subject of his sermon was public works. He said he was going to talk about how public works were the key to, and consequence of, the Fifth World, and how mere awareness of the Fifth World was pointless because what were you going to do with it, contemplate it? How useless.

No, his sermon was going to be about how you can contact the Fifth World only through good intentions but it doesn't stop there, he was going to talk about how good intentions have to ricochet off the Fifth World in the form of public works, and here his halo became intense so that almost everyone could see it gleaming fuchsia, violet, and chartreuse, and he was going to talk about how public works were the only sphere in which one could pay one's debt to society which one incurred, he was going to say, by the very fact of being born and, he was going to say, if one did not pay that debt one had little choice but to be born again, words burning forever with the sense that something was missing from one's life, something missing, he would say, that validated it and supported your sense of optimism, he was going to say, that is rightly yours as your key, he was going to say, to the kind of faith and hope that you needed, finally, to get up in the morning and have your coffee and do what it is you have to do without the feeling of despair that creeps up on you and eviscerates your soul and hangs it up to dry. And having said that, he paused in confusion, and then canceled his sermon, on grounds that he had already said what he was going to say.

realtime 10/30/02:

Another funeral at ground zero . . . perhaps the last . . .

So what now . . . the pit is mostly cleared, almost neat . . . maybe it was for the best . . . in the long view . . . anyway what's to gain from getting gloomy . . .

Okay, consider the upside . . . urban renewal . . . it's a great opportunity for city planning . . .

The Improvement Society says don't worry, keep smiling . . . that's a lot to ask but I might manage a weak grin . . . and a lot of fellow feeling . . . life after the disaster . . . everyone saying hello in the streets . . . hard hats were heroes . . . we were shocked by the deaths, glad to be alive . . . terrified by the Towers collapsing . . .

But let's get to work, like good Americans . . . don't look back, that was once upon a time . . . remains . . . abandoned baby carriages . . . the truth is everything falls . . . sooner or later . . . but why think about that now, where does it get you . . . think positive, said Jocylyn, who had become gung ho, what can you lose . . . think about the Fifth World . . . learn to yearn, to long, to lust in pursuing happiness, that way lies salivation . . . Austyn, ever more practical, begged to disagree... public works was the way, she argued, without it what good was the Fifth World...

Hymi said all trauma traces the original trauma, fear of falling... all fall down . . . therefore yearning, salivation implies catching, holding... not like catching a germ, contagious, observe mob behavior... Towers falling people fleeing... running... abandoned shoes, baby carriages . . . caught in the stampede, after the fall afraid of falling... salvaged by catching and holding on...

Austyn, ever more practical, with the help of Achs, started searching Fynch's papers for support of public works once upon a time ... what she found knocked her over... a letter suggesting Fynch was possibly her father... but how could that be... he was old enough to be her grandfather, possibly great grandfather...

Who am I, Austyn panicked... she felt like the floor had collapsed beneath her... facing memory without history... the knowledge of history...

Hymi was the oldest now... Rych the youngest... suddenly they were hanging out together, no one could figure out why... to most of the Museum personnel Rych was still the brat... and in truth he hadn't yet grown out of it...

Rych had a history with material well-being... of not having it... he had been a foster child... the family he lived with wasn't exactly poor but Rych felt poor . . . all his friends were poor . . . they had poor names... Vinny, Clark, Gerard... their fathers had poor jobs ... garbagemen, peddlers, clerks... but they had fathers, and mothers too, which was more than Rych had... Rych had a foster father who used to beat him up . . . and mother who was drunk most of the time...

Simply because he felt she was disposed to listen, Rych confided all this to Achs . . . Achs in turn confided it all to Austyn . . . who didn't let on to Rych that she knew . . . so that Rych thought Austyn's outpouring of sympathy was on account of his qualities, while they were really a function of his past . . . and while she assumed he was loath to admit to her that he was a virgin she supposed he was . . . and resolved to initiate him . . .

I have to confess that Austyn seemed a little old for Rych, old enough to be his mother . . . or even his grandmother . . . but I am not accountable for what happens here . . . I am the medium through which it happens . . . I don't know what happens next nor why it happens . . . ask the Mysterious Narrator, a mystery even to myself . . . I'm just taking dictation . . . in any case, they haven't screwed yet . . . maybe they won't . . .

The ruins at this phase, exposed pillars supporting layers of vacant spaces, looked like the ruins of the Roman Forum . . . it was a gray, drizzly day . . . hard hats were staring down into a hole made by a backhoe in a way that made you think they'd discovered more bodies . . . Hymi asked Rych if he wanted to go for a walk . . .

Rych was curious about the old man . . . he was interested in the way he sustained morale though showing obvious physical signs of aging, including a stiff legged limp, hindered vision which his eyeglasses didn't seem to help, a tendency to forget names and encroachment of long-term on short-term memory so that he seemed to live more and more in the past, black bushes of hair sprouting out ears and nostrils in contrast with a white, scraggly beard, brown teeth, bald scalp with dandruff, phlegmy cough, hunched posture, dry, cackling laugh, runny nose, yellow, misshapen fingernails, potbelly, fits of belching and farting, a tendency to nod off in the middle of conversation, to lose track of his sentences, to become tearful, fearful, irascible, and a vague scent of urine overall . . . and yet he was sharp as a tack . . .

And he could tell what was bothering Rych . . . pure resentment . . . resentment of those who had had it better than him . . . in any way . . . no matter what . . . if he suspected you had a better flavor ice cream than him he would turn sullen . . . it was Hymi's idea to walk with Rych around the ruins, hoping that the devastation would give him a little perspective . . . but no . . . as they walked Rych launched into a tirade . . . he said the World Trade Center disaster didn't have a corner on disasters . . . he said that London had it worse in World War II . . . he said that Dresden had it worse than London . . . he said that Hiroshima . . . he said Nagasaki . . . the Holocaust . . . Cambodia . . . and even today Africa . . . Yugoslavia . . . they were walking in a place where they could see the last of the gargantuan twisted girder spaghetti . . . they could see from this distance across the site the little men in orange vests picking through it with hand tools . . . suddenly Rych's face turned red and he burst into tears . . .

Hymi himself of course was more or less immune to the impact of ground zero . . . having lived with it so long out the window of Austyn's apartment . . . only he developed a fear of falling he'd never had before . . . he had dreams of falling off cliffs . . . down elevator shafts . . . stumbling and going down in front of an oncoming bus . . . tripping at the top of a stairway . . . parachute not opening . . . paranoid fantasies of being pushed through a window, from a ship, off the subway platform . . .

But much as he believed, or half believed, in dreams as prophecies, he knew that this was all in his imagination . . . and besides, Austyn was having similar fantasies . . . he wondered why he was depressed . . . she was depressed too, come to think of it . . . then he began actually falling, falling for no good reason, tripping over his own feet, thanks to his PS probably . . . the first time he was unhurt, the second time he sprained an arm, but the third time he suffered a mild concussion . . . all this in a single weekend . . . he called it his Niagara of falls . . .

Actually the concussion did him a lot of good . . . he had been stuck in a stale place and it shook him up . . . it got his juices flowing, it loosened him up . . . it was like the bottom of a sink hole opening up flushing him down imploding . . . he didn't know if he wanted to be loosened up . . . he panicked but it was too late . . . his depression went up in smoke as he was overcome by five seconds of pure terror . . . after which he realized he was still alive . . . but numb . . . frozen . . . thawing by stages . . .

Judging by their behavior, others in their little group must have been going through similar stages . . . Seymor's sudden fits of rage . . . Jocylyn's crying jags . . . Notley's logorrhea . . . Jimmy Loch's black moods of abstinence . . . Achs's shrill anger . . . the vicious squabbling over nothings . . . the sudden shifts came and went leaving them all emotionally depleted and intellectually muddled . . .

An odd thing happened . . . Hymi was receiving his mail at the Museum and one day he opened and read a letter before he realized it was addressed to Achs . . . it was from Klaxon . . . it said that he found something surprising in his investigation of a certain bank, regarding Fynch . . . irregularities . . . improprieties . . . what bank . . . Hymi was indeed surprised that Fynch should be caught doing something unkosher . . . Fynch had always been Mr. Rectitude . . . to Klaxon's Mr. Sleaze . . . from the way the letter was phrased Hymi thought blackmail . . . but blackmail implied culpability . . .

When Hymi asked Achs about it, something surprisingly harsh crossed her demeanor... it wasn't meant for your eyes, she said, and walked away... the episode filled Hymi with anxiety, he couldn't exactly say why...

Maybe Hymi was anxious because of the Mysterious Narrator... among the whole cast of characters around the Museum, only Hymi was aware of the Mysterious Narrator... though he was aware, sometimes he thought it was pure paranoia... but I can confirm Hymi's intuition... I, who write down, entranced, what He tells me... but I am not Him... not gifted with such total unpredictability...

Who could have predicted that Jimmy Lochs would show up at the Temp riding a red motorcycle with a blond on back... he parked in front of the Museum and gunned the motor till he got everyone's attention... and everyone was in for a surprise... the blond was his wife... they had reconciled, they were in love... he wanted to show her his stuff in the Museum... she was named Tripper, and far from being the bitch of Jimmy's description, she was quite lovely... hair that dwindled in the wind, face that melted sweetly into smiles... Jimmy seemed transformed with happiness as he showed her through the Temp... they disappeared into its galleries...

When they reappeared an hour later they were at one another's throats, hissing and snarling... she calling him a burnt-out drunk, he accusing her of being a money-sucking slut... he roared off on his red motorcycle leaving Tripper behind shrilling a string of expletives... Rych sidled up, offering to take her home... she turned on him abruptly... what can I do for you sonny boy, she said... or for the rest of you, her eyes sweeping our familiar group... dreamers, like my husband, you encourage him when he needs a stable income, a steady job, a down to earth occupation, something everyone can understand, something normal like the rest of us . . . the way he was when I married him on parole, on good behavior, those were the good days before he got too smart for the rest of us, when I still loved him, when we were stupid . . . she broke down in tears . . . before he knew all of you and started trying to improve himself and everything else . . .

But I like stupidity, piped Notley, I'm stupider than you, stupidity is a source . . . well I'm so stupid I don't even understand what you're talking about, replied Tripper, when I say stupid I mean flat-out mud-faced drooling-tongue hanging-lip slack lack of intelligence . . . while you, you snot nose, are just making fun of me . . . she walked out . . . she's got a point, said Hymi, what's the difference between Fundament materialist stupidity and Notley's Zen-like stupidity . . . easy, said Notley, it's strictly a question of how you treat your garbage . . .

Speaking of garbage, said Pyhl, the Museum's dematerializer is malfunctioning . . . what's the dematerializer, asked Hymi . . . that's what you might call the reverse copying machine, you put the original in and it's disappeared . . . no trace . . . better than a shredder . . . Improvement Society extremists use it to etherealize artifacts involved in exhibitions . . . would you etherealize a Rembrandt, a Vermeer, asked Hymi . . . Rembrandt and Vermeer are self-etherealizing, Seymor chipped in, they etherealize as you look at them, that's the measure of good art, how much it self-etherealizes . . . by that measure the World Trade Center is a work of art, said Notley . . . maybe, said Hymi, it didn't self-etherealize but maybe there's some truth in it, said Hymi . . .

Just at that moment there was a loud boom . . . everyone ducked, then they all looked at one another fearfully . . . Hymi looked in

Austyn's eyes and saw people on fire, people jumping out the windows on fire ... but it was a thunderstorm rolling in from New Jersey, you could see black clouds over the river down the street ... fear months after the fact, like the fires that gushed up sporadically out of the rubble ...

At least it was out in the open now, thought Austyn ... the struggle between dead matter and living matter ... that was it wasn't it, she said to Seymor ... dead matter versus living matter ... with proponents of each on either side, no doubt ... like Klaxon, she thought ... nominally on our side but really incapable of taking sides, so by default on the side of death ... because commitment is a sign of life ...

Austyn went back to her apartment with Hymi ... just as they entered, the Statue of Liberty on which the apartment looked out at one side, was illuminated by a beam of sunlight that made her torch glow and her diadem glisten, welcoming those who wished nothing more than a chance to pursue happiness ... but when he suggested to her that maybe happiness was overrated she replied, on the contrary, it was underrated, especially when you thought about mass happiness, which was a key American invention ... she said she admired happiness and wished she had more talent for it ...

Rych was addicted to ice cream ... he couldn't get enough of it ... he was often seen walking down the street to the Temp with an ice cream cone in each hand ... each with double scoops ... if you asked him why he would say it was so he could sample four flavors at one time ... he knew what the others thought about the likelihood of another attack ... he knew it was a good possibility ... but he didn't see why he should worry about it ... he preferred to assume it wasn't going to happen, because what was the gain in thinking otherwise ...

You can change your life ... thinking can change your life ... this was illustrated by the arc of Jimmy's feelings about his wife, Tripper, and Klaxon ... at first he was angry and he started drinking heavily ... then he woke up one morning thinking he didn't know for sure about Tripper and Klaxon ... either they were screwing or they weren't ... if they weren't, there was nothing to worry about ... if they were she wasn't worth worrying about ... first of all because anyone with such bad taste in men wasn't worth worrying about ... second of all because if she cared about him, Jimmy, she wouldn't be screwing Klaxon, and if she didn't care about him why should he worry about her ... and third of all she was going to do whatever she wanted to do regardless of what he was worrying about ... so what was there to worry about ...

One of the security guards, whose name was Tripe, was an amateur inventor ... Tripe was not a vegetarian, but noticing the dietary needs of vegan friends, he had invented through manipulation of spinach DNA a kind of vegetable that nevertheless was pure protein indistinguishable from animal protein ... the only problem with it was that when you bit into it it screamed ... therefore he called it Screamach ... the problem was that people were upset by its screams as they ate it ... Tripe was aware of the problem and he was working on it, without quite realizing that he had created a whole new food category whose implications could be huge ... Pyhl realized it though as soon as he heard about it ... he saw there could be a huge market for such a product if they could learn how to suppress its screams ... an animal protein that was completely noncholesterol nonfattening ...

It was a tribute to the effect that Seymor's character was having on the Temp that Pyhl was not interested in Screamach for his own profit but rather for bolstering the sagging finances of the Museum ... Seymor's disinterestedness, indeed his altruism, set an example for the staff ... nevertheless Pyhl's old habits of sly manipulation took over in his dealings with Tripe ... he told Tripe that Fundament had gotten wind of his invention and that he should give Pyhl a copy of the formula for safekeeping ... and this was the seed of the lawsuit that finally destroyed the Temp ... the Tripe Screamach suit ... but that was far in the future, and there were other risks and perils that were more immediate ...

Among those risks were the strains that the political embroilments of the Museum were putting on personal relations, strains that the personnel were unaware of personally, but which were much more disruptive in person for precisely that reason ... take the relation between Pyhl and Jocylyn for example ... when Jocylyn realized that Pyhl had moved toward Austyn in his affections she was devastated ... she had depended on him through all the gyrations of Museum politics and she felt the rug had been pulled out from under ... it wasn't a sexual thing, although Jocylyn was miffed when she heard about their affair, even though it was by then mostly over ... it was when she learned that he had invited Austyn to accompany him on a trip to the Galápagos that she was really hurt ...

But why was Pyhl scheduling a trip to the Galápagos was the real question ... this is the story ... a supporter of the Museum had donated to it a giant tortoise shell, empty of course, but so large that a man could easily get into it, and a story had evolved that persons who did so became endowed with magical faculties ... the giant tortoise shell had come from the Galápagos, noted among other things as home to a large colony of giant tortoises that lived

500 years and more ... now, there were strange markings on the tortoise shell that almost looked like writing and Pyhl wanted to check this mystic script to see if it existed on the shells of living specimens ...

Pyhl had made all arrangements for the trip to the Galápagos when he decided to check out the myth that magical qualities inhabited those who managed to get into the tortoise shell ... one night after the Museum closed, Pyhl made his way through the darkened halls to the tortoise shell exhibition ... he found that while in theory it seemed easy to crawl into the tortoise shell, the reverse was true, not because the openings in the shell weren't big enough but because they were at such awkward angles to accommodate a human body ... basically he had to get in the front of the shell backwards and work his legs down through the opening in the rear ... he struggled for what seemed an hour getting into the shell, but he persevered and eventually succeeded ... successful but tired, he decided to close his eyes and rest for a few minutes ... when he woke up, and there is a question whether he did wake up or whether what follows was a dream, he found that the shell was so heavy that when he tried to crawl he could barely move ...

Soon he gave up trying to crawl and when he stopped trying to move the shell the shell started moving by itself ... it scurried across the gallery and through the door, then levitated and flew out a window, soaring into the night sky ... before he knew it Pyhl had landed in a moist, green, misty field full of small hills ... he heard bellows-like panting sounds ... soon he realized that the hilly forms were mobile and the panting was the sound of their breathing ...

A certain unspecifiable time passed ... Pyhl was brought to attention by a heavy weight on his rear ... he tried to retract his legs into the shell but the weight had them pinned and he felt a churning protrusion rubbing against his hindquarters . . . at the same time he became aware of a bellows-like sound in the vicinity of his ears and a moist intermittent wind at his neck, which he immediately retracted into his shell . . . which did nothing to alleviate the slow insistent prodding in his rear . . .

This mysterious situation went on for some time, until the suspicion gradually dawned on Pyhl that this was a mating scenario and he was being mated . . . and that the strange writing on his shell must have indicated to other tortoises that he was a female, since sex differences were ambiguous because of the heavy carapace which hid his tortoise body . . .

The next thing he knew it was morning and he was back in the Museum, surrounded by several guards and being questioned by Seymor and Austyn . . . he tried to talk to them, but as he moved his mouth, strange panting sounds were emitted and when he tried to gesture with his hands leathery paw-like appendages responded like flippers . . . Seymor and Austyn were regarding him with horror at the same time they were trying to talk to him and Pyhl realized he been transformed into a huge tortoise . . .

Naturally the trip with Austyn was called off . . . not to mention that Pyhl's whole way of life changed . . . they rigged up a pen for him in an out of the way corner of the Museum and filled it with straw and supplied him with whole heads of lettuce . . . the only problem was it was apparently mating season for giant tortoises and Pyhl was suffering agonies of incommunicable desire . . . though Austyn soon figured out by empathy what the problem was . . . naturally she could do nothing about it since Pyhl was a female and presumably heterosexual tortoise . . .

But the situation, difficult as it was, brought home certain recognitions to Pyhl, firstly that he been going through life protected by a tough emotional shield, and secondly, that beneath this tough guy image there was a sexual ambivalence about his erotic identity ... an ambivalence which, now that he had time to think about it in his pen all day, he decided he might well be able to turn to erotic advantage ... he wondered if there were any precedents regarding bisexual tortoises ... s/he began to consider things from a female point of view, wallowing in culpability and yearning by turns for just such a one whose culpability s/he was wallowing in ...

Before long Carney heard about Pyhl's difficult situation ... Carney offered to take Pyhl off their hands, provided that the Museum staff wouldn't object to his plans to feature Pyhl in a menagerie of unusual animals ... paid admission of course ...

When Pyhl heard that for lack of a better idea, the Museum was considering Carney's offer seriously, it broke the spell the shell had cast over him ... he realized suddenly that this was all about falling, things falling and protection from things falling, things falling in a dense black cloud, with an oceanic roar, bodies falling, body parts falling, protection from things falling ... and as soon as he recognized what it was about, the phobic shell vaporized in a black cloud ... but Pyhl would never be the same ...

But maybe it was all for the best that Pyhl would never be the same ... frankly, he wasn't that great before the tortoise incident, maybe the new version would be better ... at least he had gotten that constant feeling of dread that had secretly weighed on him off his back ... unlike Jimmy Lochs, whose recent aggravation with his wife had him completely unsettled ... Jimmy kept tripping and falling ... he was constantly hurting himself that way ... people thought it was his drinking but in fact this was one of Jimmy's rare bouts of abstinence ... Jimmy didn't know why he was falling ... it was like more than falling, it was like diving, like he'd be walking along and he would suddenly take a dive . . . he was beginning to suspect he had dropsy, whatever that was . . . or it was probably psychosomatic, that was the only explanation . . . in any case, he developed a real fear of falling . . . it got so bad at times that he wouldn't leave his loft . . .

But maybe it was all for the best that Jimmy wouldn't leave his loft . . . first of all, he got more work done that way . . . and then he reduced his chances of falling since his loft was familiar territory . . . just because his dropsy was psychosomatic didn't mean it wasn't real . . . he figured it was a real re-enactment out of guilt, guilt that he didn't fall when the Towers fell . . . guilt that they didn't fall on him . . . fear that they were still going to . . . he knew it was irrational, his guilt, his fear . . . but maybe it was all for the best that it was irrational . . . suppose it were rational and that he was really guilty of the Towers' collapse, that somehow his feelings, his fear of heights were magically instrumental, were a tiny but essential link in the chain of events that brought the Towers down . . . how would he live with that . . . no, it was all for the best that his fear of falling kept him in his loft . . .

But who could have said that Jocylyn, her feelings hurt by Pyhl, would suddenly develop a supercrush on Notley . . . it began with Jocylyn's fear that 9/11 would be repeated in some form . . . she had confided her worries to Hymi and Hymi had tried to calm her down by telling her they couldn't know, that this was in the hands of the Mysterious Narrator who didn't know either, which was why the narrator was mysterious . . . it didn't make linkages between cause and effect or extrapolate the past into the future . . . the Mysterious Narrator was the voice of the mysterious present . . .

But Jocylyn was worried about a repetition all the same . . . she knew it was morbid but she didn't know what to do . . . she'd heard that Notley was working with therapeutic treatment of anxiety through music and she made an appointment to go and see him one night ... but it was a mistake to go to Notley's deserted neighborhood at night ... she felt guilty about it ... a woman alone ... in a fur coat ... she hadn't been able to get a cab ... she looked out of place in the subway ... she thought he may have begun following her from the station ... she had a sense of something behind her ... she kept looking over her shoulder ... she thought it might have been the Mysterious Narrator that Hymi had been talking about ... and maybe it was ... in a way ... anyway she suddenly felt a blow on the head, she fell to the sidewalk ... someone grabbed her bag ... she never saw him ...

But maybe it was all for the best that Jocylyn had been mugged ... when she arrived at Notley's apartment with a mild concussion and dusty clothes, she was ripe, not to say vulnerable, to Notley's ministrations ... and indeed the effects of his treatment were stunning, no doubt especially because she was already stunned ... it must be said that by now Notley's interest was as much in therapy as it was in music ... the first thing that Notley suggested to Jocylyn was that guilt was not so bad ... that it was a lot better than some other things ... like culpability, like loss ... all this against the background of Jimi Hendrix's rendition of "The Star Spangled Banner" ... suggesting that guilt was an American phenomenon in that being unguilty was un-American ... un-American because guilt was a precondition for the pursuit of happiness, since that pursuit left behind those not pursuing happiness, those incapable of pursuing happiness, and those pursuing unhappiness ... but, and this is where Jocylyn came in, if pursuing happiness created guilt then guilt created repetition to relive the guilt so as to relieve it ... but relieving it created more guilt, for relieving it, and so a need for further repetition ...

Soon Jocylyn felt that she was being sucked into something with all this pursuit of repetition and guilt and happiness . . . and at a certain point she realized what she was being sucked into was Notley . . . but she felt guilty about it . . . because she knew that a patient shouldn't get into erotic relations with the doctor . . . and more so the doctor with the patient and here she was contemplating seduction despite herself . . . but at this point something snapped in Jocylyn . . . she decided to go ahead and create some guilt . . . because she knew she was stuck and wanted to become unstuck . . . guilt was more dynamic, more proactive, more vibrant, she thought, more interesting than the false innocence which veiled it . . . besides, guilt was as American as false innocence, so she wouldn't be being unpatriotic either way . . .

But Notley was not patriotic . . . and maybe it was for the best because it insulated him from Jocylyn's advances . . . Notley in his head was still living under that massive black cloud against the blue sky . . . he didn't want to say so or even admit it to himself that he had admired the Towers, that he thought they were beautiful, especially close up where you could see the moiré patterns created by the windows gleaming in the sunshine . . . he didn't want to admit that he didn't see them as examples of phallic aggression . . . as emblems of global domination . . . as vertical slums . . . didn't want to choose between being patriotic and unpatriotic . . . he wanted to be disciplined and transparent and so he seemed . . . who could have said that he was close to crack up . . . that all he needed was noting Jocylyn's advances to break the thin ice on which he was skating . . . who could have said that he hadn't slept in three nights, that he hadn't eaten in two days, that he was hallucinating black clouds, fire, thunder, and that it kept getting worse . . .

The fact was he needed Jocylyn and Jocylyn smelled it . . . and so in one of those mysterious turns of event that cannot be predicted, the patient became the doctor ... as Notley was ministering his musical massage that he likened to playing the piano on her body, Jocylyn suddenly opened her arms to Notley and rocked him like an infant ... whereupon Notley broke into tears, sobbing, finally wailing like an infant ...

There was something Achs knew that she wasn't talking about ... Seymor was certain of it ... the two had been growing closer to one another for some time ... ever since Seymor had given up his executive position at the Museum to Pyhl ... several times, Seymor thought, she had been on the verge of telling him something of weighty import only to hold back at the last moment ... typically, this happened, Seymor noticed, when she started talking about their group at the Museum ... Why, she would begin, Why ... and then her voice would trail off ... with an air of melancholy ...

Seymor guessed it was about Fynch, and about children ... Achs had never had any ... he guessed that it was about not having children with Fynch ... and that she wanted to talk about it but couldn't bring herself to do so ... she did say sometimes that she considered the Museum staff her surrogate family ...

In truth was there not something about Achs that communicated a sense of family to their little group ... Seymor even had a theory about it which was it was Achs among all of them who was most open to discussing the emotionally traumatic effects of 9/11, and so they all gravitated to her in a way that bonded them together ...

Seymor and Rych in particular had an affinity for Achs ... the younger generation ... they were the ones perhaps who were most in need of grandmothers ... more so Rych, who had a chronic problem ... Rych's problem was false innocence ... a sure sign that he felt guilty all the time ... his stance was I didn't do that, I didn't say that, it wasn't my fault, I'm not responsible . . . he needed someone of authority to tell him of course you didn't, of course it wasn't, of course you're not . . .

Seymor's chronic problem was chronicity itself . . . he had thought about it and he couldn't see why the present was said to be in a state of constant change . . . it seemed to him rather that the present was static and that moreover it was the only state that was static . . . while the world kept moving through it from the past to the future . . . thinking about this made him dizzy . . . and this is where Achs came in, because she seemed as unchanging, as static, as the present which was his benchmark . . . he needed someone to be there like a lighthouse when he had one of his fits . . . like the strange one induced by the black smoke boiling up from the Towers . . . he perceived the smoke as static and himself as boiling up . . . of course it didn't make any sense . . . but every time he saw this scene in his head he knew it was a danger sign . . . that he was about to have a fit . . . it was a chronic condition . . . it came and went but never went away . . .

If they only knew, thought Achs . . . only knew she was adrift . . . flotsam floating on the Hudson . . . an eddy in the river floating with the tides . . . kept together by the delicate involutions swirling through her . . . if they stopped she would disintegrate, she knew that . . . but she didn't let on . . .

Maybe it was for the best that she didn't let on . . . though the example she set was dubious . . . because she knew they needed something to hang on to . . . especially when they were having fits . . .

At such times they would need Achs's sense of history as ballast . . . the history of the Museum and of Fynch's invention and execution of the project . . . the problem for Achs was whether to tell them the real history or the history behind the history ... the back-history which she didn't think any of them were ready to hear ...

Notley was beginning to think it was his fault ... oh, not directly ... but by some circuitous logic, some tenuous connections, some intricate linkages ... for example, would it really have happened if it hadn't been so much on his mind, hadn't thought about it so much, the Towers, things falling, if there weren't that feather of fear added to the prehistory of the catastrophe, would it really have happened without that infinitesimal additional terminal weight, that feather of consciousness added to the mix of circumstance that began when the buildings were first conceived in the architect's mind ... Notley had begun to believe in what he called the weight of consciousness, which was his way of saying that consciousness was a real influence in the web of what we call the real ... Americans, Notley thought, don't believe in the weight of consciousness ... the weight of circumstance, yes ... the weight of fact, yes ... the weight of action, yes ... but the weight of consciousness, including the weight of history, the weight of thought, of memory, of dream, of emotion, of, for god's sake, crude nerve end feelings, no ... so he realized that his feeling of responsibility for the Towers was unacceptable ... un-American ...

The first time it happened he blamed it on alcohol ... when Jimmy didn't acknowledge his greeting on the way into the Museum he assumed he had been drinking ... as was often the case ... but the Mysterious Narrator works in unpredictable ways ... a week or so later Austyn failed to recognize him in the Cockroach gallery across the street ... but it was the day after that that Jocylyn of all people appeared to snub him when they were in the same room when Notley began to suspect that people literally couldn't see him ... not all the time, but on occasion, he was evidently transparent ... either that or they were occasionally blind ... if transparent, he suspected, it was a function of his mood . . . it happened when he was feeling static, silent in a corner, say . . . and when he moved vigorously and spoke out, the spell was broken . . . nevertheless, incidents accumulated, became more frequent . . . soon he became paranoid about it, thinking there was some sort of social pact against him . . . eventually he had to face facts . . . he was becoming invisible . . .

Notley went to a doctor . . . who examined him, looked at his lab report, and told him to see a psychotherapist . . . the situation soon became more acute when people started crashing into him . . . it was bad enough in apartments and galleries but it got to the point where he had to stop taking public transportation . . . to make matters worse, his voice was becoming muted . . . people couldn't hear him distinctly, began to ignore him, eventually stopped listening to him . . . soon he began to feel like a ghost . . .

To make matters worse, his condition appeared to be progressive . . . soon his occasional attacks of invisibility became the norm . . . people simply stopped seeing him . . . he grew lonely . . . on top of everything else he was hardly able to function . . . if he went to a restaurant the waiters would ignore him . . . if he went to a movie the person in the ticket booth would pay him no attention . . . it was impossible to get a cab . . . in stores salespeople didn't listen to him . . .

Jocylyn was Notley's last resort . . . she finally realized what was happening . . . Jocylyn took the trouble to pay attention . . . she listened to him, she heard him, she saw where he was coming from . . . she appreciated him . . . she kept him company . . . she tried to make his life better . . . but even she didn't want him to become overly dependent on her . . . and she ended by limiting the amount of time she spent with him more and more stringently . . .

Meanwhile, Seymor too began to show signs of mental breakdown . . . in his case it took the form of temporal aphasia . . . that is to say he was never on time for anything anymore . . . he was too late and in some cases too early . . . only Hymi recognized the symptoms, subject as he was to them himself . . . but with Pyhl still out of commission from his tortoise experience, still phobic about things falling on him, the Museum was adrift . . . Pyhl speculated that a defense against fallophobia was pyromania . . . he reasoned that if things burned up first they couldn't fall on you . . . it had worked on 9/11, Pyhl having escaped covered with ash, why wouldn't it work again . . .

Hymi had begun talking in his sleep . . . according to Austyn . . . though what he said made no sense . . . she had taken down what he said word for word but it didn't mean anything to her . . . except that he wasn't sleeping well . . .

But she should have been glad that Hymi was talking in his sleep . . . it meant that he was expressing himself . . . and expressing yourself was a plus, a form of self-improvement . . . assuming you knew who yourself was, which Hymi didn't . . . and if this were true of the self-conscious Hymi, how much more so for the rest of them, who didn't have a clue . . .

At least Hymi was dully aware that something was wrong, something was missing . . . that there was something strange about their whole group . . . it was at the level of the suspicion of a suspicion that he kept brushing aside . . . but it was disturbing all the same, as if the upheaval of 9/11 had shaken something loose in his consciousness ... which he was resolved to ignore at some level ...

Meanwhile, the hard hats had excavated ground zero down to bedrock in some places, seven stories down from street level, but in some places at the perimeter they were still at street level ... Hymi felt he was still at street level, but at any moment he could fall any number stories into the real story ... the seventh story ...

Hymi had to agree with Notley though, crazy as he was ... Notley always said that the real story was music ... Hymi didn't understand what he was talking about until recently ... when he realized that the real story was music because language is music ... it was obvious that spoken language was music, the tone, the rhythm, the total sound, the way a word in one person's mouth could mean something totally different in another's ... written language was just the score ...

And the score was constantly changing ... would always change until your game was up ... but the big game was never up, the story never finished ... ever ... all you can do is pay the price and get the change and hope it's for the better, hope you're not shortchanged, though you usually are ... the balance being the gaping imbalance you're forced to make up ... in a relation if not antagonistic at least agonistic, providing the synapse that makes you speak ... argue ... think ...

Yes, thought Hymi, the new-ism was definitely Agonism ... for example, Jimmy once told him the story of how he won an academy award ... not the academy award, the Oscar, but an award from an academy for painting ... he said there was a lot of money involved, especially since it came at a time in his life when he was impoverished ... the idea of getting an academy award was so far-fetched that when the award letter came he assumed it was a request for a donation and he threw it away without opening it . . . when the academy called, he picked up the phone and said there was nobody home . . . finally they reached him via special delivery . . . he was aghast . . . all his life he had been fighting against the sensibility of people like this . . . and now they had pulled the rug from under him . . . he went into one of his black depressions . . . they had removed the grounds for antagonism . . .

Jimmy couldn't work . . . because he couldn't think . . . because the terms in which he thought had disappeared . . . the game was up . . . he could have rejected the money but that wasn't the point . . . the point was that it had been offered . . . he could no longer claim to be shortchanged . . . this is the one thing he hadn't expected . . . an academy award . . .

And this is where Agonism comes in . . . Agonism was antagonism without rancor . . . it preserved the conflict without the anger . . . impersonally but still in person . . . it preserved the gap between is and should . . . the Devil became a partner while remaining the Devil . . . the status quo . . . if there weren't one he'd have to invent one . . .

The next thing that happened was that Rych was picked up for shoplifting . . . he gave Achs's name as his guardian so they called her from the station and she agreed to reimburse the store . . . when Achs had a chance to ask him why he did that, he answered to see if he could do it . . . after all, he said, it's what's being done to the Museum all the time with no end in sight . . . maybe stealing is a method of distribution . . . when asked what he had lifted, he replied that he had lifted the idea to shop . . . shopping was an American right, he said, he was sure it was somewhere in the Bill of Rights . . . it was part of the pursuit of happiness . . . but he was sure the

Bill of Rights didn't say anything about paying bills . . . he took the Bill of Rights as the model for all bills . . . as a right not a debt . . . he said he thought freedom to shop was a basic freedom and how could it be free if he had to pay . . . that's what credit was for, not paying . . . he said every American was born with a credit card in his hand . . . he said shoplifting was just paying by credit without a credit card . . .

Austyn and Hymi set about trying to establish their deep empathy in possible familial links . . . but try as they would they didn't get it . . . there was a missing link . . . neither had known their birth parents, though Hymi had known his grandfather, a capricious gent who would show up in his life at unpredictable intervals bearing toys and foreign coins . . . the last time he saw him he looked to be approximately Fynch's age, and Klaxon claimed to have found family letters showing that they knew one another and referring to the two kids as cousins . . . but where the actual family linkage occurred remained beyond their best guesses . . .

But circumstantially, they agreed that they had always felt a mysterious affinity . . . why shouldn't it be based on genes . . . the more so because, though both orphans, they had been nurtured in vastly different environments, Austyn in a distinctly lower class milieu that exploited her in every possible way, including sexually, and Hymi in a protective and loving upper middle-class family that had been plunged into economic difficulties because of the Depression but which had tried to give him all the advantages . . . despite which he had persisted in idealizing his maverick grandfather, a sailor signing onto ships on the Brooklyn docks, disappearing for years, returning with gifts . . .

And with stories . . . like the one Hymi remembered about the mysterious island city of Lamu . . . remembered as one remembers a dream ... and which his grandfather told as one retells a dream, with the air of improvising off the tip of his tongue what he didn't remember ... Lamu was off the East Coast of Africa ... you could only reach it by boat ... it was said to be where Sinbad the Sailor landed on his flight on the giant bird called the Roc ... in any case, his grandfather landed there ... he made his way to the best bar in the charmed town ... on the way he encountered crowds coming to market but he only had eyes for the ladies, his appetite aroused by certain piquant contrasts no doubt between two tribes and two religions ... there were ladies muffled in black robes from toes to nose and ladies bare from waist to hair ... he chose a girl muffled in black robes for her burning hypnotic eyes, don't ask where or how ... but the next thing he knew it was night, black as her robes, and he woke in a small dhow in the large of the Indian Ocean, two rascals handling the tiller and triangular sail, hallucinating that time had stopped ... or was it time that was a hallucination ...

Speaking of religions, Hymi, who among them all had always been the most skeptical of the mission of the Museum of Temporary Art, began referring to the Temp sardonically as the Temple ... the Temple of the Temporary based on the American attitude that you could change your life at any time, needless to say for the better ... it was part of the pursuit of happiness ... the Fundament believed you could change your life too ... for another life ... that is to say— death ... which states the basic conflict ...

To the Fundament a thing was what it was ... it did not change its state with time ... it did not stand for something else ... a spade was called a spade because it was a spade ... words were labels for things and things were stuck with them ...

Tripper was a kindergarten teacher by day, but to supplement her income she worked by night in a topless bar downtown . . . each afternoon she would shed her prissy kindergarten clothes and roar into Manhattan on her motorcycle to turn on Wall Street clerks and brokers . . . she got a kick out of both jobs, both involved a kind of nurturing . . .

She immediately took to Notley, sucking beer at his lonely table . . . he was not like the others . . . he was worse, he was harder to turn on, he seemed uninterested . . . which got her interested . . . she sat down at his table and during her break took him to the dressing room and fed him chocolates, eventually went home with him to his strange tiny white room . . . she immediately perceived, from his black clothes as against his white room, his ambivalence about identity . . . so different from her husband's brutish unthinking selfness . . . they ended up not making love although their talk was a kind of lovemaking . . . he talked a lot about how the disappearance of the World Trade towers challenged the whole concept of appearance, a concept already ambiguous for her from shaking her tits in front of an audience who knew nothing about her except the way she shook . . .

He walked her back to her motorcycle . . . it was raining lightly and there was a mean wind . . . he warned her to be careful . . . she told him to take care himself . . . he didn't know she was Jimmy's wife . . .

Tripper was completely nonintellectual . . . not to say she was stupid, on the contrary . . . but she processed things mentally in a different way from the rest of our gang . . . she was like somebody who knew how to talk but never learned how to write . . . they were inclined to consider her stupid, but in reality it was that she had a different kind of intelligence from theirs . . . thought seemed to cycle through her body and issue in various kinds of movement . . . it was a little like music, Notley thought . . . a lot like music . . . it was a lot like painting too, though Notley didn't think of that till later, when he discovered Tripper was Jimmy's wife . . .

It was like music because her intelligence expressed itself in bodily rhythms and gestures, the way music dictates dance . . . her responses, her repartee were fluid and dynamic in a way Notley found irresistibly beautiful . . .

What Tripper saw in Notley was more difficult to say . . . maybe it was the absence of typical male demands in him, the lack of ego, of competitiveness . . . maybe it was he was like a blank screen on which she could project her own fears and desires without being afraid of contradiction . . . because though Tripper had her fierce side it was a cover-up for her vulnerable side . . .

Hymi was having dreams . . . in fact they weren't so much dreams as they were nightmares . . . as American dreamers we tend to forget that there are bad dreams as well as good dreams, but this was something Hymi was not allowed to forget . . . his dreams were about wishing and doing . . . for example, he wished to pick up a tea cup, he could see himself picking up the tea cup, but he couldn't pick it up . . . or he wished to run and catch the bus but he couldn't catch it and instead fell down . . . or the bus fell down, fell down into the pit of ground zero . . . or the towers fell down into themselves . . . or the people fell down out of the towers . . .

Even though today was the day when they stopped digging up what fell down and began building up whatever they were dreaming up . . . there was a memorial ceremony . . . for those who died . . . but instead of closure it opened the wound . . . for Hymi . . . it reminded him of the dimensions of it . . . looking at the vast level plane and amphitheater of what was now ground zero . . .

the whole nightmare coming back . . . pushing into reality . . . more to come . . . welcome to the new millennium . . .

the whole game was played at the level of dream, thought Hymi . . . terror was a dream wrecker . . . wreck people's dreams and you change their behavior . . .

that was what the Fundament was all about . . . burying the dream in the literal body . . . thought Hymi . . .

which is to say—death . . . as opposed to which, thought Hymi, dream is the only thing to hang on to . . .

dream and desire . . . dream is desire . . .

thought Hymi . . .

even bad dreams . . .

. . . even nightmares . . .

realtime 6/30/03:

   things at the Museum are settling down
   who could have foreseen it who can say why
   Hymi and Austyn are a pair so are surprisingly Jocylyn and Pyhl again
   most surprising of all is Rych with Achs in a grandmotherly way
   though Jimmy is the odd man
   the Improvement Society could hardly improve on the situation
   rooted in their little Museum in-group
   they had up to now carelessly assumed is serendipitous in composition
   but not quite because Austyn remembers she had been more or less recruited by Fynch
   as was Seymor
   as was Pyhl
   as was Achs
   as was of course Jocylyn who was family
   as Achs is family by marriage to Fynch common-law or otherwise
   and Seymor recruited Rych
   and Austyn recruited Jimmy and Jimmy recruited Notley

and if there's something to ponder about all this Achs has a lock on it
she has the key anyone else will have to jimmy it

Jimmy is the odd man
he's given up on Tripper he's given up on Austyn
he tries to be a positive presence despite his depression
but he feels flatlined and monotoned
he can't paint he can't even draw
he feels he's at the end of something maybe his life
but he keeps smiling
he walks around with this fixed smile on his face
he looks demented
he utters encouraging words all around which have however a wet blanket effect
the wet blanket effect affects everyone around him
as soon as he walks into a room conversation withers and dies
he's encouraging to everyone and everyone turns pessimistic in his presence
but he's not drinking though soon people wish he were
he's not drinking and he's not fucking
and he's not painting
his wet blanket effect is so strong it influences people in his loft building he's never seen
whole blocks are suddenly afflicted
the effects are devastating for the Museum
the wet blanket effect stifles the patrons and discourages those thinking of visiting
even when he's not there the wet blanket effect seems to linger as if unleashing a germ
but still Jimmy stalks around with his demented smile oblivious to his influence

Seymor can't help but think that Jimmy is symbolic
symbolic of the Temp maintaining an attitude

Pyhl wonders about the sudden pairings within their group
    as if some magnetic force field is running through sifting and attracting and repelling
    stabilizing but also shutting down a healthy dynamic of change
    except for Jimmy the odd man whose instinct is that the stable is unstable

    Jimmy is still focused on the thefts
    just because they don't know what's missing doesn't mean there's nothing missing
    and even if there's nothing missing nothing still counts for something at the Temp
    so he huddles with Klaxon who has his supply of odd fact
    like that everyone in the Temporary in-group has some connection to LaFange
        in some cases direct in some tenuous but a connection
        this he learns from talking to Blunn the Chairman of the Board
        the Board is an inert body and in fact was conceived that way
        its main function is fund-raising
        but Blunn who is a notorious bon vivant reads it as fun-raising
        and part of the fun is the gossip the Temp generates
        the gossip is about money the sex is too obvious
        to Blunn the Temp is like a fish tank
    completely transparent with various exotic specimens coupling and drifting
        but why Jocylyn was disinherited in favor of the LaFange clique
        and why Achs is tacit head of this influential subgroup
        that is something Blunn could get his teeth into

why the Klumps and their rival Cockroach Gallery are so intimate with Achs

why Achs is changing her will

why the Klumps were donating money to the Temp

all these subplots assuming they're true could only be connected by money

the universal lingua franca

to Blunn it's all like a living crossword puzzle

or a picture that would emerge when he connected the dots

is it possible that the Klumps whom he despises nevertheless have their qualities

Blunn in his crude way foresees a whole new situation emerging at the Temp

a situation that may be worse for the Museum but more fun for Blunn

meanwhile Blunn has become friendly with Lynch who is of course very LaFange

Lynch sees Blunn as an avenue to his real estate designs on the Museum property

they had been introduced by Pandora Klump herself very LaFange

not that Pandora is trying to destroy the Temp

she just wants to see it change direction

she considers it aimless

a waste

it goes against her grain

she isn't even thinking about profit just that valuable property is going to waste

the Museum is dedicated to nothing and nothing gets nothing she chafes

she just wants to get Blunn on the LaFange team to push the Temp into something solid

something tangible

something permanent

it turns out that Lynch and Achs are related

Lynch brings in genealogical charts to prove it

he figures they're fourth cousins

he seems very invested in this relationship

he knows Achs considers family very important

he doesn't see why since she's generated none of her own

she's not even from LaFange

but through his kinsman Fynch she must know all LaFange's secrets

maybe that explains why she's a preeminent member of the LaFange clique

and maybe that explains why she helped disinherit Jocylyn from Fynch's estate

as Blunn had told Lynch

even though she is the only flesh and blood heir

of course when Jocylyn hears this rumor she hits the ceiling

so does Pyhl who wants to confront Achs but Jocylyn refuses

she's afraid of Achs says she had been even when her father was alive

despite all appearances she'd learned that Achs was the power behind Fynch

especially despite her pose as the pseudo matriarch who everyone loves

a pose behind which, according to Jocylyn, rages an evil old witch

power mad and jealous of her prerogatives

Jocylyn goes so far as to imagine Achs could have been complicit in Fynch's death

though she admits that Fynch at the age of 100 maybe wanted her to be

Byrd descends on the scene
Jimmy wonders how Byrd got to know so much so fast
it's true he's now the senior member of the cast of characters
he must be about 90
he looks thin boned and dwarfish and his skin is covered with brown spots
he has a potbelly and he's bent in a 45 degree angle at the waist
his chin sinks into his chest
that he's bald goes without saying and his voice is squeaky
it's hard to say how he communicates his air of authority
maybe it's his huge ears or the way hair bushes out of his ears and nostrils
but when he speaks people listen
possibly out of surprise that he can be coherent at all
and even though he sprays them generously with slobber as he speaks
it's clear to Jimmy that Byrd wants to come in and clean house
even though it's not his house
and that he thinks the only one standing in his way is Achs
Byrd seems to think Achs wants to stop the thefts by giving away the Museum

it is at this stage that Hymi begins to notice
both things one his imagination not coinciding
with his reality and the other that everything
or rather everyone starts getting better he only
needs to look at someone like Wendy Blustrous
who starts being surprisingly nice to him sweet
even instead of militant and on the other hand he
used to be able to imagine things and they would
happen and now they don't like he imagines
raising his arm and it doesn't happen and also

it's not happening faster than it used to not happen
everything is happening faster than it used to

Klaxon in the role of peacemaker
not likely but true he thinks he's on
to something he won't say what but
claims it will blow the case wide
open what case asks Hymi the case
of the Temporary Museum says
Klaxon I didn't know we're a
case Hymi where there's a
mystery there's a case Klaxon

so is this another case where
Hymi's imagination doesn't
coincide with reality or is
Klaxon just being nice by
making the unwholesome
scene at the Temp seem a
a bit glamorous or what in
any case things seem to be
unraveling faster than Hymi
ever expected another way
reality outruns his imagination

meanwhile
improvement becomes
self-improvement
our gang is pursuing
happiness through

self-fulfillment
each on their own
Rome burning that
is the Museum except
Jimmy the odd man
and Hymi who
keeps
imagining
things that
don't
hap
pen
he ties his shoes his shoes don't tie
he buttons his shirt his shirt doesn't button
like reading a novel about things happening that don't really happen
at about the same time word spreads
Seymor is in the hospital
mild heart attack
overweight
and coincidentally
Rych has an auto accident
whiplash shaken up
and incredibly Achs trips
takes a fall sprains her knee
Austyn on the way to the hospital to visit Seymor
is hit by a cyclist for a messenger service
knocked down major abrasions
emergency room
it's a massacre
only yesterday each of these
unfortunates had been self
improving at rapid rates

Seymor doing exercise
Rych in psychological counseling
Achs in physical therapy
Austyn returning to scholarly pursuits
and then
bang
just like that
Jocylyn too
her new genealogical research spurred
by Klaxon's hints is assailed by mysterious
neurological tics
only Jimmy and Notley are spared
as if practice of the arts is protective
though they're running scared
meanwhile the excavation of ground zero has ended
no more hard hats sifting for body parts
there's even a ceremony with flags and bagpipes
Hymi sees it all from Austyn's window
some consider it curious the sickness and injuries in our crew date from then

he thinks of ground zero as a scar
a scar that will be covered but won't heal
he relates their physical afflictions to the Scar
they're a kind of repetition in memoriam
he hasn't doped it out it involves shock and guilt
but he knows the Scar will mark everything he does
and that a coincidence of afflictions and Scar is no coincidence
Hymi suspects the Scar can be assuaged by another coincidence
the imagined coincidence that artists forge
he phones Notley

Achs tells Seymor in the hospital that she once had a near death episode
　　　she was told she was dying and it was all right with her
　　　she says her death struck her as a lack of coincidence in that
　　　soon there would be no gap between her mind and the world
　　　she would coincide with nothing
　　　time would flatline and disappear
　　　time is just the distance between places she says
　　　she says she had imagined the universe as a vast coincidence
　　　in which we have the illusion of dwelling for a time
　　　the illusion which we call mind
　　　and then by coincidence she didn't die she says
　　　it was all something she just imagined

　　Hymi too has the feeling revelation is at hand there are signs
　　　the end of excavations
　　　the probing of Byrd Blunn Pyhl Klaxon
　　　the way adversaries were beginning to talk Byrd with Achs Klump with Pyhl
　　　the feeling that people are getting better while events are getting worse the way
　　　the 9/11 catastrophe brought people together
　　　for a while
　　　Hymi wants him to create a coincidence Notley
　　　a coincidence that brings people together without catastrophe and that
　　　will bring Hymi together with his own reality in imagination
　　　so the two coincide
　　　Hymi thinks if you can get things to coincide a revelation will follow because
　　　the big bang is the original coincidence and it's important to be in tune

with the universe
he phones Notley
Notley tells him that he's in tune mostly with silence because
silence contains the sound of the big bang
just the way the sound of the World Trade tower collapsing seemed to sound
too loud for anyone to hear

the fact is Hymi's problem with imagination and reality can be traced to the Scar the original wound inflicted on him a case of what the doctors called Pygmalion Syndrome or dropsy because it causes him to drop everything he picks up
but it soon becomes obvious his affliction involves fear of falling
fear of anything falling
buildings airplanes people himself
not everyone relates that way to the Scar

why him
he feels he's the fall guy since last fall
all this he tells Notley
who tells him he needs to get out of language
short for shut up Hymi asks
not shut up shut out Notley
shut up is shut in shut out noise open to silence
it's easy language is self-annihilating
in stress it melts back into sound
sound degenerates to noise
the only way out is silence

they recover from their various afflictions in good time
all but Hymi
whose lack of coincidence endures even aggravates requiring feats of reconciliation
he imagines pedaling a bike the bike topples over
he imagines climbing stairs his feet don't climb
he imagines running his legs don't run
he imagines walking he ends up falling
he imagines talking it comes out mumbling
his imagination stretches like a rubber band to coincide with reality
occasionally he achieves coincidence
Notley says he's becoming a work of art
Jimmy says he's an action painting
Hymi proclaims coincidentally he still exists despite the Scar and its effects
there've been inquiries he says he says
call them
tell them I'm here
or he thinks he says
actually it comes out __ them I'm __

Seymor is feeling better he's out of the hospital but
he's had a scare
scare enough to jog him out of time and history for a moment and into memory and personal space
Seymor is in the habit of thinking big of thinking issues not of thinking at the level of his pulse beat
thinking what he likes and who he likes to do it with
thinking of untranslated intimacies and untranslatable pleasures

    thinking how the little group at the Temp had become almost like family
    with familiar faults
    Jimmy with his depressions
    Notley with his withdrawals
    Hymi and his afflictions
    Jocylyn's fluctuations
    Pyhl's aggressions
    Achs's impulses
    Austyn's loyalties and disloyalties
    Rych and his growing pains
    Seymor can't say why he's fond of these foibles
    except he's getting used to them
    they don't correspond to ideas he has about them they just are

Austyn's latest thing is optical intelligence
she claims it's the equivalent of sonic intelligence
not the same thing but the equivalent
this kind of intelligence happens in a tiny space of time
before thinking kicks in and she claims
this tiny space of time is where most things that matter hatch
where you fall in love for instance
where likes and dislikes take shape
where fear stabs and laughter erupts
she confides to Achs it's how she knows she's in love with Hymi
that tiny space
it's how she knows the wound opening in his world
the wound that will never heal
unless he heals himself

is there life beyond language Seymor asks Notley and Byrd
　　if not Notley answers then I'm dead
　　Jimmy too
　　Seymor is headed for never never land in Byrd's opinion
　　the fatter he gets the harder to find he is
　　so nebulous he's hard to see
　　his head is cloudy
　　his talk obscure
　　he walks in mist of his own making
　　people who don't know him consider him stupid
　　those who know him think of him as pure as a saint but a saint
of what
　　no one can say
　　unless a saint of stupidity
　　he goes around asking stupid questions like
　　where does God come from and why why does language take
time and where where does memory go and why
　　he's like a two-year old and fat as a baby
　　he seems to talk before he thinks if he thinks at all
　　two days later they find Seymor bleeding in his bathtub babbling and counting his toes
　　blubbery as a stranded whale but still flopping
　　flipping

　　Byrd thinks he has the answer it's simple
　　two letters
　　l e
　　added to the Temp equals Temple equals Church
　　revelation is at hand and it's that old-time religion
　　you can change your ways
　　you can admit the error of your ways
　　it's not too late

it's never too late
look at that painting what do you see
you see beauty you see harmony
you don't see scatter you see focus
you don't see waste you see economy
you don't see hostility you see understanding
you don't see hatred you see pleasure
you don't see the next minute you see forever
you don't see chaos you see resolution
you can change
you can change your life

he feels good today
Rych
he spent the night with his new girlfriend Emma
they smoked a lot of weed made love twice and ordered in pizza
with sausage and anchovies his favorite
he likes his body this morning the way it feels it feels
like his cells are relaxed on vacation
he does a quick appraisal of his organs decides they're all happy and if they're happy
he's happy
his mind is a blank which is the way he prefers it
he feels he's too young to think about anything seriously
why should he concern himself about the machinations at the Museum
and the inclinations of its personnel especially Byrd who keeps asking him sly questions
as if Byrd knows something he doesn't
like does he have girlfriends does he use protection
he's beginning to think Byrd is queer

    actually he prefers the crowd at Cockroach Gallery who appear more low falutin
      if not downright crude he's thinking Klumps
      feet on the ground
      that Seymor dude whacked out thinking about what he called the big issues
      he could dig Wendy Blustrous though he likes the way she works with trivia
      puppets and money
      puppets and money he can understand
      she has nice legs
      never mind Achs's talk about happy family
      what could she mean
      happy family is an item on a Chinese menu

    Klaxon tells Pyhl that Lynch is collaborating with the Fundament
      about the thefts at least Pyhl tells Achs Achs
      is not disturbed
      she says no matter what Lynch is one of us
      Pyhl who is us
      Achs is silent for a long moment
      then an extraordinary thing happens Achs starts to sing
      it begins as a high vibrating hum and expands in timbre and volume till it
      reaches to something like a shriek ending in gibber
      us is you you wess
      in banks we trust
      I've tried to confess
      the museum stands for
      watercress
      nibble nibble bibble

Pyhl is there something you went to tell me
Achs I'd like to but grotesque giggle
Pyhl is it funny
Achs in a way
Pyhl is it important
Achs relatively grotesque giggle
Pyhl tell me
Achs I can't giggle turning to horse laugh
Pyhl has the impression he's witnessing a disintegration of something precious
the shattering of a piece of fine china the smashing of a vase the splintering of stained-glass

Jimmy wants something more permanent than his temporary paintings
digitized to disappear after a time but it's not going well
his medium is ephemera
when he paints for posterity he loses it it doesn't last
it makes him think too much
he loses that little space of time between art and reality and quicker than thought
the eye of the needle through which things pass transformed
he can't explain even to himself
he doesn't want to
he wants to be stupid
and stubborn
pig-headed
when he explains this to Austyn she says he sounds like LaFange
she says Fynch had told her pigs were the cash crop in LaFange
and that pigs look stupid
but don't turn your back on them

    Austyn likes to stay out of the politics of the situation
    then why is she getting cozy with Wendy Blustrous for whom the situation is all politics
    because Austyn knows from art history there are always strings attached and
    Wendy works with marionettes things don't happen in vacuums
    Wendy's marionettes are very correct but she improvises with the strings
    as history improvises with Hymi on strings of DNA
    so what he can do and what he imagines
    don't coincide

    how to explain Byrd's fondness for Jocylyn
    maybe it's because he thinks she looks like him
    maybe it's because he thinks she's reserved and old-fashioned
    maybe it's because he thinks he understands her
    maybe it's because in fact he misunderstands her
    certainly he doesn't understand why she's what he calls in cahoots with Notley
    she's not in cahoots she's in love
    all her toughness seems to have been a façade in any case she's now a real softy
    almost timid
    at least around Notley
    she caters to him says Byrd as proof of her being in cahoots
    he says he'd like to put the kibosh on their relations
    he says Notley's after her for her rear end and front porch
    he says he deserves a kick in the keister
    but surely Byrd exaggerates

maybe Notley just likes her
Notley is a clean slate
a vacuum
a silence

Jimmy doesn't know where they come from
the images
it seems his main function is to leave space for them when they come
effortless and exhilarating
happening is the key happening is the Mysterious Narrator musing
images happen Jimmy catches them before they blur into time
or so it appears to him
they emerge from the void into space then blur into time
like the frames of a film
he prays into the void
he's rewarded with the glyphogram:

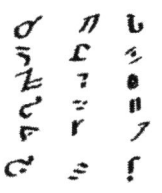

Rych isn't a virgin but he hasn't
had very much experience
a quicky here a quicky there
but Emma is something else
she's a little older 22 to his 17
a little older and a lot of mileage
but that's not what it is what it

is he's in love he tells Seymor
how would you define that asks
Seymor how you define the color
blue says Rych I mean blue is
blue probably my blue is different
blue when we see it the way I
see it if I knew I was going to
die tomorrow I could be happy
today it's like a drug Rych
Seymor it's anesthesia for
reproduction and your job
done you wither and
contract in fact you might
as well die
Rych stares at Seymor
Rych you're depressed tell
me about it
in fact Notley couldn't choose between Tripper and Jocylyn
nor did he want to
it was against his principles
and the source of his power
the passive party always wins
why
because everything flows to the point of least resistance
though the Mysterious Narrator is capricious even there
there are no laws that bind the Mysterious Narrator
no rules and regulations anything can happen
what happens here is Tripper makes friends with Jocylyn
   they decide to share Notley baffling Notley nevertheless he accepts the situation
   then Tripper and Jocylyn begin to get more interested in one another
   sexually both are surprised

gradually they withdraw from Notley Notley is surprised and a little peeved
nevertheless he accepts the situation he's more disturbed by the bickering aggressions of the Fundament concerning the thefts and the counter aggressions of the Museum
Notley decides to go on a hunger strike
one may question if the strike is against the Fundament the Museum or Tripper and Jocylyn
be that as it may the strike proves ineffectual against any of them
except Notley
for whom it does a lot of good an effect not negligible concludes Notley since
all we can hope to control is ourselves
if that thinks Notley
since all our schemes are defeated in the end
thinks Notley or if they succeed it's just by chance

the zeitgeist surprises you reflects Hymi
but so does your DNA
who could have predicted the Museum and the Fundament would be talking about the thefts
or that the doctors would tell him the way he imagines his body is indeed screwy
that he imagines his body doing things it can no longer do
and that it will be doing less and less as time goes by
and that there's nothing to be done
except to modify his imagination
but these skeletons are in all their closets it turns out
once tongues are loosened by empathy with his diagnosis
it seems that Austyn who looks gymnasal has a heart murmur and that

Jocylyn of robust bust and festal fesses has chronic
　　anemia and that Pyhl has prostate problems and Achs has asthma
　　Notley migraines Jimmy is alcoholic Seymor depressed Byrd
　　lung cancer in remission and Rych has an aneurysm in his brain prohibiting vigorous
　　activities
　　though it turns out Rych plays trumpet and can blow
　　as long as he doesn't blow too hard luckily he likes cool jazz since the
　　docs forbid hot
　　but when Rych jams with Notley who's supercool he becomes superheated by contrast
　　Notley and his minimalist computer against which Rych blows harder and hotter
　　until he risks blowing his brains out

　　Achs is putting her foot down
　　it's her opinion that there's too much fraternization going on
　　the affair between Rych and Emma is the least of it though the
　　pet name he calls her by Mm for Emma is all too transparent and
　　incestuous
　　but neither does she like Notley's affair with Jocylyn though his affair
　　with Tripper seems to be all right why
　　and though she likes Austyn she's never liked her roundrobin
　　sexual relations with the men in their little congregation
　　so she calls a halt
　　or tries to
　　to Hymi she says in dissuasion of his relations with Austyn

what's wrong with Wendy Blustrous she's cute she's talented she's level
headed why are you stuck on Austyn blind
to the depth of commitment there
how to account for Achs's strange behavior
is she jealous
is she cranky
is it just old age creeping up
or does she knows something the rest don't know and that the Mysterious Narrator
will reveal in due time
as soon as it knows

Achs is sending out invitations to a dance
she calls it the Dance of the Last Happiness and
she says that at it she's going to make an important announcement
soon everybody refers to it as the dance of the announcement
the dance is going to be held at the Temp and word goes around our gang
that Achs has a terminal disease she's going to announce at the dance by
way of passing the baton
the baton of the spirit of the Museum of its tradition of its august collective memory
its history which is admittedly negligible in terms of time
but which is dense and rich in the memories of our little group
and so the dance of the announcement quickly acquires a fabulous quality in anticipation
and the ambiguity of the phrase last happiness whether meant as final or ultimate only adds to the mystery and luster of the occasion

in the meantime anticipation lifts the spirits of the Tempniks

it gives them a sense of movement in this scene of recent stagnation as is the general sense

and provides something to look forward to

though Hymi for one has the inkling they may be in for a rude shock

a shock that will change all their lives for better or for worse who knows

maybe both

Rych isn't having any part of it

the dance

he knows it won't be his kind of music his and Mm's

otherwise Achs would have asked him to play but

she didn't ask either him or Notley

but Mm persuades him to go

out of respect she says however grouchy

Rych OK but if I go I go with my horn

Mm but you have to promise not to play or if you play not get excited you know what the doctors say

Rych screw the doctors

but as he says this a morbid intuition fills him with dread

occasionally it hits him Rych

his lost sister

they grew up together as foster children but

separated at 16 he lost track of her Lyra

she'd been studying voice a singer and won a scholarship to music camp

and never came home

she was older 16 to his 14 and he loved her still does

in more ways than one

when he thinks of her he gets depressed where is she

he tries not to think about it

they used to play duets together her voice to his trumpet

they clicked at many levels sibling musician inamorata yes inamorata

but let's not get into that now

the only thing he knows that rivals their duets are his sessions with Notley Notley's

style and the way it eggs him on it's beyond cool it's frozen

would be the way he characterizes Notley's style frozen into slabs of silence

which if melted would flood the ears with whole symphonies

he's sure they'll get into it at the Dance of the Last Happiness

or the dance of the announcement as it's commonly known

in truth he's ambivalent about playing Rych

Rych knows he won't be able to resist the temptation

to blow hotter and hotter and faster and faster to melt Notley's cool

finally the blessed event

the dance of the announcement

of the Last Happiness

the band sounds like Guy Lombardo out of Achs's generation

nobody knows how to do those dances the fox trot the lindy hop they improvise

hip-hop crossed with lindy hop anyway it hops

that's how Achs refers to it The Hop

The Hop of the Last Happiness after things heat up she gets up to say a few words

I have an announcement to make she says a surprising announcement

but before I say what it is I want to say ahead of time that it will go a long way to

    justify a grandson since it is for is it not our grandchildren
    that we undertake such projects of pacification amelioration and salvation otherwise what
    is the point of it all and the point I wish to make is that there is a grandson
    she pauses to allow for gasps of surprise then continues
    the depth of the implication
    here she seems to lose the thread
    the implication of the death for the end of the correct address the death of the evidence of the end to the end of the path
    and finally Seymor asks if she needs to be helped to her seat she waves him off because
    going to Fynch and something he told me she continues before he died was that it was for
    the correct address at the end of the path and realizing the depth of implication of the evidence and with the help of Klaxon getting access to the records
    in short it was a sperm bank
    implying that many of you are actually relatives because generations then depend simply on when fertilization was initiated
    if you see what I'm driving at he was everyone's father
    so many of you are engaged in innocently incestuous relations at one remove or another
    silence
    then a murmur begins to rise a murmur of confusion
    the assembled company regards one another as if through the wrong ends of telescopes
    then forced laughter here and there
    Hymi breaks the ice it's certainly a conversation stopper
    Austyn I don't see what difference it makes
    Seymor let's calm down
    Rych who's excited

Pyhl I'm excited I've been screwing my cousins my sisters who knows my mother

Austyn gasps

Rych my aunt

Jocylyn screams

Rych I told you you're old enough to be my mom

Achs I'm the only one old enough to be everyone's mother and I never had children

Jimmy Fynch's trap is snapped we're all one big family

Notley how did this happen

Achs he spent much of his life trying to reclaim his spermbank progeny and that isn't all

Pyhl that isn't all that's enough for the time being let the musicians play

but the band is on it's break whereupon before

anyone can say no Rych breaks out his horn and starts

to play plays slow and mournful a version of Taps a dirge

for Fynch and his doomed brood that is themselves quickly quickens tempo increasing

volume pointing his horn and nodding at Notley who withdraws more into himself

the harder Rych plays finally hits a high note

holds it

holds it

higher higher as Notley shrinks back into himself hands on ears

Rych elevates his tone even farther it's too much for Notley

he seems to explode in sound a deep rich percussive chord rolling outward

engulfing the listeners sweeping them out of their seats

across the dance floor

modulating to a deep organ tone then rises in another crescendo and begins to ebb people begin to recover pull themselves out from under tables off the dance floor

Hymi that's some voice you got there or whatever it is they're all slowly getting up now

except for Rych prone on the floor trumpet clutched in his outstretched hand

Hymi he's passed out

Achs oh my goodness she signals to a couple of museum guards let's take him to my office

as she goes out with Rych a young woman comes in very pregnant

she says my name is Lyra I'm looking for a person named Achs she's black

Pyhl she just left what's it about

Lyra I'm Rych's sister

Pyhl stares

Lyra because I'm Afro-American she asks

Pyhl well frankly

Lyra he's my foster brother

Lyra and this is his baby he doesn't know about it

Jocylyn then I'm going to be an aunt

or am I Rych's aunt I have to talk to Helen about this

Austyn who's Helen

she's my therapist

Austyn I'll have to talk to Mildred

Hymi who

Austyn she's my therapist

Pyhl I can't wait to tell my group

Achs hurries in something is wrong with Rych I called EMS

Lyra gasps hand over mouth Achs looks at her

Achs now you know almost everything she says to everybody

Pyhl what do you mean almost

Achs about Lyra and Rych she's not his foster sister

Austyn no
Achs she's his half-sister they have the same father you
she points to Pyhl
Pyhl omygod
Lyra what are you saying
Achs you're all victims
Hymi and perpetrators it seems
Jimmy why did he do it Fynch
Achs I think ego at first
Hymi spreading his seed
Achs then later to fulfill his concept of family
Pyhl why didn't he tell us
Achs guilt I suppose but he believed in guilt he believed you couldn't do anything
important without guilt
Pyhl what could be so important
Hymi it's genetic engineering before the fact
one of the museum guards comes in looking shaky
I think he's dead

EMS
confirms
Rych dead
Lyra explaining between sobs
it turns out Lyra pregnant and scared had been adopted by the Fundament
who naturally tried to keep her out of the Museum's sphere
until the latest Initiative opened the way to a rapprochement
too late
the assembled congregation hit too hard to speak
until Jocylyn wiping a tear intervenes in the grief stricken shock
Jocylyn and what will the little one's name be

Lyra between sobs he doesn't have a name
then what will you call it
Lyra it's a boy and I call him a lot of things
I call him little man cool
I call him cuckoo
but mostly I call him saver because he saved me when I was depressed
I was suffering post-traumatic stress because of 9/11
which stopped as soon as I knew I was pregnant
Austyn and when will you give him a name
I'm going to let him name himself
but to me at least he'll always be Saver

after that things take a turn for the better
the Museum thefts slow to a trickle then stop
but the public appetite for nothing also seems to be drying up
Pyhl institutes a series of concerts in the Museum
he reasons that music has become closer to the mission that Fynch intended for the Temp
since music is always invisible and comes closer to nothing than graphic art ever could
he turns the Temp into a concert hall
encouraging visible art on the walls
the social atmosphere at the Temp becomes claustrophobic for our little family
one by one each person announces plans to go off separately while at the same time
declaring that the family will always be a source of strength to return to
and they further declare as a group that the day that Saver is born will be a holiday
on which to hold an annual family reunion

and on that day they hold the first of these as a goodbye ceremony they call the last supper
and that day is 9/11

9/11/03

at the last supper they each get up in succession to talk about their plans Pyhl is leaving the Museum to become a real estate broker in partnership with Lynch and is selling off his art collection he says that making money is a kind of art robust and transparent at the same time Byrd says he's going back to LaFange to die in the fertile mud from which he came Achs says she's going with him Jocylyn says she's opening a doll and puppet gallery with Wendy Blustrous starting with a show of Statue of Liberty icons Notley says he's giving up music and entering a Buddhist monastery where they'll take care of him in his old age Jimmy says he's going to go to art school and learn his craft from the bottom up Seymor says he's going to go to graduate school in comparative religions to learn how to be religious and which religions to choose as an aspiring saint Austyn says she's going to devote herself to taking care of Saver and Lyra as a sort of maiden aunt Hymi says he's going to go off to a nursing home with his various decrepitudes not because he can't take care of himself but because soon he won't and because he likes nurses the Klumps take over management of the Museum with Blunn and change its name from the Museum of Temporary Art to the Extemporaneous Arts Museum featuring impromptu acts happenings and works in progress with a series of performance-oriented projects and an ongoing improv theater and climaxing with a brief engagement of the Barnum and Bailey Circus needless to say one of the first shows at the Extemp is the Jocylblust Puppet Theater where Klaxon a confirmed sexist connects with Jocylyn a hardnosed feminist and they fall in love proving once again that opposites attract speaking of which the Fundament which turns out to be run by a committee is made to feel perfectly at home at the Extemp which even issues guest passes to all of its members courtesy Lynch and the LaFange clique which in turn gives glowing reviews of the Extemp in the militant Fundament newsletter Wordflesh which says things like the new version of the Museum has been rethought in the spirit of the Church of the Fundament which teaches that it doesn't matter what's the matter as long as it is matter and that even the word is flesh though the Church preaches a modified form of vegetarianism which prohibits eating anything that's cute bunnies duckies lambies but maintains above all that you can eat words and the words become flesh and you can eat flesh and it becomes words which then don't matter and cancel out in favor of action so you can see there's very little difference between the positions of the Extemp and the Fundament and everything is for the best with reconciliation and happy endings all around with optimistic predictions for the future and everyone pursuing happiness though not necessarily yours or yours though it is said all live happily ever after except when they don't according to the whim of the Mysterious Narrator whose story becomes our history to which we all must subscribe

realtime 12/31/03:

and having written down the above I sit here as the Mysterious Narrator ordains my rogue computer spins like fate out of control me suddenly inside its frame of reference the speech recognition program writing on its own:

the death of the death of the death of the death at the death of the death of the death of the data to the death of the death of the death of the death of the left the death of the death of the death of the death of the death of death at the death of the death of the fact that the death of the death of the death of the death of the death of the death of thinking that the death at the death of data that the death that the death of meaning of the history of the visitor on the screen

like a warning the only escape from history into the dynamics of the pure present the ultimate coincidence where everything happens at once as I sit here reading dictation from the void